Escape Over The
Iron Curtain

ESCAPE OVER THE
IRON CURTAIN

CRISTINA ROSI

iUniverse, Inc.
Bloomington

ESCAPE OVER THE IRON CURTAIN

This is a work of fiction. All of the characters, names, incidents, organizations, and dialogue in this novel are either the products of the author's imagination or are used fictitiously.

iUniverse books may be ordered through booksellers or by contacting:

iUniverse
1663 Liberty Drive
Bloomington, IN 47403
www.iuniverse.com
1-800-Authors (1-800-288-4677)

Because of the dynamic nature of the Internet, any web addresses or links contained in this book may have changed since publication and may no longer be valid. The views expressed in this work are solely those of the author and do not necessarily reflect the views of the publisher, and the publisher hereby disclaims any responsibility for them.

Any people depicted in stock imagery provided by Thinkstock are models, and such images are being used for illustrative purposes only.
Certain stock imagery © Thinkstock.

ISBN: 978-1-4759-8423-1 (sc)
ISBN: 978-1-4759-8424-8 (ebk)

Library of Congress Control Number: 2013906402

Printed in the United States of America

iUniverse rev. date: 04/15/2013

PART ONE

BY CRISTINA ROSI

CHAPTER 1

1970 BUCHAREST ROMANIA

It was the spring of 1970 in Bucharest, Romania. In the living room, my family gathered around a large table under the dim light of an old, iron chandelier. Against the walls tall bookcases with glass doors kept under lock and key by my father, displayed rare books and archeological findings that he passionately dug out from various sites. Byzantine and Russian Icons as well as all sorts of religious relics were canvassing the remaining walls. A Turkish fireplace in the corner was especially designed to store more heat in the winter. In front of it, an ornate iron crucifix was standing tall reminding everybody that the church was still powerful though we lived under a communist regime. The windows were covered with velvet curtains bordered with intricate embroidery on the edges giving the living room a timeless feeling. Everything was dark in that room except for the immaculate white tablecloth.

My mother, father, aunt and boyfriend Phillip were sitting in silence. Father did not touch his food. Neither did I. Mother served dinner in her best dishes. We drank wine from her favorite purple crystal cups embossed with real gold leaf flowers. Feeling feverish with a cold I only had a few sips of wine.

On my way to the front door I turned around to have a last look at them. My mother didn't get up. They were quietly watching me leave. My father gave me a hug, his eyes full of tears. I didn't want them to come to the train station. It was easier if I left alone. The oppressive silence in the room was charged with anxiety. My mother's face frozen in time was watching me leave, without words. For a second I looked into her green eyes. They were glossy, cold and confused. Deep lines on her forehead gave her an expression of sadness and grief. That image will stay with me forever.

"If everything goes well," I said, "I'll send you a postcard as soon as I get to Italy."

"I hope to hear from you soon," my aunt said.

Phillip helped me with the small suitcase where Mother packed all kinds of useless things among which a yellow velvet gown and a lace evening dress. I had some franks hidden in the lining of my jacket. Foreign currency was difficult to obtain and dangerous to possess. I opened the door and stepped out into the dark evening.

After putting the luggage into the trunk of the cab, Phillip grabbed my arm.

"Anna I need to talk to you, it's something important!"

"Ride with me to the train station, we can talk in the cab."

"No," he said, "it's not a good idea to be seen together at the train station. Let's go for a walk."

"We'll be back in a minute, please wait," I told the cab driver and we walked up the street.

"In a month I'll be in Paris," Phillip said.

"I can't believe it. How come you didn't tell me?"

"Nobody knows it yet. I'll write you as soon as I get there, but please send me a note when you arrive in Italy. Don't use my name. When you write to your parents refer to me as Louis."

"I will, don't worry . . . It's easier to leave knowing that I'll see you again."

"You'll join me in Paris as soon as we can. Please, be very careful and ask for 'political asylum' when you get to Italy. Those are the magic words, don't forget."

"Of course I won't forget. See you soon," I said and squeezed his hand tightly. The cab driver was getting impatient and started honking his horn.

"I have to go Philip." I ran to the cab. "Please take me to the train station."

As the cab turned the corner, I looked at the small two-story house with wild rose bushes growing over the old wooden fence. The front door was open. I can still see my father standing there watching me. He was a small man with sad eyes, thick eyebrows and wrinkles on his forehead. He always had a suntan from spending a lot of time outdoors. My father was an artist. He painted religious frescos in churches and most of the time lived in small villages or monasteries where he worked on his projects. Those projects would usually last for a year or more. During my vacation, Mother and I would join him for the entire summer. As the cab turned around the corner, I was saddened not having had the opportunity to get to know him better and learn more about his life. He never talked about his past.

We drove by a long brick wall of a large stadium where outdoor movies were projected on a big screen every Saturday evening. From my window I could hear the sounds and see the blurry images. I would spend hours looking at the fuzzy shapes from faraway, wishing I could be there.

We turned right and drove by my grandmother's house. For the first six years of my life Mother, Father and I, Aunt, Grandmother and many cats and dogs, lived in that small two bedrooms house. My grandmother and aunt resented my presence in that over-crowded dwelling. They didn't try to make me feel welcome.

I loved the animals, especially the cats. Muki was a big, gray tiger cat. He let me play with him watching me lovingly with his big, yellow eyes. He had a toy bed with embroidered pink sheets and little pillows. Sometimes he wore a white hat left over from an old doll with holes for his ears. He looked funny with his big ears sticking out. Loving every minute and purring loudly, he slept in the little bed with his tail hanging out, sometimes waving it when he had a bad dream. Muki followed me everywhere. Often I gave him chunks of meat from my plate. One day, I came home from playing on the street and found Muki stretched on the floor in front of my door, dead with foam around his mouth. He had been poisoned. I held him in my arms crying hysterically and didn't want to let go. My aunt forcefully pulled him away. His true friendship I will never forget.

"Where are you traveling Comrade?" the cab driver asked.

"In vacation to Yugoslavia," I said.

"Are you a student?"

"I just finished High School. It is a good time to take a break."

"Where do you want me to take you the front or back of the station?"

"I don't know," I said, "take me to the front."

"I am sure you'll have a great vacation," he said. "I wish I was the one going to Yugoslavia."

"Come with me," I smiled . . . It was a long ride to the Station. I lit a cigarette. "Would you like a cigarette?"

"Yes," he said.

"Good cigarettes, where did you get them?"

"From a friend, they're American."

"May I have another one please?"

"Here," I said, "have a couple. I've got plenty." I had a whole carton of Pall Mall my favorite cigarettes in my green army backpack. I inhaled the smoke deep into my lungs. Instantly a numbing sensation spread over my brain. It was fine, because I didn't want to feel anything.

We arrived at the train station, a massive construction built from large slabs of granite. The tracks were covered with an old glass roof and the missing panels replaced by plywood boards. An inconspicuous door led to the only restaurant open all night in the entire city. That reminded me of my sixteenth birthday.

My parents were away and I decided to have a big party. There was wine in the cellar brought by my father from the village where he worked. Everybody came with bottles of vodka, cognac and wine. Loud Rock 'n' Roll music was playing on a tape recorder as big as a suitcase. The tapes were about six inches wide. Every now and then I had to shut it off, when overheated and when it was emanating a strong smell of burned oil. That night I invited everybody I knew and their friends. Someone brought me a bottle of gin. I loved gin, and drank more than half of the bottle. Around one o'clock in the morning

I collapsed. A couple of guys dragged me to my bed. There was a woman doctor at the party. When I started to pull the blankets over my body, I remembered her saying, 'If she pulls the covers over her, she is out of danger'.

Suddenly there was a big commotion downstairs. "Your father just came home!" somebody yelled, shaking me vigorously. The news instantly sobered me up. Everyone was astounded by my miraculous recovery. They were afraid not knowing how my father would react. He wished me 'Happy Birthday' and asked everybody to join him to the restaurant by the train station for a late dinner. Most of us went and continued the party until daylight. My father was unpredictable and I never knew what to expect from him.

I stopped in front of the restaurant, turned around and went inside to have a last look. It was noisy and full of people. On my way out I reached into the back-pack for my ticket. I could see the train behind a multitude of people, some sitting on their suitcases, others carrying baskets on top of their heads, children running and screaming and many military men dressed in long kaki coats patrolling back and forth. On the international platform nobody could pass through to the gate without a ticket. At the entrance, a man dressed in railroad uniform was checking the tickets and two soldiers were standing next to him. I showed them my ticket. The railroad man looked me up and down and made a vague gesture for me to pass through.

I climbed aboard and walked from one compartment to another until I found a window seat. It was an old train with benches covered in dark blue velvet and matching curtains. After I put my suitcase up on the shelf, I noticed a handsome young man seated right across from me. He had longish hair with dark skin and brilliant blue eyes. I was trying not to look at him so I opened the curtains watching the busy station with people rushing everywhere. The train filled up with many passengers standing in the corridors loaded with baskets, packages and suitcases. I was lucky to find such a good seat. I could sense him watching me and turned around to face him. He smiled.

"Good evening, I'm Lorenzo. What's your name?"

"Anna . . . You have an accent," I said, "where are you from?"

"Italy, a small town near Roma. My grandmother was from Romania."

"Unfortunately I don't speak Italian, but you speak Romanian quiet well."

"Well, just a little Romanian," he smiled. "Where are you going?"

I was startled for a moment and didn't know what to say. "I am going . . . on vacation to Ljubljana."

"How old are you, if you don't mind me asking?"

"Nineteen," I said "how about you, where are you going?"

"I traveled through East Europe and I am going back home."

"Italy must be a beautiful country."

"Come and visit, my parents have a big house. They used to tell me to marry a Romanian girl."

"Thank you for the invitation," I said, "but I don't think I am ready to get married yet."

"See, you have a beautiful smile," he laughed.

"Seriously now, it's not so easy to travel to Italy. Only a few people can get a visa."

"I know," he said, "what a shame."

I kept quiet knowing better than to start a political conversation in front of everybody. The train began to move so slow that I could hardly feel it. When I looked out the window, I was under the impression that the train from across the platform was moving. Soon, when we picked up more speed I realized it was us moving faster and faster. For a moment I panicked.

"Anna you're all right?" Lorenzo asked. "You look so pale."

"I'm not feeling well, I have a cold."

"Would you like some hot café au lait, maybe?"

"I didn't know they serve café au lait in this train."

"In the international trains they do. I traveled a lot in local trains too, but this is different."

"Thanks, it's nice of you."

"We Italians are the friendliest people in the World," he said.

"And modest too," I smiled.

"I'll be right back." He disappeared into the crowded hallway.

Suddenly I felt alone in a compartment full of people. I sensed their eyes scrutinizing me and turned my head toward the window. We were still traveling through the suburbs of Bucharest, with smaller houses and farther apart from each other. The telephone poles were following the train tracks. Soon everything was dark except for the lights projected on the ground by the speeding train. All I could see were silhouettes of telephone poles rushing into the night. I felt dizzy and put my head down. The blood rushed into my head and I started to see sparks of light. Soon they disappeared and I lit a cigarette. Lorenzo came back bringing a tray with two big cups and few slices of poppy seed cake, a Romanian specialty. I was happy to see him.

"Thank you Lorenzo, you shouldn't have."

"It's my pleasure," he said. "Anna, pull out the table please." "Of course," I said, pulling the folded wooden table from under the window. He gently placed the tray on it.

"Why do you smoke those cigarettes? They're so strong." He seemed displeased.

"I like them strong."

"You're a tough girl," he smiled and handed me one of the cups.

The hot coffee with a lot of milk was relaxing, and suddenly I felt very tired.

"Lorenzo, I don't think I'll be great company. I can't keep my eyes open."

"It's all right," Lorenzo said, "I'll watch over your things."

My mind was drifting. I thought about Alexander, my secret love. When lonely, I always felt him close by. The thought of never seeing him again brought tears to my eyes. Somehow Lorenzo reminded me of him.

CHAPTER 2

ALEXANDER

I remembered the magical effect Alexander had on me the day we met. He was a painter and one of my father's students. I was about twelve years old. Mother and I went to visit my father in a small village where he was restoring the frescos of an old medieval monastery. The church was still functioning, but the monastery had been closed since the end of the war. It was a solid building on two levels with very thick walls and rooms lined up on one side of a long dark hallway. The worn out stairs going to the second level were carved from large slabs of stone. The rooms and hallways with vaulted ceilings and brick walls had been painted white sometime ago, but now the paint was chipping off. The monastery formed a U shape around a large courtyard. The church was standing in the center. At the entrance to the courtyard two big towers erected on each side of an old iron gate, witnessed the tumultuous history of the last 300 years. The monastery was built on top of a hill, close to the village. My father showed me four or five empty rooms on the second floor.

"Choose any room you want," he said.

I decided on a corner room. It was bigger than the rest. The room had thick wooden beams under the high ceiling, and narrow windows with brick arches fanning into half circles. A rounded wall gave the room an odd shape. The smooth and uneven stone floors had been finely polished by time.

"This is my room," I said to my father.

"I'll send Isaiah to bring you a bed," he said. In a while Isaiah, one of my father's students, came dragging a metal frame and asked where to put it.

"Over there, close to the door please," I said. "By the way, my name is Anna."

"I think I've met you before when we all stayed at your house in Bucharest, a few summers ago."

"Yes of course," I said embarrassed.

Isaiah brought a thin mattress and put it on top of the frame.

"I'll be right back," he said and ran out the door.

From the window I could see far away the rolling fields melting into a distant blue light. They were spotted by patches of trees and some small houses. The fences were tall so I could only see their slanted roofs. Smoke rising from the chimneys, made me think the inhabitants were cooking or baking bread, unaware that outside their little village a big mysterious world was stretching beyond the horizon.

Isaiah came back bringing a pile of sheets and some blankets. The sheets weaved from soft unbleached cotton didn't match but had beautiful hand embroidered borders. I made the bed and found a crate, using it as an end table. I took two empty bottles from the kitchen and put them in each window with wild flowers. There was no electricity and the old oil lamps that we used, had a mirror to amplify its brightness. In one of the empty rooms, I found an old wooden bench and put it right in front of the window. When Father came by, he was surprised.

"Your room looks very nice," he said.

"It feels like home in here."

"Come to the church, we just cleaned the most beautiful fresco. You must see it."

"Yes," I said all excited, "I'll be right there." I wanted to investigate around the monastery to see what else I could find to put in my room.

"Annie, I have something for you," Father said. I followed him to the other end of the corridor. He pulled a big, iron candleholder from under his bed. It had three arms with intricate metalwork and was very old.

"Here," he said, "I just discovered it today in of one the towers. It's yours if you like it."

"Thank you Father." I took it back to my room and put it on top of the crate at the end of my bed. Sitting on the bench by the window I admired the beautiful room, the old brick walls and the embroidered sheets on the bed. Strangely like in a dream everything seemed so familiar.

A long time ago, I was waiting for my lover in a similar room full of excitement and anticipation for us to be reunited. Could the present be just a repeat of a past experience, or maybe a dream? Everything was not quite the same in the distant past, so hard to pinpoint somewhere beyond my fading memory. I savored that moment of anticipation, and bowed to this imaginary person. "Hello," I said, "you can leave your sword by the door!" . . . Awakened by the sound of my own voice I ran out into the courtyard and stopped in front of the church looking at two thick columns painted with different scenes from the Bible. On the bottom of the left column, I was surprised to see strange scenes depicting hell with devils carrying long forks, torturing little people upside down, pulling naked women by the hair, all surrounded by flames.

Inside the church, the air was always cool no matter how hot the weather. Right under the main tower a wooden scaffold with many levels was rising about thirty feet into the air. Each level had a different ladder going up. I used to climb ladders for as long as I could remember. I climbed without stopping all the way to the top. The first thing I could see was a dirty pair of shoes and soon I was face to face with Alexander. He had a pale aristocratic face, with perfectly chiseled features and deep blue eyes. His mouth was sensual with a dimple in his chin. The disheveled hair and unshaved face added to his bohemian charm. He looked just like the imaginary person I've seen in my room. For a moment I lost my balance and almost fell off the ladder. Luckily I regained it quickly but the scare made my blood rush to my head.

"Annie," my father said, "did you meet Alexander? He's a very talented painter, learning fresco with us."

"I don't think so," I said not being able to take my eyes off him.

"Alexander this is my daughter Anna. She wants to be a painter."

Alexander's face lit up in a faint smile. "It's nice to meet you Anna, what do you like to paint?"

"I don't know," I said, "maybe things that I cannot see." They were all surprised by my answer. So was I.

"She came here to paint," my father said.

"I'd like to see what you paint," Alexander said looking deep into my eyes.

"I'll show you as soon as I get something done, I just got here."

"Look at those beautiful frescos," my father said.

The frescos were remarkable. Each scene was painted in muted colors from a variety of earthly tones, with vibrant accents here and there. The background architecture was skillfully depicted with colorful fabrics covering the roof terraces. Stylized trees and flowers looked like nothing that I have ever seen in nature on this Earth, and personages were dressed in the most beautiful robes with a rich variety of flowery designs. It was an art in itself to depict the folds on those fabrics.

"This is the most beautiful fresco I've ever seen."

"Let's have a toast for the fresco," Father said. "Isaiah, bring some glasses and the wine we received last evening."

"Yes Master," Isaiah said and rushed down the ladder. Father wanted his students to call him Master.

In a short while Isaiah came back carrying a basket with two bottles of wine and a bunch of glasses. My father poured everybody a glass, but only half for me, and we toasted. The wine was delicious, a sweet new wine.

Isaiah and Alexander were good friends. They met in art school and Isaiah came to study with my father a few years ago. He brought Alexander one day to show him what he was doing, but Alexander never left. He refused to go back home. His parents came to get him but they too decided that staying at the monastery was the best thing for Alexander, keeping him off the streets. They drank many more bottles after which Father decided to cook dinner. He was a great cook.

I went back to my room, arms full of paper, paint and other things they had given me and painted a woman on an empty street walking arm in arm with a shadow. One could see the cobblestones through the bluish shadow. That evening I showed them the painting over dinner. They were intrigued.

"You are a painter," Alexander said looking at my painting with a sad expression.

"Who is the shadow?" My father asked.

"I don't know," I said, "When I was little I could always see him, now I don't see him anymore." There was a moment of silence.

"She's got a vivid imagination," Father said.

After dinner I retreated for the night. My room was quite isolated and I was too excited to sleep. Alexander made a deep impression on me. He was a ray of sunshine illuminating my cloudy existence. Maybe I should have done something about it, let him know how much I cared . . . it was too late now.

CHAPTER 3

IN THE TRAIN

Swayed by the rhythmical movement of the train I drifted into a deep sleep. When I woke up, Lorenzo was dozing off. For a moment I was afraid that my luggage disappeared, but everything was in its proper place. I looked at my watch and two hours had passed. When I stood up to stretch my body, Lorenzo opened his eyes.

"Anna, you're up. You slept for a long time."

"You slept too," I smiled.

"No," he said defensively, "I was just thinking."

"Lorenzo I feel so stiff, please accompany me for a walk."

"Sure," he said "why not?"

An old lady sitting by the door was looking at me from under her thick glasses.

"Would you watch my luggage for a few minutes, please?" I asked her. "I want to stretch my legs a little."

"Yes, Comrade, don't worry," she said "you were very tired. I watched you sleep. I wish I could sleep like that."

"I was tired and I have a cold . . . I feel much better now."

"Don't worry," the old lady said, "I'll watch over your luggage."

We went into the narrow corridor and I looked around. There was a group of people a few compartments away smoking, but I didn't think they could hear us.

"Lorenzo, I need to tell you something, but I couldn't tell you in front of all those people. I am planning to escape. I will be crossing the border into Italy."

"Are you crazy? That's too dangerous!"

"I know," I said, "but I am not going back to Romania no matter what."

"Oh, Dio mio," how do you think you can get away with it?"

"Maybe I made a mistake by telling you. My mother was right when she said I couldn't thrust anybody."

"It's up to you, but since I am Italian what interest would I have to keep you from escaping? I would be happy if you end up in Italy. Please, you can definitely thrust me on this one."

"Well . . . by the Yugoslavian border close to Trieste, the border patrols are cooperating to let people escape into Italy. That's how so many Yugoslavs are able to cross the border. It's true. I know this from a good source."

"I don't know," Lorenzo said, "maybe some of the guards are humane enough to let people escape, but I am sure not all of them. If they get caught they can go to jail and you know, if they catch you, you go right back to some jail in Romania!"

"Lorenzo you don't understand, I hated my life at home! I am not going back there. Maybe I'll be better off in jail!"

"Oh, that's ridiculous," Lorenzo said very worried. "I've heard a lot of bad things about jails in communist countries. They torture people, you know."

"I am not worried about that. Why would they torture me? I am not a spy."

"I should hope not," Lorenzo smiled. "Let's go to the restaurant. I am hungry and we'll talk some more." We started walking through the long corridor toward the restaurant.

"Lorenzo," I said "it's better if we don't talk about this at the restaurant. They could listen to everything we say."

"I doubt that, but if it makes you feel better, we'll talk about something else."

It was an old fashioned restaurant with benches and windows covered in dark blue velvet showing signs of wear and tear. The tables were covered in white tablecloths and the napkins starched and well ironed. In overall everything looked clean and inviting. We sat facing each other. A waiter handed us a menu written in Yugoslavian and Russian. We both looked at the menu but couldn't understand anything. He asked us in perfect French if we were ready to order. I ordered in French for both of us.

"What did you order?" Lorenzo asked.

"You'll see. It's a surprise."

"I like surprises," he smiled.

The waiter came back bringing a hot metal plate with fried Swiss cheese covered in bread crumbs, a basket of bread, butter and a small bottle of wine.

"The Swiss cheese is my favorite," Lorenzo said.

"Mine too. You can eat this in every train in Romania."

"I know it's delicious."

"How do you like the wine?"

"Everything is great!"

"Oh, I don't know if I believe you."

"You make everything wonderful."

"It must be the wine," I said.

After dinner we went back to the compartment. The lights were off and most passengers asleep. The old woman by the door was still awake.

"I watched your luggage," she said.

"Thank you so much," Lorenzo said. "Wait here," he told me and ran back to the restaurant. Soon, he returned with a small box of fried cheese for the old lady. At first she said "No, no," but then she thanked us and started to eat the cheese with a smile, savoring each bite.

We sat quietly waiting for something to happen but everything was calm except for the rhythmical, monotonous sound of wheels rubbing against the metal tracks. The train began to slow down and then stopped. It was dark outside and I couldn't see much, except for a shabby building that looked like a warehouse. Some of the passengers started to search for their passports. I assumed we were at the border.

Two men dressed in military outfits opened the door and began to check our passports. They carefully examined each passport wishing each passenger a 'Safe Trip'. They looked like they had just woken up. I handed them my passport trying to look calm but my hands were shaking. I smiled to cover up my anxiety even if I knew that everything was in order. After checking my passport they gave it back to me without any problems and left whishing us a 'Good Trip'. We heard a commotion down the corridor. The two officers were dragging a young man down the hall. Nobody paid any attention. I looked at Lorenzo but we didn't say anything. The train began to move and Lorenzo squeezed my hand with a sigh of relief. Everyone in the compartment got comfortable and went back to sleep. Propping my head against the soft curtain I closed my eyes.

"I'll wake you up when we get to Ljubljana," Lorenzo said. "We are in Yugoslavia now!"

I took a deep breath, finally being able to relax for a while. Going in and out of sleep, time seemed to be standing still. Lorenzo woke me up by gently stroking my hair.

"Anna, it's time to wake up," He whispered in my ear, "we'll be arriving soon."

"Did I sleep all this time?"

"Don't worry," he said, "I watched over you. You are beautiful when you sleep."

"Thank you, Lorenzo, someday I'll return the favor." I carefully put my things in the backpack making sure that I don't forget anything, when the train came to a halt.

CHAPTER 4

LJUBLJANA

We arrived in Ljubljana. I was ready to say good bye to Lorenzo when he whispered:

"I am getting off with you. I can't leave you here alone."

"I don't know what to say Lorenzo, are you sure?"

"I want to help. Let me get the luggage for you, please."

"I don't know if this is a good idea," I said. All eyes were watching us and I was afraid that somebody would report me to the authorities. But of course they didn't know who I was. It was an irrational fear . . . or maybe not.

"It's a very good idea," Lorenzo said with a faint smile from the corner of his mouth. He grabbed my suitcase as well as his and started walking towards the door. I could feel everybody's intrigued looks. At the door I turned around and with a forced smile I wished them 'Bon Voyage'.

The old lady seated by the door grabbed my hand and said "Good Bye," with a worried voice. She was wearing a black scarf tied under her chin. Her face was full of wrinkles and her skin leathery and dark from the sun. She was probably a peasant that worked all her life in the open air on the fields. I grabbed her hand.

"Thank you and good luck to you, too!" Her hand was rough and strong in spite of her age.

Lorenzo opened the door. "Come-on Anna we must hurry! The train will take off any minute now."

We rushed through the crowded corridor and got off just in time. The train started to move slowly and then picked up speed and disappeared. On the street in front of the station a few cabs were parked waiting for customers. We got into a cab and Lorenzo asked the driver to take us to an international hotel. The cab driver mumbled something and had some trouble getting the engine started. The car was moving slowly shaking and screeching every time it hit a pothole. Cabs in Yugoslavia were just as bad as the cabs in Romania.

"Let's leave the luggage at the hotel and I'll take you to dinner," Lorenzo said.

"Thanks, I am really hungry."

"By the way, I am going to tell them at the hotel that we're married."

I smiled giving him a kiss on the chick, "Good idea." He grabbed my shoulder and kissed me on the mouth. My whole body warmed up and for a moment I felt better.

"That felt good," I said and Lorenzo laughed.

The cab pulled in front of a massive old building constructed maybe in the thirties or forties. It was brightly lit and we walked into a large lobby with high ceilings and columns decorated with bas-reliefs of stylized leaves gilded in gold. In the back of the lobby a man dressed in a blue jacket was standing behind a huge mahogany desk waxed to a perfect shine. Groups of plush chairs and coffee tables were symmetrically arranged around the room. In the middle of the lobby a large crystal chandelier was hanging from the high vaulted ceiling. The windows were covered with heavy curtains. The lobby was impressive and I felt out of place. Lorenzo went to the desk and I sat on one of those big chairs sinking into the soft velvet. In a few minutes he came back dangling a key on a long cupper chain.

"Let's take the luggage to the room," Lorenzo said smiling.

We walked down a long hallway on the dark blue carpet. The walls were covered with fabric, and crystal sconces were illuminating the way. We entered a large bedroom.

"I told him we're married," Lorenzo said.

"I know . . . what if he asked for my passport?"

"I took a chance."

"I bet you've done this before," I said jokingly.

He became serious. "Anna this is a very unusual situation, don't you think?"

"Let's go and eat, I am not feeling too well."

"You'll feel better after a good dinner. By the way, how are we going to share the bed?" Lorenzo said kissing my hand.

"I suppose you'll sleep on the floor."

He looked like a hurt puppy. "I swear I'll sleep on the edge of the bed and I'm not going to touch you. It's an enormous bed."

"I trust you," I said smiling and went into the small bathroom to wash my face. I didn't recognize myself. I was very pale and had big circles under my eyes. I probably never looked so bad. I didn't understand what Lorenzo could see in me. After some lipstick and makeup I looked more like myself.

"Oh Signorina, you look ravishing."

"Liar," I said, "let's go." We were both hungry.

Suddenly everything felt like a dream. I began questioning the reality of my situation expecting any minute to wake up in my room back in Romania. Aware that I could never turn back I had to be focused on the present. We went downstairs to the restaurant. It was an old fashioned room with tables covered in red cloth touching the floor, and white plate mats. Each table was set for dinner. The plates were white with a thin golden trim, and masterfully folded napkins embellishing the thick crystal glasses like red flowers.

"Please don't talk about my escape here or anywhere in the hotel. We'll go for a walk after dinner to talk," I whispered to Lorenzo.

"I think you're exaggerating, but it's up to you Anna, maybe you know better."

"You don't take me seriously," I said.

"Oh, I do. What if I didn't sit in front of you in the train, if we never met?"

"Lorenzo, let's talk about this another time."

"Where would you like to sit?" He asked.

"Anywhere, I don't care."

He took my hand and we walked to a table by the window. "How about this table?" he pulled a chair for me and sat across the large table.

I was feeling very self-conscious and uncomfortable.

"Please sit next to me," I said.

He sat in the chair next to me holding my hand. "Feeling better now?" he asked smiling.

"Yes, thank you, I guess I need you close to me tonight," I said embarrassed.

"Let me order this time," he said.

The waiter spoke Italian. We had steak with fried potatoes and a salad.

"How did you know this was my favorite food?"

"Everybody likes steak and fried potatoes in Romania."

"I thought you were psychic."

"Maybe I am. Would that scare you?"

"I am not afraid of you," I smiled, "you don't look like a dangerous man."

"Appearances can deceive," he said.

"Not this time, I trust my intuition."

"Anna, let's go for a walk. We need to talk." We walked in silence for a while. Many cabs lined up in front of the hotel. The streets were empty.

"Are you sure you want to cross the border? You know, you are taking a big chance."

"I am very sure," I said. "Nothing will stop me from trying! I want to start my life over, I want a new life."

"It might not turn out as good as you think," he said.

"Why are you trying to discourage me? Of course I am scared, but I have a good plan."

"Those plans don't always work out," Lorenzo said.

"Lorenzo, how do you know this won't work?"

"I am older than you, I have more experience."

"Mister knows it all. Please help me! I never asked anybody for help. At home they always told me what to do."

"You didn't turn out that bad."

"I am not as good as you think. You just don't know me," I said.

"What do you want me to do?" He asked, suddenly becoming serious.

"You need to get me a train ticket to Italy," I said in a soft voice.

"What?"

"Yes, that's what I said. I need a train ticket to Italy."

"I don't know," Lorenzo said. "I am afraid for you."

"Maybe was better if I kept my mouth shut! I don't know why I felt I could trust you?"

"You can trust me, but I want you to be safe."

"Look, I am not going back home! I will try to escape with or without your help. Nothing will make me change my mind, nothing!"

"Okay Anna, I'll get you a ticket. I just wanted to make sure you were willing to take the risk. It's up to you, it's your life."

"Thank you Lorenzo, I'll never forget this." I was tired and cold. "Let's go back and get some rest," I said. He took off his jacket and draped it over my shoulders. "Please don't forget to get the tickets tomorrow morning."

"Of course, don't worry about anything. Things will work out, they always do."

"Not in my life."

"Anna you're so young, you have the whole life in front of you. You can do anything you want."

"Some of us don't have many choices."

"Don't talk like that, you're too young!"

"What age has to do with anything? I am nineteen, it's not that young."

"Believe me I know what I am talking about."

"I hope you're right." We went back to our room. "Lorenzo, you sleep on the floor."

"I don't want to sleep on the floor," He said defensively.

"Okay, but don't come to my side of the bed."

"I'll stay on my side if you stay on yours, I promise."

"You're a good man."

"I am not that good," he said facing me. We locked in a tight embrace that brought me into the present moment. I lay in bed with all my clothes on. He did too next to me. I could feel the heat of his body attracting me like a magnet. I moved closer and hugged him tightly. For a while, we both forgot ourselves. I slept in his arms the whole night with my head on his chest trying not to think about the future. This was the last night where everything was predictable. From then on the whole future was a question mark. I was going to take a dive into the unknown and at this point, nothing could to stop me. My only touch with reality was feeling Lorenzo's warm body.

Next day when I opened my eyes I didn't know where I was. Slowly the reality began to set in and I felt a knot in the pit of my stomach. Lorenzo was gone. I found a note on his pillow: 'Anna I went to get the tickets. I did not want to wake you up. Wait for me. I will be back in an hour.' The note was not signed. I tried to go back to sleep when Lorenzo returned.

"I have the tickets," he said catching his breath, "and I brought us some lunch from the market. We have cheese, fresh tomatoes and fresh bread, and hot tea for you."

"Thank you Lorenzo. You're an angel, my guardian angel."

"Nobody called me an angel before."

"There is a first time for everything."

After lunch Lorenzo touched my forehead with his lips.

"Anna, you seem feverish. Why don't you sleep in the afternoon and I'll go out to see the city by myself. I hope you don't mind."

"Of course I don't mind, you did so much for me. I'd like to go with you, but I really need to rest. Sorry for being such a bad companion."

"You are the best thing that happened to me in a long time," he said smiling.

Lorenzo left and I took a hot shower, got dressed and went back to bed with all my clothes on. I closed my eyes and fell into a deep sleep. I had a strange dream. In my dream I was part of a ski competition. It was happening in a concentration camp. There were three of us. The winner was allowed to survive and the losers were to be tortured to death. After a long slalom downhill, I won the competition. Suddenly I found myself in an airport in front of a huge screen that was playing a movie about the future. I saw myself approaching a city of the future covered by an enormous dome of glass brightly lit by millions of lights. I landed on a street corner. It was a busy intersection. All the cars were small, box like, basically a chair in a box on wheels.

A noise woke me up. It was Lorenzo storming in from his escapade. "We have to go right now," he said, "the train leaves in forty-five minutes!"

"Oh, my God, I'll be ready in a minute!" I jumped out of bed feeling dizzy and packed all my things in a hurry.

"Are you ready?" He anxiously asked.

"Yes, let's go!" I said looking around the room to see if I forgot anything. We rushed out. The cab was waiting in front of the hotel and took us to the train station. We were about fifteen minutes early and sat on a bench impatiently waiting. Lorenzo was nervous.

"I got you a ticket to Trieste. If they stop you at the border tell them that you wanted to visit Trieste and didn't know you needed a visa. Maybe they'll buy it." I took the ticket and put it in my wallet. He also gave me some liras. "That's all I have," he said, "hide it well until we get to Italy."

"Thank you Lorenzo," I took the money and put it in my sock.

"Just in case we get separated here is my phone number," he handed me a piece of paper which I carefully folded and put it in my wallet.

"Thank you Lorenzo for thinking of everything. Honestly, I don't know what I'd do without you?"

"There is the train." Lorenzo said.

We approached the edge of the platform and he helped me with my luggage. In the train, we walked for a good while looking for two seats next to each other. Finally, we found two seats in a compartment at the end of the train. All eyes were on us and I said: "Hello!"

"Buonna sera," Lorenzo said smiling.

In this train people looked much cleaner and they were better dressed. A few smiled and said hello. We sat in silence. Neither of us wanted to talk. I didn't know what to say to him. So much had happened between us, but in a way we were strangers. I did not know anything about his life, and he didn't know much about mine. The more I was trying to find something to say, my mind become a blank. I was concerned about what people would think about us. I wanted us to appear to them just like a regular couple, but I couldn't say anything about the little we had in common. The tension between us was growing. Lorenzo realized my dilemma.

"How are you feeling?"

"Better," I said. "I really needed the rest. Where did you go?"

"I went to a museum."

Lorenzo began to realize the dangerous situation I was in and didn't know how to deal with it. We both sat quietly neither of us being able to carry on a conversation. Looking out the window I couldn't see anything but darkness. Faint lights of scattered villages appeared once in a while. I couldn't tell how much time went by. I was approaching a point where my life could take a bad turn. There was no going back now and Lorenzo knew that. He grabbed my hand holding it tightly.

Chapter 5

AT THE BORDER

The train began to slow down and soon came to a stop. "The Yugoslavian border," Lorenzo said with apprehension.

I sat motionless trying not to disturb the direction my destiny was taking. Two men dressed in army uniforms opened the compartment door and asked for our passports. My hands were shaking. One of them looked at me while I pulled my passport from my backpack and handed it to him. He noticed that I was trembling. He looked at my passport and hesitated for some time, then showed it to the other man. They both looked at the passport again and looked around the compartment. Finally he closed it, handing it to me with a smile. I was shaking like a leaf, waiting for them to grab me, but nothing happened. They left and closed the door behind. Lorenzo looked scared. I knew that I wasn't out of the woods until we were on Italian soil. It took another half an hour for the train to start moving.

Lorenzo grabbed my hand. "We'll be home soon," he said.

I squeezed his hand but couldn't say a word. The train didn't pick up speed. It was moving slowly in between the two borders. I was immobilized with fear, expecting anytime to be arrested and returned to Romania, where prisons were completely secret. No one knew their exact location and people would disappear in the middle of the night, never to be heard from again. There was no trial or a proper defense legal system.

During the Second World War, two brothers, friends of my family were taken prisoners, one by the Germans and the other one by the Russians. The brother from Germany lost his legs and was in a wheelchair. The brother from Russia ended up in Siberia. He was submerged in icy cold water and left there to freeze to death. Against all odds they survived and after twenty years were reunited. The thought that I would be put in jail for trying to escape was chilling. The train was moving so slow, I didn't realize when it stopped in the middle of nowhere.

"Why are we stopping?" I asked Lorenzo.

"It must be the Italian Border," he whispered in my ear, "hang in there, and be strong."

We waited in silence for a very long time. Two men appeared at the door and asked for our passports. I handed my passport with shaky hands. They looked at it for a long time talking to each other and left, taking my passport.

"It doesn't look good," I said to Lorenzo.

"No," Lorenzo said."

One of them came back with an officer. The officer said something to me in Italian. I looked at Lorenzo. He talked to them in Italian and I couldn't understand anything. He looked worried, pulled my luggage off the shelf and handed it to me.

"They told me you have to go back," Lorenzo whispered.

"What? I am not going back! They'll put me in jail in Romania."

"They want you to follow them off the train," Lorenzo said. "I can't go with you, they won't let me. Call me if you need to."

"I will . . . Good bye Lorenzo, I hope to see you soon."

"Andiamo," The officer said.

I took my luggage and the backpack and followed them through the crowded corridor. Everyone was watching the scene. I got off the train. It was completely dark. They helped me across the tracks with a small lantern illuminating the way that lead to a barrack. Inside the dimly lit room with couple of old metal desks, some chairs and shelves full of folders an older officer was seated at a desk watching me behind a pair of thick glasses. His gray hair was parted to the side and a small mustache gave him an austere look.

"Do you speak Italian?" He asked me.

"No." I said.

"How about French?"

"Oui" I said, "Je parle un petit peux."

"Most Rumanians speak French. I wonder why?" He said, in broken French. "You must go back, Segnorina. You do not have a visa! There is a train going to Romania in one hour."

"I am not going back," I said, "I want to stay here!"

"Segnorina," he said, "you cannot stay here! No! You must go back!" He was gesticulating with both hands.

"I am requesting political asylum," I said.

Suddenly he started to smile and changed his attitude completely.

33

"Why didn't you say so from the beginning?"

They gave me some forms to fill out and offered me a cup of coffee. I did the best I could. After some time I heard a car approaching. I was told me to follow them. A flashlight was pointing at the car. It was a Jeep and two officers got off and put my luggage in the back. They sat me next to one of the officers. I had no idea where they were taking me. We drove for about an hour. It was so dark that I couldn't see anything except the road in front of us illuminated by the headlights. We were in a mountainous terrain and the Jeep was taking many turns. As I was getting used to the darkness I could distinguish silhouettes of trees by the side of the road, black phantoms rushing into the night. The Jeep stopped by a brick wall with barbed wire on top. A large gate opened and we drove in.

They took me up the steps into an old, poorly maintained building. There was a metal door with a small opening and iron bars going across. I couldn't understand a word of Italian. They put my luggage inside the room, and locked the door behind. It was a good size room brightly lit, with about twenty beds, all empty. I was the only one there. The windows facing an alleyway had thick metal bars, so close together that only a cat could squeeze through. The beds had no sheets or blankets, just empty mattresses. Everything seemed like a bad dream. I was feeling feverish and exhausted and wasn't sure if I was hallucinating. The room had no light switch so the lights stayed on the whole night. I rolled up my jacket and put it under my head on top of the mattress. It was warm in the room so that gave me a sense of comfort and I fell asleep.

CHAPTER 6

TRIESTE

The following morning I opened my eyes and didn't know where I was. Everything seemed unreal. I sat at the edge of the bed waiting for someone to come. An officer finally came to the door. I conveyed to him that I was ill with a fever. He left and soon returned with a woman guardian. She helped me with my luggage and took me to the infirmary. It was a small office full of boxes of medicine on the shelves. A very young nurse greeted me with a smile. She took my temperature and gave me a shot and some pills. With a full infirmary, the only bed available was in the children's section. Most of them were very young. The nurse gave me a small plastic purse with soap, toothbrush and toothpaste, talc powder and a thin, cotton blue gown. Finally I was able to take a shower. The hot water felt good on my tired body. I put on the blue gown and my body smelled fresh like talcum powder. In spite the noise made by the children I was able to fall asleep and felt safe.

When I woke up at lunchtime, there was a tray by my bed with a bowl of vegetables soup, bread and some small cubes of cheese. I was famished and the food tasted really good. A woman walked in and addressed me in Romanian.

"Hi, my name is Mona. They told me you came in last night. I am so sorry you're ill, what's wrong?"

I was happy to hear someone speaking my language. Mona was older, maybe about twenty-five years or so. She had dark hair and big, black eyes. She was wearing a red sweater and brown corduroy pants. Tall and slender, she was moving slowly like sleepwalking. Her skin was dark and there were big, dark circles under her eyes.

"Hi Mona," I said, "I'm Anna. I arrived here late last night, and no one could tell me what's going on. This looks like a prison, why am I here?"

"Oh my dear, it's not a real prison. It's a camp for refugees. Everybody like you and me coming from a communist country, crossing the border illegally is brought here. We stay here for a month."

"One month, you must be kidding. I have to get out of here as soon as possible. I want to join my relatives in Switzerland."

"Unfortunately, those are the rules. They have to investigate your case. Let's say, they want to know if your passport is real, or if you have committed any crimes back in Romania. It takes time, Italians are very slow. Do not think about anything. You are alive, and that's the most important thing. Just rest and get better."

"For how long you've been here?" I asked her.

"Three month."

"Why so long?"

"There were some complications and I had to start the emigration process from the beginning. I wanted to go to England. I had a boyfriend there but he changed his mind about sponsoring me. Now I applied for Australia. Everybody says they don't have enough women over there. It's easy to get a husband and I want to get married."

"Oh," I said, "there must be a way I can get out of here. I am going to write to my relatives in Switzerland to get me out of here."

"Just relax," she said, "you need to get better. I'll come back to see you again and we'll talk more about everything."

The nurse walked in pushing a cart with coffee, milk, bread and small cubes of butter and jelly. I took two slices of bread and a handful of jelly.

"The jelly is very good, have some butter with it too," she said putting couple of cubes of butter on my plate. "I have to go now, if you need anything ask for me. Everybody knows me here."

"Bye, Mona, thank you so much for coming. Tell me this is just a nightmare."

"I am afraid it's all very real . . . Eat now, you need the strength."

That night I couldn't sleep. I was thinking about Phillip. Would I ever join him in Paris? I felt utterly alone and couldn't visualize myself living in Paris with Phillip, wondering how much he really cared about me.

Time was going by slowly. I was well taken care of and started to feel better. As my health improved I became more impatient. Medication in Italy was very effective, especially the Aspirin.

One morning the nurse walked in with a big smile on her face.

"Get ready! You are getting out today, you're well now." She handed me the bundle of clothes, my backpack and my luggage. "You can get dressed, and Mona will help you out."

"Molto grazie," I said.

"Good luck to you," the nurse said gently caressing my head.

Mona walked in. "Anna, you're finally better! Come, I'll show you around." She took my small suitcase and my backpack. "That's all you have, such a small suitcase?"

"Yes," I said "and everything in that suitcase is useless stuff. I keep it because it reminds me of home. Maybe I should get rid of all that."

"No, keep it. You might appreciate it later."

"I doubt that."

"Let's go," Mona said and walked out the door. I followed her into the yard.

The large courtyard was surrounded by concrete buildings, two stories high. In front of each building, rectangular patches of grass were enlivening the otherwise dull environment. Over the tall, concrete wall that surrounded the whole camp, one could only see trees on the other side.

In the center of the complex a square building without any windows had a big, red sign above the door spelling the word 'Cantina'. It was sort of a convenience store where one could find delicious mortadella and cheese sandwiches, cappuccino, sodas, and all kinds of sweets and small bottles of Campari. At the same time they sold pens, notebooks, magazines, soap, toothpaste and just about anything essential. At the entrance there was a pinball machine for the sports oriented people.

The Cantina was managed by an older Italian woman with grayish hair pulled back in a bun. She always wore black, shapeless dresses. Living in Trieste she drove every day back and forth between taking care of her three children and attending to the store. Once in a while she employed some of the refugees in exchange for food and drinks.

Cantina was the focal point of the camp where refugees from many Eastern European Countries used to gather. Albanian women were easy to spot. They covered their heads with a scarf and wore dark colored long dresses. On the other hand the Polish women were the most sophisticated.

There was a payphone in the Cantina, and when we walked in I turned to Mona.

"I need to make a phone call, it's very important and I need to change some franks."

"You can change money here, but they give you less than the banks."

"I don't care," I said.

"Give me the money. I'll see what I can do."

She came back with a big stack of paper money, and a handful of coins showing me how to use the telephone. I called Lorenzo and my heart was pumping. The phone rang, but nobody answered. An answering machine picked up and I left a message.

"Thank you Mona, I called an Italian friend. I hope to hear from him soon."

"One thing you need to know about Italian men is that they lie and cheat."

"I hope that some of them are different."

"Don't bet on it," Mona said, "let's go! I'll show you to your room."

Each building had two levels. The dormitories were small with four to six metal beds. Every refugee received two sheets, one blanket and a pillow from the laundry room. Refugees could work doing the laundry for 400 liras per day. For that amount one could get one mortadella sandwich and a cappuccino, or a bar of soap and tooth paste and a small bottle of Campari.

I was sharing the room with Mona, a Polish woman named Erica and another older woman from Romania. Her name was Dina. Erica was very ordinary looking. She had light brown hair, gray eyes and an expressionless face. When she got dressed up to go out with her Italian boyfriend she looked dashing. Her nails were always impeccable as well as her hair. We were never supposed to leave the camp but everybody did. In the back of the camp on top of the fence there was a large hole in the barbed wire through which one could easily climb to the other side. The Italian guards were too lazy to reinforce the rules.

Dina was a short, stout woman with a prominent chest and black curly hair cut very short. She was about forty years old and used to be a journalist in Romania. She was constantly talking about politics and listened to her radio all day long. She was aggressive and blunt and sometimes offensive, but underneath all she had a good hart. Dina became very protective of me, telling me with whom I should or should not talk to.

I spent one month in that prison. It was about half an hour drive from Trieste. A few times I climbed over the fence and hitch hiked a ride to Trieste. I sat in a café and savored a cappuccino with whipped cream. For a few moments I felt like a human being. Other times I used to sit on the grass in the middle of a field of yellow flowers right outside camp, admiring the beautiful mountainous landscape. They were moments when I forgot all my worries.

One morning I was called into the office. The old, Italian man running the camp, politely told me to pack my things because the following morning I had to leave for another refugee camp near Rome called Latina. Every month, a van was transporting refugees from the Trieste camp to Latina. The news filled me with hope. The van was leaving at six in the morning so the evening before I said good bye to my roommates.

The following morning I put all my things in the back of the van and sat next to another woman that looked familiar but I never talked to. She was about forty years old, looking good for her age. She was slender but well built with long red hair, penetrating brown eyes and classical features. Her name was Daniela. She had a husband and two daughters back in Romania. Waiting for her visa to immigrate to Australia, she was planning to take her family out of Romania at a later date. Daniela believed that she could find a rich man in Australia to take care of her.

CHAPTER 7

LATINA

We drove for about six hours and finally arrived in Latina. It was a small town built during Mussolini's regime with lots of concrete buildings, blend looking uninspired architecture. We pulled inside the camp and all of us had to register at the office. I was given a key and the number of my room. Later I picked up a foam mattress, bedding and an aluminum bowl. We were not allowed to have knives in the camp, so I was given a spoon and a fork. My room was all the way in the back. Rows of concrete barracks were lined up on the pavement, with rooms on both sides of a long corridor. The atmosphere was not as friendly as Trieste and the camp much bigger. Some offices were located on the second floor of a small building. The Cantina, a large dining room and a kitchen were on the ground level, and the storage room in the back of the camp.

I tried to get some cleaning supply but the office was closed. Too late for lunch I had to wait until later in the afternoon. I returned to the storage room, where a small man with shaved head and thick eyebrows gave me a bucket and some soap. I had to fight for an extra blanket. After scrubbing the floors and cleaning the only window that opened into the yard, I washed the blankets and dried them in the sun. A blanket went on the bed and the other one on the floor. I could see the sky from the window. It was such a brilliant blue, unlike the pale blue sky that I grew up with. I was restless and decided to go for a walk around the camp and see what was going on.

It was easier to climb out the window than walk through the dark corridor. In the front of the building, shabby looking men were drinking and smoking with women dressed in skimpy outfits. On the way back to my room I picked up an empty bottle from the garbage and some weeds with small white flowers. I sat on the floor looking at the flowers, admiring their unassuming beauty, thinking that people walk by and never notice their existence. I fell asleep on the floor and when I woke up the room was bathed by the moon light. I sat for a long time looking at the shadows on the walls. The warm air against my skin gave me a sense of comfort and again I fell into a deep sleep.

The following morning I called Lorenzo. He owned a small restaurant on the side of the road somewhere close to Rome. The phone rang for a long time. I almost hang up when he answered. At first he didn't recognize my voice.

"It's Anna," I said.

"Oh, Anna," he sounded surprised, "I thought you already left. Are you still in Trieste?"

"No," I said, "I stayed in Trieste for a month. Now I am in a camp near Rome, waiting for my visa. It might take six month or so before I can go anywhere"

"Where exactly are you?"

"Latina, in the Profughi Camp . . ."

"O my God! I know where you are. Latina it's not too far from my restaurant," Lorenzo said and paused . . . "Come and have lunch with me. I'll pick you up."

"Lorenzo," I said, "I can't wait to see you."

"Let's see . . . I am very busy right now, but what about four o'clock?"

"That's good." I had the feeling that something wasn't right.

"When did you arrive?" He asked in a low voice.

"A few days ago, this place is a real dump."

"I know, I know, but, I have to go now," Lorenzo said. "I'll see you later."

I was disappointed hoping that he would invite me to his house but something was definitely wrong. Maybe he was married or had a girlfriend. I was going to find out soon enough.

Back in my room, the sun was projecting the shape of the window on the floor. The conversation with Lorenzo left an uncomfortable residue. Since I left home nothing was turning up the way I planned. Right now I was supposed to be in Switzerland with my relatives. Instead, I was waiting for my visa to immigrate to the United States, in an Italian Refugee Camp that looked worst than a prison. I had no money or any marketable skills, Lorenzo did not seem too happy to hear from me and I couldn't count on him. On top of everything, Phillip found a new girlfriend in Paris and made it very clear that he didn't want me to join him. Thinking about the future made me dizzy and I felt immobilized with fear. I took a deep breath repeating over and over; "Let go of the past, let go of the future, be here now . . ." Slowly the fear diminished and closing my eyes I drifted into a light sleep.

When I opened my eyes it was already 3:00 o'clock. I got dressed and went outside to wait for Lorenzo on the street in front of the camp. A tall concrete wall with barbed wire on top surrounded the courtyard. I had plenty of time and sat on the sidewalk leaning against the wall, watching the cars go by and letting the warmth of the sun melt my anxiety.

"Anna," I heard Lorenzo's voice. When I looked up, he was smiling from behind the wheel of a small, yellow truck. His eyes were bright and he looked healthy and suntanned. "Jump in," he said. I got into the truck and he gave me a hug, kissing me on the chick.

"You didn't think you'll ever see me again," I said. Lorenzo paused a little embarrassed.

"What happened," he asked, "I thought you were in Switzerland by now?"

"No, unfortunately my so called relatives didn't want to sponsor me, and I couldn't immigrate to Switzerland. I applied for a visa to the United States."

Lorenzo straightened his back looking embarrassed. "I am sorry," he said. His voice was cold.

"What's the matter? You are married, aren't you?" He looked at me startled.

"Let's not talk about this. I am happy to see you."

We drove about twenty minutes and I was getting impatient. "Where is the restaurant?"

"Just a few minutes from here, on the highway," he seemed distant and kept silent for a few minutes. "Do you want to work at the restaurant as a waitress?" He asked unexpectedly.

"Sure . . . but I don't have any experience."

"I don't care, it's easy. Our waitress just quit a few weeks ago, I'm having a hard time replacing her."

"Why did she quit?"

"Oh, she found a job closer to home. She was a good waitress."

"I guess it's just my luck." There was a faint smile on the corner of his mouth.

"I need you four hours during lunch, from 11:00 in the morning to 3:00 in the afternoon. I can pay you 2000 lire per day, plus tips and all the food is free. What do you think?"

"Sounds great, when do I start?"

"How about tomorrow morning? I'll pick you up at 10:00 in front of the camp."

"You seem changed. Something happened, I know it."

He turned toward me smiling, his eyes beaming the way I knew him in Yugoslavia.

"You are so pretty," he said, "I hope you'll be happy working at the restaurant."

"Of course, what are you doing tonight? Let's do something!"

"I cannot tonight. I have some things to do."

"Do you have a girlfriend?"

"I don't want to talk about me."

"Oh," I said, "you are a mysterious man."

He smiled and we drove in silence for a while. "I missed you," I whispered. He didn't hear me, looking at some distant point, lost in thoughts.

We were driving along the deep blue sea spotted with boats. The road was carved into the steep rocky mountain and we were looking down at the sea from up high. The beauty of the sea transfixed me. It was a perfect moment and I wondered if I would ever be back on that road again, free of worries. The reality of my situation was daunting. Where was I going to live? How to survive in America . . .

so far away? Suddenly I felt alone in the Universe. He made a sudden turn and we parked on the back of a small building next to a gas station.

"This is my restaurant, how do you like it?" He asked with the excitement of a child.

"Very nice," I said.

"Doesn't look like much, but being next to the gas station it's always busy with lots of truck drivers. They leave very good tips. Let's go inside."

The restaurant was a large room with square tables, checkered tablecloths and baskets of bread on each table. A few customers were drinking cappuccino and Campari. The freshly baked bread emanating a delicious fragrance, made me hungry.

"Ciao Lorenzo, ma que bella raggaza," one of the men said looking at me.

"She is my new waitress," Lorenzo said, "Her name is Anna."

"Ciao Anna," the man said, "you'll do well here, Lorenzo is a generous man."

Not knowing what to say I just smiled. Lorenzo asked him if he wanted something to eat.

"It's almost dinner time," the man said, "I can't eat here tonight. My wife wants me home for dinner. What can I do? You understand Lorenzo, don't you?"

"You better not be late!" Lorenzo said and patted him on the back. "Excuse us. Let's go to the kitchen, Anna." We walked through a swinging door into the kitchen, a rather small room but clean, well lit and well organized.

"Be careful with the door," Lorenzo said, showing me how to open it slowly. "We usually leave this door open. I don't know who closed it."

In the kitchen a corpulent woman was cooking in front of a large cast iron stove.

"Ciao, Bella," she said scrutinizing me from top to bottom. "Comme ti chiama?"

"Anna. I am the new waitress. I hope you don't mind my accent."

"No problem, you speak well enough. Come closer per favore." I went closer and she handed me a spoon with tomato sauce. "Taste this," she said. I took the big wooden spoon from her wrinkled hands and tasted the tomato sauce.

"Delicioso," I said "the best I ever had."

She winked at Lorenzo with a big smile of satisfaction rinsing the spoon and dried her hands on her old apron. That apron was a patchwork of all kinds of materials added over the years by mending all the rips and holes. She noticed me looking at the apron.

"This is my lucky apron," she said, "I've been wearing it for twenty five years. I couldn't cook without it."

"Maria, please show Anna what to do. She doesn't know much about being a waitress. Anna is from Romania and she is staying in the refugee camp."

"Oh, Dio mio, Anna, have a seat over there," she said pointing to a stool behind an old wooden table, in the middle of the kitchen. The tabletop used as a chopping counter over the years was thinner in the center and much thicker around the edges. I sat on the tall stool and watched her throwing all kinds of spices in the sauce.

"I have to go now," Lorenzo said. "I'll be back in half an hour to pick you up. By the way did anybody call?" He asked Maria.

"Your wife called. She asked me to tell you that she was going to Rome to do some shopping and you can eat at the restaurant." Lorenzo looked embarrassed. I was not surprised. I knew that something was going on with him.

"See you later Lorenzo," I said smiling. He ran out the door without looking at me. I knew that something was up because during the month I spent in Trieste, he never called. For a moment I thought of saying something, but I decided to keep everything to myself. Maria noticed that I felt uneasy. I guess she'd seen Lorenzo having affairs with younger girls before.

"Watch out, he is a ladies' man," Maria said, "lots of girls fall in love with him, but he loves his wife and children, he will never leave them."

"Thanks for your advice," I said. "Lorenzo is a very nice man but I already have a boyfriend." She took a breath of relief and handed me a white apron.

"Lorenzo likes his waitresses dressed in black with a white apron. You should wash it often and iron it."

"I don't have an iron," I said. She looked at me surprised. "I don't have anything. I left home with small suitcase full of junk, and that's all I've got."

She came closer and gave me a hug. "Don't worry," she said, "I have lots of children. I will bring you some clothes and an iron tomorrow. Here," she dug into her deep pocket and handed me 500 liras.

"Thank you Maria but I can't take your money. You work very hard for it. It's for your family."

"Take it! Take it," she said stuffing the money into my pocket. "I have extra money. I am a rich lady."

"Thank you," I said and felt like crying. "You have a good heart."

"Don't mention it," she said, "let me show you around." She showed me how to write the orders, where they kept the clean and dirty trays, where to put the dirty dishes and silverware. She was a diligent teacher, repeating everything over and over. She was probably thinking that I couldn't understand Italian as much as I did. Lorenzo was late therefore I helped Maria with cutting vegetables and making the salads. I did take an order from a couple of old tourists. The job was really easy and the tourists gave me a generous tip of 200 liras. I was rinsing some dishes when Lorenzo walked in.

"Sorry I am late," he said and looked at me with an apprehensive expression. "How do you like the job? I hope you're not ready to quit just like the other girl. I need you here!" He had an imploring look in his eyes. That look melted all my anger and disappointment. "Maria," he continued, "do you need anything for tomorrow?"

"Let's see . . . we need zucchini and tomatoes, linguini, milk and potatoes. That's it."

"Would you close up tonight, Maria? I don't think I'll be coming back."

"Si Signore," she said, "I always have to do everything around here!" Lorenzo gave her a hug.

"Maria you're the best," he said looking straight at me, "she runs the restaurant. I would be lost without her." Maria had a big smile. When she smiled with her eyes almost shut on her wrinkled face, she looked like an old cat.

"Are you ready to go?" He asked me.

"Yes, of course," I said, "let me wash my hands and pick up my bag."

I picked up my cloth bag, and hugged her. "Buona notte, Maria, thank you for everything."

"See you tomorrow," she said. "Don't be late!"

We stepped outside. The truck was parked in front of the restaurant. I felt awkward sitting next to Lorenzo.

"Are you hungry?" He asked.

"Yes. Very much so," I said looking straight in front of me to avoid his eyes.

"I'll take you to dinner."

"I know, since your wife is shopping in Rome, you don't have to eat dinner at home," I said with a touch of sarcasm.

"Let's not talk about my wife, please!"

"Sure," I said.

"Please don't be angry with me," he said in a soft voice.

"I am not angry, just wish things were different."

He ran his fingers through my hair. "Your hair is so soft." I closed my eyes feeling his hands caressing my hair and my neck.

"Lorenzo, please pay attention to the road."

"Si, Signorina," he said, but I could see that he was nervous because he started to drive much faster.

We passed Latina, kept on driving south and stopped in front of a little restaurant facing the sea. "What a beautiful sunset," I said. It started to get dark. The sea and the sky bathed in shades of deep reds and pink were breathtaking. Above us, the sky was a brilliant blue. On the terrace, each table had complete privacy being separated by tall bamboo dividers.

"The owner is a good friend of mine," Lorenzo said.

A middle-aged man approached us. He was rather short, with long black hair hanging down to his shoulders.

"Lorenzo, how good to see you!"

"Hi Vincent," Lorenzo said hugging him. "This is Anna, my new waitress."

"Hello Anna, it's nice to meet you," he smiled. "Don't work for him, he is no good! You can work for me anytime."

"It's nice to meet you too," I said. "I am just starting to work for Lorenzo and I know how bad he can be, but I'll keep that in mind."

"See what kind of friends I've got?" Lorenzo said. "They always want everything I have." They both laughed.

"What would you like?" Vincent asked Lorenzo.

"Well . . . What's good tonight?"

"Let's see . . . we have spaghetti with peas and shrimps, green noodles with asparagus, polenta with mushrooms and lamb with tarragon sauce. That's about it. Everything is good but polenta is great. I highly recommend it."

"Anna, what would you like?" Lorenzo asked me excited about the menu.

"I don't know, you order for me please."

"Bene, we'll have the lamb and the polenta. It's all right with you Anna?"

"Too good to be true," I said smiling.

"Make it the same for both of us," Lorenzo said.

"Subito," Vincent said looking at me with a smile, "Lorenzo knows the good things in life." Vincent left and Lorenzo took off his sandals.

"You can walk barefoot in this restaurant. Would you like to dance?" He asked grabbing my wrist.

"I'd love to," I said taking off my flip-flaps.

We walked into a small courtyard. The floors covered with sand felt warm from the heat of the day. Candles were hanging from a grid of beams above. One could see the sky between the wooden beams. The jukebox was playing a slow song and we danced in a long embrace. I was enjoying a great sense of comfort feeling Lorenzo's warm body so close, when a waiter came to tell us that dinner was ready. We continued to dance until the song was over and returned to the table.

The sea was a dark blue with just a pink line across the horizon. I tried to savor each detail of that evening in the bliss of the moment, suspended between past and future. During dinner Lorenzo kept on touching my feet and was completely lost into the moment as well.

It was getting dark and we decided to leave. We started on our way back toward Latina. The sky was illuminated by millions of stars. Lorenzo was driving with one hand, and holding me tight with the other.

"I missed you," he said squeezing my shoulders.

"Lorenzo, you're married," I said.

"Well, you told me that you have a boyfriend, and you'll be joining him in Paris," he said a little irritated.

"It's not the same thing," I said, "and I am not joining him. I am going to New York."

"I am so glad you called," Lorenzo said. "I thought about you a lot but because of my situation it was better if I didn't call you."

"I understand," I said.

"Let's stop for a moment by the sea and sit on the rocks," he said, with his eyes beaming with intensity. I didn't say anything. He stopped the car and we descended some narrow wooden steps to the sea. Big waves were crashing into the rocks at even intervals, projecting white foam high into the air. A mist of sea water was raining over us. We sat on a rock watching the waves appearing and disappearing with the perfection of a clock.

"This is a perfect night," I said pulling Lorenzo close. We lay on the warm rock watching the sky studded with millions of stars. A brilliant star, sliding across the sky left a luminous tail behind.

"When a star falls somebody dies," I said.

"In that case hundreds of stars should be falling every day."

"I believe they are, but too far away for us to see them. I wonder how many people die every day."

"I don't know but we are still alive," Lorenzo said and pulled me closer, holding me in a tight grip. The repetitive sound of the waves was hypnotic. I closed my eyes and was able to let go of everything as I inhaled the cool salty air. There was a moment of complete peace where I thought that time stopped. The waves were crashing into the rocks for millions of years. They were ageless, just like this moment which I hoped would last forever.

Suddenly Lorenzo jumped. "Oh, Dio mio, nine thirty! We must leave right away," he said. It was an abrupt awakening. We rushed, climbing the steep stairs back to the truck. I sat close to Lorenzo. He was driving as crazy as all the other Italians competing with each other. Soon we took a turn toward Latina.

"Will you pick me up tomorrow around ten or so?" I asked.

"I'll pick you up at nine thirty. I have to be there at ten to get everything ready. Oh my God! I forgot to do the shopping. We have to do it tomorrow morning."

We were approaching an intersection and the light just turned. We engaged. A car was coming from the right, speeding, and couldn't stop when the light changed. It was charging toward us. I yelled: "Lorenzo!"

It all happened in an instant. Lorenzo hit the brakes. It was too late and the other car hit us from the side, luckily toward the back of the truck. We both came to a short stop. I hit the windshield but my reflexes were good enough that I was able to put my arm forward and protect my head.

"Are you okay?" Lorenzo asked.

"I think so," I said, "how about you?"

"I think I hurt my leg," he said. In a few minutes the police was there and Lorenzo had to get out of the truck to fill out a police report.

"Are you okay Segnorina?" The officer asked me. "I'll help you get off the truck." He gave me a hand and supported my shoulder.

"I am all right officer, my wrist hurts. Thank God I didn't hurt my head." I shook my body a little to see if everything was in place.

"Do you need to go to a hospital?" the officer asked me.

"No, I am really fine."

Lorenzo's leg was bleeding. "It's just a scratch," he said to the policeman. After we filled out a police report, Lorenzo drove me to the camp. He was quiet and I didn't feel like talking much. It was an uncomfortable silence.

"We are lucky to be alive."

"You better believe it," Lorenzo said. "He came from nowhere and didn't stop at the light. What an idiot! People like that shouldn't be driving! He should go to jail! They should revoke his license!" He was angry. "I just painted the truck. Now it's full of scratches and I have a big dent on the side."

"I am so sorry Lorenzo, at least we are alive." We arrived in front of the camp. It was about eleven o'clock and Lorenzo was very nervous. I didn't know what to say to make him feel better. "It was just bad luck," I said and got off the truck.

"Ciao, Anna," he said in a faint voice and drove away slowly. I watched him disappear around the corner.

Walking into my room, a peaceful feeling was permeating the air. The moonlight shinning through the window was illuminating everything like daylight. I sat on the floor facing the window, thinking about the evening's events, trying to calm down. I was still shaky from the accident and couldn't help thinking that it was a sign from God for both of us.

The following morning Lorenzo didn't show up. Later in the day I called the restaurant.

"What happened?" I asked.

"I am sorry Anna, but you cannot work here. I am so sorry," he said. "The accident appeared in the local newspaper and a friend of my wife called her and told her about it. She became crazy when she found out that I was with a girl in the truck. It's better if we don't see each other for a while."

"I understand, Lorenzo," I said, "I am sorry too."

"I've got to go now, ciao," Lorenzo said and hang up the phone.

I stood by the public phone in the Cantina thinking that my career as a waitress was over before it even started. My relationship with Lorenzo was over as well. At that point Dina walked into the Cantina.

"Where were you last night? I was looking for you."

"Don't ask!" I said.

"That bad?"

"Worst, I met Lorenzo last night. It was a disaster."

"What happened?" She asked worried.

"First, he is married. Second, we had a car accident, and third I lost my job working in his restaurant."

"My God, are you okay, did you get hurt?

"I am fine."

"When did you decide to work in his restaurant?"

"The day before, he asked me to."

"Everything happens for a reason," Dina said with a mischievous look in her eyes. "I was looking for you because I wanted to introduce you to a nice man. Please don't say no. He is a young journalist from Czechoslovakia, a very nice guy. He told me he wants to meet you."

"I don't know, after what happened with Lorenzo, I don't know if I want another boyfriend."

"You can just be friends," Dina said.

"Ye right," I whispered.

"Come, let's go and look for him."

"You go. I don't feel like it. You like him because he is a journalist, like you."

"Maybe that's part of it," Dina laughed, "but he is too young for me."

"I think I'll have a cappuccino and a mortadella sandwich. I am going to splurge. This lady gave me five hundred Liras last night at the restaurant."

"I'll be right back," Dina said.

The mortadella was on a fresh piece of bread and tasted delicious. I was drinking the cappuccino slowly to savor each sip. I took out my notebook from my backpack and started doodling. There was a crowd of men around the pinball machine making a lot of noise. The loudspeaker was playing some Italian songs repeating the same songs over and over. Everywhere, I could hear the same songs.

I tried to block all the noise and concentrate on designing a sculpture where a person could stand inside a box being exposed to specific colors and sounds that would influence their mood. I had done some research on the influence of colors on the human emotions. Philip landed me a book by a German psychologist that had done research on this subject. From a deck of cards of different colors, you had to choose the colors you liked the most, arranging them next to each other. Each color represented a certain emotion. This way he was able to analyze what the person was feeling and reveal his unconscious tendencies. It was an inspiring book, and now I needed something to take my mind off the present.

I was absorbed in my project when Dina came back accompanied by a tall young man on the thin side. His very light blond hair parted on the side was covering his eye. He was constantly running his fingers through his hair pulling it back. Dina waved to me and both came to my table.

"This is Yuri," Dina said.

"Hello," I said

"This is my friend, Anna," Dina Smiled looking intensely into Yuri's eyes.

"Hello Anna, I've seen you around the camp. I'm happy to meet you."

"How long you've been here?' I asked.

"Five month. I am waiting for my visa for Australia. My uncle has a publishing company in Melbourne. I will be joining him soon, I hope."

"How exciting," I said. "If you don't mind, I'll see both of you later. I need to go now."

I needed to be alone and went back to my room. Lying on the floor, I was enjoying my solitude when somebody knocked at my door. When I opened the door a tall, well dressed woman was standing in front of me. She looked so familiar.

"Hi, I know you from somewhere," I said.

"Buon giorno," she said, "my name is Arianna. Dina told me about you. I am from Bucharest . . . you look quite familiar too. Where did you live in Bucharest?" It turned out that we lived close to each other. I remembered her. She worked in a hair salon as a hair dresser and she was a great cosmetician as well. Everyone in the neighborhood knew her. She was also new in Latina but she came from a German camp. Her daughter was still in Romania and Arianna was planning to help her leave the country. She was tall, well built with brown shiny hair and dark, penetrating eyes. She moved gracefully and every man turned their heads to look at her. We instantly became friends. Arianna was always involved with some boyfriend. Men were crazy about her so she did not spend much time in the camp.

Life in the camp was monotonous. I was getting tired of the same minestrone soup and triangles of cheese, every day. I was hungry all the time and didn't have money to buy mortadella (salami) sandwiches from the Cantina. As I was sitting outside, eating my cheese triangles with coffee, a girl approached me and said hello. She was a heavy set girl, with a neat hairdo and perfect makeup.

"My name is Andrea," she said. "Comme te chiama?"

"Anna," I said, "how long have you been here? I've seen you around the camp."

Andrea smiled. She had healthy white teeth and a nice smile. Her hair was chestnut brown with lighter highlights same color as her almost yellow eyes. It made me think of a jaguar or a wild cat. In spite of her weight, her movements were swift and precise.

"I've been here for almost a year," she said.

"How come so long?"

"Well, it's a long story, I come from Cuba."

"Cuba?" I asked in disbelieve. "It's so far away, how did you get here, swim across the ocean?"

She lowered her eyes with a sad smile. "I came in a cargo boat. I was told that the boat was going to California but I ended up in Spain. They were planning to turn me back to Cuba. They wouldn't let me off the boat. In order to get off the boat I drank a considerable amount of laundry detergent. They had to take me to an emergency room on land. They pumped my stomach and I was severely ill for about a week."

"Oh, my God," I said.

"The boat left," she continued, "and they wanted me to take the next boat back to Cuba. I had to wait two weeks. As soon as I felt better I went to the police station and demanded political asylum. There was a problem because Cuba was never part of the agreement signed after the Second World War. My father lives in California and all I wanted was to join him. But instead of California I was in Spain, without a visa or a passport. He sent me some money and advised me to go to Italy and ask for asylum. I had to hitch-hike a ride because I couldn't board a plane without a passport. At the border I hid in the trunk of the car and ended up in Milano where I asked for political asylum and they sent me here almost a year ago. My situation is still unsolved. At least now I don't have to go back to Cuba. They don't seem to find a legal venue for me to immigrate to the United States. My father is trying everything he can."

"God, I would go mad if I had to stay here for a year."

"You get used to it," she said smiling.

"Aren't you hungry? I am hungry all the time. This food is horrible. I am so tired of the same soup and cheese."

"Go to Mr. Lombardi. He is a nice man and likes to help young girls. Tell him that you are sic and need a special diet. Ask for steak and salad, mention that I sent you. He is my friend.

"Thank you Andrea, you're a life saver."

"We have to help each other. You seem like a nice girl. Pay attention to the kind of people you talk to. You'd be surprised how fast some of them take to drugs and prostitution."

"I've noticed," I said, "I'm always careful."

"Better safe than sorry," she said.

"Where is your room?" I asked.

"I am in room 24 right in front of the camp. I work in the office every morning till 12:00. I get paid a little, it helps. You can come by if you want."

"I will, Andrea, you're very kind to me."

"By the way, I know where your room is. It belonged to a Hungarian woman involved in drug dealings. She slept with a gun under her pillow. One night somebody tried to force his way into her room and she shot him in the leg. The carabinieri (police) came and took her away."

"Oh my God, I wonder how safe is for me to stay there?"

"I don't know," Andrea said, "I don't think so, what if somebody comes looking for her?"

"I better find another room."

"There is one empty next to mine," Andrea said. "They don't like it when people switch rooms but you say that your room is all the way in the back, and you're afraid at night."

"I am going straight to the office," I said.

"Good luck," Andrea said, "let me know what happened."

I had no problem switching rooms and began moving my things into the new room. Borrowing a bucket from

Andrea I spent the whole afternoon scrubbing and cleaning. She was impressed. That night I sat on the floor watching the tree in front of my window. It was the first time I got a good night sleep since I arrived in Latina.

The following morning on my way to the Cantina, I ran into Mona. I was so glad to see her. She told me she just started to work in a restaurant in Terracina, a small town by the sea about twenty kilometers south of Latina. She cleaned, cooked, served at tables six days a week from morning to night. She was happy because the pay was good. Mona invited me to visit her in Terracina.

"How can I get there?" I asked.

"Hitch-hike. Remember never get into a car with a man driving alone!"

"I know," I said, "I remember that from Trieste."

She told me that an Italian family that owned a pensione by the beach was looking for a girl to take care of their two children, two young girls. Mona asked if I wanted the job. I thought about it and being sic of the camp I accepted the offer. We decided that I'll be going there at the end of the week to meet the family.

That Saturday I woke up late, dressed in a hurry and ran into the street to hitch-hike a ride to Terracina. When traveling, I kept everything in my pockets and never carried a purse. Few cars went by in the opposite direction. I started to get anxious when a big truck stopped. A young man was driving it. On his way to Napoli he was passing through Terracina. He looked harmless to me so I decided to climb into the truck.

"Ceao," he said, "comme ti chiama?"

"Anna," I said, "e tu?"

"Enzo. Where are you from?"

"From Romania, I am staying in the refugee camp, and you?

"From Rome, I drive this truck transporting olives. Do you like olives?"

"Yes I do, but in the camp we don't get to eat olives very often."

"It's a pity," Enzo said, "Italian olives are the best in the world!"

"I am sure they are," I said.

"How is life in Romania?"

"Not so good, that's why I left."

"I meet many refugees. I drive the truck every week from Rome to Napoli and pick up hitch-hikers. Many of them refugees like you from behind the Iron Curtain. Are you planning to stay in Italy?"

"I really love Italy but I can't get a visa to stay here."

"Why not?"

"I don't have any relatives here or anybody to sponsor me. It's difficult to stay in Italy"

"Where are you planning to go?"

"I think, maybe America. I can emigrate to Sweden, Australia or the United States. Those countries have organized emigration policies, makes it easier to get a visa."

"You speak Italian very well, how about English?"

"No, not really, I don't speak any English."

"Maybe you need to learn a little English before you go." Enzo said.

"Maybe I should . . . Do you transport only olives or other things too?"

"My father is in the olive business, I help him out. I am also going to school to be a movie producer."

"I like Italian movies." We were driving along the sea shore. The water was shimmering in the bright sunlight. "Italy is a beautiful country," I said.

"I traveled a lot but this is my favorite place . . . I am getting kind of hungry, would you like to join me for lunch? It's my treat."

"I don't know . . . I guess, maybe. I am a little hungry too."

"Don't be shy," he said, "you are like a sister to me."

"Thank you Enzo, but I cannot spend too much time because I am meeting a girlfriend in Terracina about a job."

"I am also in a hurry. We can have lunch in Terracina. Later you can go and see your friend."

"It's a good plan," I said.

"I know a good restaurant right before we enter Terracina. They make the best pasta."

"Sounds perfect," I said.

We stopped at a small restaurant on the side of the road. It was a rustic old house with wooden tables and benches. We sat outside under a tree. The waitress said hello to Enzo and asked him how he was doing.

"Anna wait here for a moment please, I need to get a box out of the truck. I deliver olives to this restaurant every week." He went to the truck and came back with a box of olives, taking it into the kitchen. I sat on the bench waiting, and he came back with a happy smile. "It's an easy job," he said, taking a seat across the table. "I like to help my father with his olives. I stop here for lunch every week."

"What would you like today?" The waitress asked.

"Pasta with Calamari please, for two." He whispered in my ear; "I hope you like Calamari. The sauce is the best, better than my mother's."

"I never tried it but I love sea food." He was pleased and the waitress came back with two big plates full of spaghetti. A mound of pasta on each plate, and the sauce mixed into the pasta.

"This is the biggest portion I've ever seen. Hopefully I can eat everything."

"Of course you can," Enzo said. "I would be very disappointed if you don't," he added laughing. "You eat as much as you want, but please, tell me if you like it!"

"It's the most delizioso pasta, ever," I said after eating the whole plate.

"You eat like an Italian woman," Enzo said.

"If I eat like this every day, I would be as big as a house."

"Oh, don't worry about that, you're so skinny, you need to put on a few kilos. I guarantee you'd find a husband right away."

"That's all it takes?"

"That, and a few other things," he added.

"Thank you, Enzo. This was the best meal I had in a long time."

"My pleasure," he said. "Anna, we must go now. Where are you meeting your friend? I can take you there." I gave him the address and he let me off where Mona worked. "Ciao Bella!" he said and was on his way.

Mona came outside in a hurry: "What took you so long?"

"I had lunch with the truck driver," I said.

"I told you never to get into a car with a stranger!"

"I know, but just couldn't find another car, it was getting late. Enzo looked like a nice guy."

"You can't tell just from looking at somebody who they are," Mona said.

"Well," I said, "I can."

"Don't be so naïve, let's go. They are expecting us at the pensione."

We walked for about fifteen minutes on the side of the road. The pensione located right by the beach, had a big red sign 'Pensione Primavera' above a yellow door. We went in and Mona introduced me to the owners, a middle age couple. His name was Marcello and his girlfriend Erika was from Germany. They were in love and she used to spend every summer in Italy with her two girls. Hilda was seven years old and Greta was five. Marcello was crazy about the girls, and they were very spoiled.

Erika wanted me share the room with the girls and take care of them. I had to make sure they were dressed and had breakfast at eight o'clock every day. The rest of the morning we would be spending on the beach. Marcello served lunch in a small dining room with only six tables and he rented four rooms for the summer. The tenants were devoted customers and Marcello was taking good care of them. He asked me to serve lunch as part of my job. The girls were spending the afternoon with their mother. Every evening I had to serve them dinner prepared by Marcello. Afterward I could sit at the table with them and have dinner. Marcello loved to cook.

They were offering me food and ten thousand liras per week. I was happy to get out of the camp and live in such a nice place, plus the food was so much better. They decided to hire me right away. I needed two days to go back to the camp and bring my things.

After the meeting with the owners Mona invited me to her room. We walked back to the restaurant where Mona worked. She lived right above the restaurant. We went upstairs and Mona pulled out of the closet a bottle of Campari and two small cups. We had a toast for my new job.

"They are very nice people," she said. "I'll tell you something but please don't say anything to anybody."

"I won't!"

"Erica is married in Germany but they are separated. She doesn't want a divorce until the girls grow up. She spends the summers in Italy and winters in Germany."

"Not a bad arrangement," I said.

"Erica is very rich. There is nothing in the World that she wouldn't give to those girls. They are good friends with my boss. That's how I found out about the job."

"Thank you, I can't wait to get out of the camp."

"How much do they pay you?"

"10.000 lire a week."

"Oh, that's not enough, you must ask for more."

"It's an easy job. They're giving me enough money."

"It's your choice. Why don't you stay and have dinner with me? I have plenty of food from the restaurant. Wait here, I'll be right back." She came back carrying a tray with cheese, olives, tomatoes, prosciutto and fresh bread. "The food is really good here. I put on a few kilos."

"Mona, you look great. Hard work is good for you."

"I am not complaining," Mona said. We eat everything and a bunch of fresh Cannoli for desert.

"This was really good," I said, "I think I eat too much." When I looked outside, it was already dark. "Mona, I have to hitch-hike back to Latina, it is dark outside."

"Oh, my God, how will you get back? It's so dangerous!"

"It's not more dangerous than during the day."

"I think it is. Look, I have an idea," Mona went to the kitchen and brought back a big kitchen knife. "Take this knife, just in case!"

"Are you crazy?"

"No, no, take it!

"Okay, I'll take it but where can I put it? I don't have a bag, or a purse, or anything."

"Let's see," Mona picked a large envelope from the dresser and put the knife inside the envelope. "Good, the envelope is big enough. You must bring me the knife when you come back."

"Look, this is crazy. I don't know what to do with the knife."

"Just give them a good scare, that's all. I'll wait until you get into the car."

We both went out to the street and the traffic was very slow. Most cars didn't pick up hitch-hikers at night. When we almost gave up, a small Fiat stopped. A middle age man was driving it.

"I'll take it!" I said to Mona. She was reluctant to let me go. When she saw me getting into the car she wished me good luck. I sat in the front next to the driver.

"Dove vai?" He asked.

"Latina," I said, "the refugee camp, where are you going?"

"Roma. It's a long ride, I don't mind some company."

"It's not that long of a ride," I said.

"I am coming from Salerno. Do you drive?"

"No. I don't know how to drive a car. I am from Romania. Very few people have cars in Romania."

"I see, life must be tough in that part of the World."

"Everything is better here in Italy."

"Italy is the best country in the World," he added proudly.

"I think so too."

Looking out the window while observing all his movements I came to the conclusion that he couldn't be a bad person. If he only knew what I was hiding inside the envelope . . . Even if I had to defend myself, I couldn't use the knife. Holding the envelope with much care, I was terrified that the knife might poke a hole into the paper.

"What were you doing in Salerno?" I asked.

"My wife lives in Salerno. I live in Rome."

"Are you divorced?"

"Oh, no. We are separated, we cannot get a divorce."

"Why not?"

"We are not allowed to get a divorce by the Catholic Church."

"That makes no sense, if you don't live together what kind of marriage is that?"

"You're right, but there is nothing I can do. I go to see my children every weekend."

"My father was away a lot,' I said. "In Romania is very easy to get divorced but my parents didn't want a divorce."

"You're not Catholic, are you?"

"No, I am Greek Orthodox."

"What's the difference?" He asked.

"I am not really sure, maybe because we believe in the immaterial spirit of God, or the Breath of God. We pray to the Father, Son and the Holy Spirit. I think!"

"Have you been to the Vatican?" He asked.

"So far I wasn't able to. I don't have a work permit and I am waiting for a visa to the United States. I think I will be able to work off the books."

"Doing what?" He asked.

"A family hired me to take care of their children in Terracina. I'll be starting in couple of days."

"You must visit the Vatican before you go. The most beautiful place in the world! Every year millions of people visit the Vatican."

"Maybe I will." We drove in silence for some time. We were getting close to Latina.

"We'll be there soon. Everybody knows the Latina camp. I'll take you to the gate. It's too late for you to be walking around alone."

"Thank you," I said, "I really appreciate that."

Italian men were so protective of their women. In the afternoon one could see mostly men hanging out in the sidewalk cafés while their wives were home making dinner. We made couple of turns and stopped in front of the camp.

"Thank you and have a safe trip," I said getting off the car.

"Ceao Bella," he said and drove away.

Only after he disappeared I realized that I forgot the envelope with the knife in the car. Thinking that he might come back I ran all the way to my room. That night I slept well.

For the next few days I packed all my things, put a lock on the door and found a refugee couple to give me a ride to Terrecina. The couple had relatives in Napoli. Spending most of the time there, they came to the camp just for the day to check on their emigration status. They drove me to the pensione.

Marcello was happy to see me and helped with the luggage. Erika and the children were out shopping. Marcello showed me to the children's room. My bed had clean sheets and a fluffy blanket and next to the bed was a small dresser. I put my luggage under the bed.

"They'll be back for lunch," Marcello said. "If you wish, come to the kitchen with me and I'll show you how to serve lunch." He showed me where he kept the trays, plates and silverware and how to set the table. They used a fork and a spoon for pasta, rolling the pasta around the fork while holding it steady with the spoon. It was easier to eat pasta that way.

"You can start tomorrow. Erika will show you everything. I'll serve lunch today so you can watch me."

Erika and the two girls came back loaded with packages. She was happy to see me and diligently showed me everything I needed to know. The work was easy and the girls were a delight. I was spending most of my time with the girls. We were all a happy family. One day Erika asked me to accompany her on a shopping trip to Rome. I was very excited to go. She drove her new Mercedes and I sat in the front. She was a good driver and I had no fear being in the car with her.

"Do you have any other shoes?" She suddenly asked me, "I see you wearing these rubber flip-flaps every day."

"Yes," I said, "I have a pair of tennis shoes but it's too hot to wear them now."

"I'll buy you a new pair of sandals," she said. "I know we don't pay you much, but you should save all your money for when you go to America!"

"Thank you so much, I don't know what to say, I am tired of these sandals."

"Don't worry. A girl should have at least a pair of nice shoes. I know all about it, I have to two girls, you know."

"You're so lucky," I said, "Hilda and Greta are so well behaved. I love them like my little sisters." I could tell Erika was so proud of her two little girls. She looked out the window.

"I love Italy," she said. "My girls love it here too. I wish I could spend all year around in Italy."

"I know, I wish I could stay here too."

"You're such a young girl," she said. "What are you going to do in America?"

"I am not sure. I want to be an artist."

"Artist, what kind of artist?"

"I want to paint and build things, maybe a graphic artist."

"It's hard to make a living as an artist. If I was you I would study computers and make art on the side."

"What's that? I never heard of computers before."

"It's a new area of technology. Briefly . . . machines that can think. It's the beginning of a New World. Most of the work that people are doing now will be replaced by machines."

"How do you know all that?"

"My husband works in the field. He is very excited about it. If I had to work that's what I would do. My husband and I are good friends, but it didn't work between us. He fell in love with another woman and left. But as you know, it was all for the best. I am very happy with Marcello. I would like to live here but I am waiting for the girls to grow up. They go to school in Germany and they also love their father, so we only spend summer vacations here in Italy."

"Do you miss Marcello during the winter?"

"Of course I do and also it's so cold during the winter in Germany, I don't like cold weather."

We arrived in Rome and got stuck in traffic around the Coliseum. The streets were very busy with lots of people, bicycles and cars. Erica was concentrating on driving through the colorful mosaic of cars of all shapes and sizes, trying to outrun each other. It took a long time driving North on side streets to avoid the more serious traffic gems.

"We are very close to Piazza Di Spagna," Erika said. "You'll like it! Lots of young people from all over the World gather on the Spanish Steps. Around here we need to walk. There are too many people on the streets and it's impossible to drive."

From the car, we walked for a while and suddenly arrived on the top of the Spanish Steps. The view was magnificent. A cascade of steps opened in front of us, covered with a colorful blanket of people. We zigzagged our way in between all kinds of people, to the bottom of the steps.

"See this whole area in front of us? It's the best shopping in Rome," Erika said, "my favorite place to shop."

We walked on Via Condotti looking at the windows, going from shop to shop. Erika bought me a pair of sandals. She ended up with her hands full of boxes and I helped carry some of them. Something caught my attention. A white embroidered dress was glowing on the dark background of a window. I was fascinated. Erika grabbed my arm and we went into the store.

"Do you like that dress?" She asked.

"I've never seen such a beautiful dress."

Erika went to the counter and returned holding a pink box. "Here, this is for you," she said handing me the box. "The dress is yours. I know how much a beautiful dress matters to a young girl."

"I don't know how to thank you . . . I'm going to keep it for a very special occasion."

"One thing," Erika said, "don't tell Marcello about this dress. He has very different ideas about money than I do."

"I won't tell anybody. I'll keep it in my luggage until I go to America."

Back at the pensione, I hid the dress on the bottom of my suitcase. Sometimes I would take the suitcase into the bathroom and look at the dress. I worked at the pensione for couple of month, and one morning I decided to go back to the camp. I wanted to be free. After breakfast I told Marcello that I needed to take care of my visa and had to go back. They were all sorry to see me go. I was too, in a way.

Back to Latina, the door to my room had been forced open and everything stolen. I had to make up a story, that I was robbed while eating lunch. Nobody was allowed to leave the camp without a special permit issued by the Central Emigration Office in Milano. To get such a permit took several weeks or more. No one followed those rules. Refugees left the camp whenever they pleased. The Italians never kept count of the refugee's whereabouts. After I cleaned the empty room and furnished it with the usual metal bed frame and a foam mattress, I hang a scarf that Erika gave me on the wall behind the bed. I locked the door and pulled the 'White Dress' out of my suitcase. After putting it on, I knocked on Andrea's door. She was startled to see me back, dressed like a princess.

"Anna, when did you come back?"

"This morning," I said. "I needed some time off from work."

"How did you get that gorgeous dress?"

"It was a present from Erica, my employer."

"When are you going back?"

"I don't think I'll be going back. I want to stay in the camp for a while."

"Are you crazy? You're so lucky to have gotten this job. You know how difficult is to find a job without a work permit?"

"I know, but I'm happy to be back here. I don't have to get up in the morning and spend every minute with the kids. I need my own space." Andrea was disappointed with me quitting that job.

"I'll see you later," I said and went back to my room. That afternoon, I spent most of my money on a pair of red sandals that matched my red corduroy jeans.

One morning, the guard knocked at my door. "Signorina, please come to the office right away!" I followed him to the office. Some people were already there, waiting. Arianna was there too. "Your visas for United States were approved," the camp director said, "you will be leaving next Wednesday from Rome. You should be here and ready at six a.m. Our bus will take you to the airport. Good luck!"

"Let's celebrate!" Arianna said. We went back to her room and she pulled out a half bottle of Campari. "Cin, cin!" she said and we ended up drinking it all.

I was so happy my life in the camp was coming to an end. The day before leaving I went for a walk around the camp to say "good bye" to everybody I knew. Back in my room, I sorted through my bags and got rid of a lot of useless things including my two evening dresses from

Romania. I wondered why my mother packed these dresses for me. What was she thinking? I realized how much she lived in a dream world, so far from my reality. I finished packing.

I was going to be an American. In my mind, American women had short hair. I cut my hair and styled it parted on one side to look like a hairdo I've seen in an American fashion magazine. I left out my red corduroy jeans, red sandals and a white blouse to wear on the plane. The following morning the camp director gave each of us an envelope with the airplane tickets. I put it in my backpack and boarded the bus. Arianna was already seated in the front row. I gave her a hug and went to the back of the bus to find a seat. Everybody was excited about leaving the camp.

As we were pulling out, I felt a sense of ease. The heavy load I was carrying on my shoulders melted away. A feeling of freedom overwhelmed me. My life became a blank screen with nothing projected on it. We drove along the blue sparkling sea in the bright sunlight. I will always miss the brightness of the sun and the deep blue sea of Italy. I decided that someday, I will return to Italy under different circumstances, when I will be able to enjoy the beauty and rich history of this magnificent country.

We arrived at the airport. It was mainly a military airport but I could see many private airplanes lined up along the runways. I showed my emigration card together with the ticket, and boarded the plane.

CHAPTER 8

OVER THE ALPS

Arianna and I were able to find seats next to each other. The airplane was full of people, refugees from all over Eastern Europe, traveling to the United States. It was the first time in my life flying in an airplane, and on top of that an international flight from Rome to New York. Before we embarked, everyone received an envelope with twenty Dollars. It was a gift from some nonprofit organization. For me it was a blessing because I had no money left. Arianna was very secretive about money so I had no idea how much she had but definitely more than me. Before we boarded the plane she went to the duty-free shop and purchased a bottle of whiskey.

"We're going to get blasted," she said smiling.

"It's okay with me."

It was a long wait until we finally took off. The stewardess came along with refreshments. I got a can of coke and put it on the little table in front of me to let it warm up. I didn't like cold drinks. We left Rome behind, flying in and out white puffy clouds. The sky was spectacular. In a while the clouds cleared up and we were flying above a mountainous area.

"I think we are above the Alps," I said to Arianna. "Look, you can see the mountains."

"I am afraid of heights," she said, "I can't look down."

"It's the most amazing spectacle I've ever seen!"

"I think I'll have a sip of whiskey," she said getting the big bottle out of her bag. She opened it and took a mouth full straight from the bottle, passing it to me. I didn't feel like drinking but I took a sip just to please her. After that I poured some coke in a plastic glass. The coke was good but still a little too cold. I turned my head toward Arianna.

"Isn't it amazing that we used to be neighbors in Bucharest and now we're sitting next to each other, on the way to New York?"

"Yes, cheers to that," Arianna said and took another sip of whiskey. She pushed the bottle toward me, "Come-on, have another sip."

"Hey Arianna, look at this," I said.

"What?"

"Look at the coke in the cup."

"Well, is kind of shaky," she said.

"I think something is wrong with the airplane."

"You can't be serious!"

"You see the ripples in the cup? Well, my friend Dodi, who used to be a pilot, told me that if you see ripples like this in an airplane it means that something is wrong with the motor."

"That's ridiculous," she said handing me the bottle after she had a few mouthfuls, but I could see fear in her eyes. "Here, have some whiskey, if we go down at least we don't feel anything." She gently placed the bottle on my lap.

"Okay, I'll have a drink but I think we should be praying instead."

There was a voice on the loudspeaker: "Please fasten your seatbelts, we will be having some turbulence!" We looked at each other with fear. The stewardess walked directly towards us and stopped in front of our seat.

"Do you need help?" she asked with a fake smile.

"What's going on?" Arianna asked.

"I don't know, I only follow orders," the Stewardess said drily.

"Is something wrong with the motor by any chance?" I asked.

"Please fasten your seatbelts and stay calm," she said and swiftly turned around toward the passengers across the aisle. We fastened ours seatbelts and Arianna looked at me.

"If I don't make it, will you please write to my daughter and help her if you can?"

"Of course I will, but Arianna don't talk like that, nothing will happen." In reality I was quiet scared. I looked at the bottle and about a quarter of it was gone. "Let's save some of the whiskey for later," I said.

"What later?" Arianna asked with a touch of sarcasm.

There was agitation in the plane and other passengers started to question what was going on. We heard the voice on the loudspeaker again.

"Bon jour, this is your pilot speaking. We are having some technical difficulties. There wasa change in our flight plan. We are in France flying towards Paris. We will be landing in Paris within one hour. Everything is under control. Keep your seatbelts fastened, please!"

"Maybe we should get off and stay in Paris," Arianna suggested.

"I am going to New York. There is nothing for me in Paris. My ex boyfriend found another girlfriend, a French girl."

"I am sorry," Arianna said, "maybe that wasn't such a good idea, but I would rather stay in Paris than go to New York. Anyway, I can't wait to touch ground. Let's drink some more. I'll buy another bottle in Paris. I don't care!"

"Okay," I said but the whiskey made my mouth very dry, and the flight was becoming bumpier.

"It's like riding a horse," Arianna said.

"I would rather be riding a horse anytime."

"Me too," she was pensive for a while. "Who did you say your pilot friend was?"

"Dodi," I said. "He used to live up the street from my house."

"I remember him, an older guy riding a motorcycle."

"Yes, that's him all right."

"I wouldn't bet on anything he said, he was a nutcase," Arianna shook her head with distrust.

"He liked young girls a little bit too much, but he had a good heart. My girlfriends and I used to have a lot of fun with him."

"He was taking advantage of you," Arianna said motherly.

"Maybe, but we had fun together."

"How are your ripples in the coke?"

My coke spilled everywhere. I drank the last sip with regret. "No more coke," I said.

"What else Dodi told you about the ripples?"

"Nothing, it indicates something wrong with the motor. He used to fly small military airplanes."

"Well, maybe he knew what he was talking about."

"May be so . . . Look, if nothing was wrong we wouldn't be landing in Paris," I said.

"How about another sip of whiskey?" Ariana said, taking a mouthful.

"Be careful that you don't break your teeth when we hit a bump." I said. After she checked how much whiskey was left, she gave me the bottle. I drank a whole mouthful. It was burning my throat on the way down.

"I can't get drunk,' Arianna said. "I am too scared to get drunk. I can drink this whole bottle, what the hell!"

"I hope you'll be able to walk, because I can't carry you."

"I never get drunk," she said defensively.

"I don't believe you."

"Try me, let's have a contest."

"I don't think so, I already feel a little dizzy."

She turned her face toward me and her eyes were bloodshot. "You're lucky you don't have to spend much money on booze."

"Not as much as you." We heard the high pitched voice of the stewardess on the loudspeaker.

"We are getting ready to lend. Please keep your seatbelts on, and put your head down. There are oxygen masks hanging from the ceiling. If you are instructed please put the oxygen masks on."

"What the hell we need oxygen masks for? We are going to die, anyway," Arianna said.

"We made it all the way here, maybe we'll survive."

"Maybe someone in this plane is lucky, not me!"

"Arianna, you're drunk."

"Maybe a little bit," she admitted it, "so what?"

"Dodi told me, the most dangerous time is at the takeoff and landing."

"You didn't have to tell me that!" She said a little annoyed.

"I am not thinking straight right now."

We were hovering over Paris. We couldn't see much, but an endless stretch of buildings.

"Paris is a big city." I remarked.

"It's the biggest."

"I think New York is bigger."

"Maybe,' Arianna said "but Paris is bigger than Rome."

"Whatever."

We started to descend and I could feel my ears popping.

"Say a prayer!" Arianna suggested.

"May we lend safely," I said and wrapped the blanket around my head.

"Good idea," she wrapped the blanket around her head as well.

The stewardesses were watching us in disbelieve. We heard the screechy voice on the loudspeaker.

"We are landing within the next ten minutes. It may be a little bumpy so hold on to your seats."

"Oh, Dio mio," Arianna said. There was a big bump when we touched the ground.

"Bon jour, we just landed at the Orly airport in Paris. Everybody stay seated until next instructions. Please keep your seatbelts on." We looked at each other with relief. The plane was speeding on the ground like there was no tomorrow. Everything was shaking and luggage flying off the shelves. Everybody was protecting their heads.

"What the hell is going on?" Arianna said.

"Maybe they are looking for a parking space."

"That's not funny." We finally came to a stop. Arianna sketched a cross sign over her chest.

"I didn't know you were religious," I said.

"Not necessarily, only in extreme cases."

Suddenly the voice of the Pilot came clearly over the loudspeaker.

"Everybody stay seated please! We made an emergency landing successfully. We have some technical problems. We will be staying in Paris until tomorrow afternoon for repairs. Everybody should be back at the terminal by two o'clock tomorrow afternoon. There are free accommodations at the Hilton Hotel near the Airport. You will be given temporary visas to go and visit Paris. A bus will drive you to the hotel and back. Have a nice stay in Paris!"

"Would you like sharing a room with me at the hotel?" I asked her.

"Definitely, we have to celebrate. I don't want to go to New York. I want to stay in Paris!"

"Don't be silly, you cannot stay in Paris without a visa. They'll send you back to the camp in Italy. I think you are just afraid to fly over the ocean."

"I am terrified," she said, "I never want to fly again, ever!"

The captain was standing by the exit greeting each of us. When our turn came, Arianna looked him in the eyes.

"Captain, you did a great job! You saved our lives, we owe you one!" She got closer to him. "Tell me, was anything wrong with the motor?"

"As a matter of fact you're right. One of the motors broke down but we were in no danger at anytime," he assured Arianna. "How did you know that?"

"My friend here," Arianna said, "she is the expert." The pilot looked at me surprised.

"It's a long story," I said, "thank you Captain!"

"Have a great time, girls! Don't be late tomorrow."

We all boarded the bus. The Hilton Hotel was less than five minutes away. There was a long line in the lobby by the registration desk.

"I cannot believe that we are staying in such fancy hotel."

"Things are looking better and better," Arianna said."

After registering both of us went up to our room. Arianna opened the door and we hesitated for a moment.

"I think I'll take off my shoes," she said, "such a clean carpet."

"Me too," we both kicked off our shoes and tip-toed into the room.

"I'll give Phillip a call. I never told him I was planning to go to New York."

"Why would you want to call that creep?"

"Well, I don't know, I want to see his face. I don't care that much about him, I really don't."

"Anna, you let people step all over you. Tell him to go to hell!"

"You had one too many."

"So what, I am still a lady, not like that ex boyfriend of yours."

"I'll call him anyway," I said and went to the telephone.

"Do whatever you want but don't cry on my shoulder."

"I am tougher than you think."

"You are young and naïve, but life has a way of teaching us the hard lessons."

"What am I supposed to learn from this?"

Arianna gave me an exasperated look taking the bottle out of the bag. It was almost empty.

"I think I'll go to sleep early. There is no more whiskey," she said shaking the bottle and then collapsed on the large double bed, sinking into the soft pillows. "Go ahead call him, what the hell."

Digging into my backpack, I finally found my phonebook and with shaky hands I dialed Phillip's number.

"Alo," a female's voice answered.

"I would like to talk to Phillip."

"Just a moment," she said. Phillip picked up the phone.

"It's Anna," I said. "I am in Paris." A moment of silence on the other end . . .

"Where are you?" He asked startled.

"At the Hilton Hotel by the Orly Airport."

"Oh, I know that area. I'll come by. It'll take me about an hour to get there. Meet me in the lobby."

In about forty-five minutes the front desk called announcing that Phillip was waiting in the lobby. I grabbed my backpack on the way to the door. Arianna propped by four pillows in the middle of the bed, gave me a big smile.

"Au revoire," she said, "don't do anything I wouldn't do."

In the well lit lobby Phillip was pacing back and forth. "Phillip," I said stepping out the elevator. He turned around, looked at me and froze.

"Anna it's good to see you. I didn't expect you so soon, why didn't you tell me you're coming?"

"Well, you have a girlfriend. Do you live with her?" He seemed surprised and embarrassed, not knowing what to say.

"I live with her now . . . let's go to a café and talk. A lot happened since you left."

"Phillip, I am just passing by. I am on my way to New York."

"What?" He said in disbelieve. "How come you didn't tell me anything?" His face became very pale and stood in front of me stunned, watching me.

"Oh, I don't know, maybe things are better this way," I said, "let's go and have something to eat and we can talk about this."

"I know a good Middle Eastern restaurant. It's very popular and the food is great." We went out in the humid, oppressive air. Phillip hailed a cab. We were silent for some time. He turned toward me: "I can't believe you're going to America!"

"What am I going to do in Paris by myself?"

"What are you going to do in America? You don't speak any English."

"I don't know," I said, "I'll survive!"

The restaurant was in the Arab section of Paris, gem packed with mostly Arabs.

"This is an interesting place!" I said.

"It is! The food is great and prices are okay. It's the best Moroccan food in Paris."

Moroccan rugs were hanging on the walls and oil lamps burning on the old wooden tables.

"This place looks from the Middle—Ages."

"It does," Phillip said, "its owners are an old Moroccan family. They go back over five hundred years."

Phillip was right about the food. I had lentil soup and lamb with chickpeas. The spices were very subtle. I never tasted anything like it. It was a culture shock.

"It's really amazing," I said and Phillip smiled.

"I knew you'd like it!"

"I am a little apprehensive about New York," I said. "I heard there is a lot of violence on the streets, and is dangerous to walk around at night."

"Nonsense," Phillip said. "Natalie, my girlfriend, goes to New York every year. It's perfectly safe."

"Is she rich?"

"She comes from wealthy family but she is very modest. You would like her."

"Maybe," I said. We finished our meal and I was beginning to feel exhausted from the challenging events of this long, emotional day.

"I am very tired, Phillip. I want to go back to the hotel and get some sleep, before I leave tomorrow."

Another sleepless night. The whiskey bottle was empty and Arianna sound asleep. All the events in the last twenty-four hours were spinning in my head. I was worried about crossing the ocean, worried about was I going to do in New York with twenty dollars in my pocket, felt rejected by my family in Switzerland and by Phillip. I couldn't enjoy the fancy hotel or the night in Paris. In the morning we went to the airport. Arianna, full of anxiety checked out the plane.

"This is the same plane, isn't it?"

"It looks like the same one but they all look alike," I said.

"No, this is the same one."

"How do you know?"

"I just have a strong feeling about it. I am not flying across the ocean in this piece of junk!"

"They fixed it. I am sure of it."

"I am going to the duty-free shop. Will you watch my luggage, please?"

"Sure," I said, "don't forget to come back."

"I wish!"

I waited for a long time worried that she'll take off and I would have to fly alone, but she came back holding a bottle of Bacardi.

"This has to last us till we get to New York."

"I don't see why not?" I said.

We boarded. Arianna asked the stewardess about the plane. It was the same one, and she assured us the motor was fixed, and running like new. We both felt doubtful about the outcome of this adventure. We sat next to each other and Arianna started to prey.

"Dear God, please help us arrive in New York in one piece."

"And alive," I added.

'Thank you God, Amen."

"Amen."

The flight was boring and uneventful, but there was tension. We started passing the bottle back and forth. I was sipping and she was taking a mouthful each time. We slept and drank all the way and forgot about everything. Suddenly we were awakened by the loudspeaker.

"We are approaching the JFK Airport in New York. Please fasten your seatbelts and stay seated until further instructions."

I looked out the window. It was evening and millions of flickering lights were illuminating the sky as far as one could see. It looked like another world, an unearthly sight.

"Look at this, Arianna, the nights will never be dark in New York. We've made it!"

"Our new home," Arianna said with tears in her eyes.

Our airplane was hovering over New York for more than thirty minutes. An ocean of lights was stretching below us surrounded by a purple haze. Everything else was black. The voice on the loudspeaker recommended that we keep our seatbelts on.

"We will be landing at the JFK Airport in New York".

"I hope nothing goes wrong," Arianna said.

"We made it across the ocean, we'll be fine." I said.

"Anna, you better come with me. I know you don't have any money, we'll stay together."

"Okay," I said not being able to envision what was going to unfold after arrival.

"We are descending," I said.

"How do you know?"

"My ears started popping, that's how I can tell. We are losing altitude."

"You know a lot about flying, considering this is your first flight."

"It was all theory until now . . . I wonder what New York is like," I said, "I heard so many crazy things about this city . . ."

"What did you hear?"

"Well, I was told if you walk around after eight o'clock at night you can get shot."

"Where did you hear that?"

"From this Cuban girl in the camp, she said that New York is the most dangerous city. She was waiting for a visa to go to Los Angeles."

"We can fight them back!" Arianna said full of self confidence.

"You're joking."

"I am half joking, but I wouldn't mind having a gun like in the movies. I am strong, you know, if I punch somebody in the face they won't like it."

"I don't know if I can do that, but I can run." I said not too proud of myself.

"That's good too." We felt a jolt when the airplane touched the ground. The voice on the loudspeaker said:

"We successfully landed at the JFK Airport. Please stay seated, we will call you when is time to leave the airplane. Each group will be guided by an agent to the exit."

We looked at each other, waiting for our group to be called. Groups were called by nationalities in alphabetical order.

"All refugees from Romania should exit now. Please gather around a man with a sign that says 'Romania' right after you exit the plane." I grabbed my luggage and backpack.

"Wait for me," Arianna said. She had a lot of luggage. "We must be very careful with spending our money."

"It's not that hard," I said, "I only have twenty dollars."

Arianna shook her head in disbelief, and we walked through the corridor into a huge waiting room. People of different nationalities were gathered in groups. We walked to the group from Romania.

"Where are we going?" Arianna asked the man holding the sign.

"I'll take you to a hotel. It is paid by the church that sponsored you to come to the United States. You can stay there for one week."

"How much are the rooms?" She asked.

"Twenty dollars per day," The man said.

"Do we have to pay it back?"

"Of course, but later on when you get a job."

"Twenty dollars is a lot of money," she whispered in my ear, "tomorrow morning we have to look for a cheaper hotel."

"I agree, if we stay for one week we will own the church $140. I don't need to stay in such a fancy hotel."

We followed the group through the airport to a small bus. The airport was huge. It took about twenty minutes to drive through the labyrinth of terminals, many cars, busses and traffic jams.

The ride to the hotel took about one hour. We drove through poor neighborhoods with two story houses next to each other, and boarded building complexes that seemed abandoned. We entered a long tunnel brightly lit with fluorescent lights. Suddenly, we were in 'The City' with tall buildings as far as one could see. A lot of them were built in the beginning or mid century. I expected a futuristic city, but that wasn't New York. It was evening but I could see people walking everywhere and many restaurants, diners and coffee shops open for business. A constant stream of busses, cars and bicycles were going in all directions. People looked ten years behind the fashion compared to Italy. Most of them were dressed haphazardly without any sense of style.

"This is not what I expected," I said to Arianna, "this city looks much better from the airplane."

We turned into a side street and stopped in front of a hotel about ten stories high. It was an old, red brick building. The windows on the ground floor had been painted brown so one could not see inside. Some of the paint was peeling off. We waited in the lobby until everybody received their keys. It was a poorly kept lobby with a reddish-brown carpet full of stains. Our room was at the sixth floor.

Arianna and I stuffed our luggage into a small elevator. Arriving at the sixth floor, we walked into long and narrow corridor with rooms lined up on both sides. Everyone had to share their rooms. I opened the door and the room was small with two single beds covered with brown blankets. Two small windows were facing the street. I tried to open a window for some fresh air, but was stuck.

"I wonder if they will charge us twenty dollars each."

"I think so," I said, "but this is not a luxury hotel."

The bathroom was small, and the tub had brown and green stains, especially by the faucet. Water was dripping and I had to turn the faucet really hard to stop it.

"I guess Americans don't care to turn the faucet all the way," I said.

"It's better than the showers in the camp."

"That's true, but those showers were free."

The door to the bathroom was hanging loose and wouldn't close. Arianna with couple of good kicks was able to close it.

"See, that's how you do it!"

I had a small radio that somebody gave me in Italy. I turned the radio on and someone with a deep voice was speaking so fast, that I couldn't understand a single word. It sounded like they were speed talking. That's how I realized that I was in a foreign country.

All night long I was awakened by the loud sound of sirens coming from the street. In my half awake state I panicked being afraid we were being attacked.

"It sounds like the alarms during the war," I said to Arianna.

"How do you know, you were born after the war?"

"I just know. My mother told me,"

"Your mother had no business frightening you like that!" She was getting edgy.

"My mother said that the war was easy until the Americans started bombing."

"Would you stop talking about the war," she said all annoyed. "America is a big country, very well protected. You are safer here than in Romania."

"Well, I don't feel safe."

"Just go back to sleep. Tomorrow we have a long day."

The following day we went to look for a cheaper hotel. I was able to rent a small room for $10 per week on the upper West Side 110th Street, in Harlem. The room was very narrow with a single bed and a chair. There wasn't enough room to put the chair in front of the bed so the best place was near the door. The only window with a great view of a fire escape and a brick wall wouldn't open. After a examining it, I noticed that the frame had been painted over with multiple layers that sealed it closed. When I wanted some 'fresh' air I had to prop the door open. The common bathroom was at the end of a long hallway, and sometimes I had to wait in line.

Arianna's room was in the same building, but at a higher floor. She was paying $15 per week, but she had her own private bathroom, a rusty metal shower and a toilet with no sink. She would allow me to take a shower in her bathroom when she was at the hotel, which was not very often.

The common bathroom on my floor was filthy, with a shower that was constantly dripping and a bathtub covered in layers of rust and dirt. There was no shower curtain and water would splash all over, so one had to be careful not to skid on the slippery floor.

I wasn't feeling well. My upper jaw had been infected for a few months. The infection was caused by a molar but now the whole side of my upper jaw was puffy. I was feeling nauseated and feverish. I had no money for food and Arianna was worried about me. We decided to go to the Romanian church and talk to the priest about finding me some work.

The priest also lived in the upper West Side, close to Central Park in a better neighborhood. The street was quiet, with big trees and brownstone buildings most of them five or six stories high. He owned an entire brownstone and the church occupied the whole basement. On the first floor the bedroom had been transformed into the priest's office, and the living room was now a waiting area, where Romanian emigrants gathered to talk to the priest about all kinds of problems.

As we were waiting to see him I started a conversation with an older woman and she gave me the address of a Russian dentist that was inexpensive. After we talked to the priest, Arianna insisted that we go and see the dentist. On the way to the dentist we stopped by McDonalds and shared an order of French fries. They tasted pretty good to me. Arianna was fussy.

"My French fries are better," she said proudly.

The dentist was within walking distance. We entered an old building and went to the second floor in a small elevator that looked like an iron cage. I expected some kind of an office, but it was a regular apartment. The bedroom was also the 'Dental Office' and I sat on a regular dining chair. Boris the 'dentist' was a young man and his girlfriend played the role of his dental assistant. The only equipment that I could see was an old drilling machine. When he looked into my mouth was shocked by the stench emanating from my severe infection.

"You need Antibiotics," he said, and turned to the 'nurse', "Lara, please give her the red pills." He put his hand over my shoulder. "I cannot do any work until you take the pills. Come back when infection is gone. I have to pull the molar. It's too far gone to be saved."

Lara put some red pills in a plastic bag and gave me a glass of water. "Take one pill right now. Infection is very bad. Take pills every four hours. Don't skip. Come back in five days." I took the pills and asked Boris how much I owed him.

"Nothing," he said, "You pay me when we're finished."

The priest recommended me for a job in the jewelry business and I started working immediately.

After five days the infection was almost gone and I went back to see Boris by myself. He told me that he was a dental student in his fourth year back in Russia but left the country and now was saving money to go back to school in New York. In the meantime he was working mainly to get experience and help people like me that couldn't afford a regular dentist. Considering the rudimentary equipment, he was an okay dentist. He pulled my molar and gave me a tea bag to bite on.

"It will stop the bleeding," he said, "keep on taking the antibiotics and come back on Tuesday, the bridge will be ready."

"I am sorry, but I cannot come on Tuesday. I just got a job and I work six days a week."

"What about evenings? Can you come Tuesday evening?"

"Yes. I can come at seven."

"What kind of job did you get?"

"I work in a jewelry factory cleaning rubber molds. They don't pay much."

"How much do you get?"

"Well, they pay me twenty dollars a week."

"They are taking advantage of you. They pay you less than minimal wage. You work in what they call a 'sweat shop'. How did you get this job?"

"The priest from the Romanian church recommended me. I don't know . . . I need the money."

'I know," he said, "see you on Tuesday."

I have been working at the jewelry job for about a week. Every morning at seven thirty sharp I had to be at my work place. It was a big room with folding tables and metal chairs so close together that I could touch the person next to me with my elbows. An older woman was seating on my left side, wearing a gray apron with a big pocket. She had salt and pepper hair rolled in a bun on the back of her head. Above her upper lip she had a big black mole that she kept on touching. Her name was Vaida. She was a senior worker in the factory constantly watching my every move. Being an expert she was getting twice as much work done as I was. Once in awhile, she would inspect the mold that I just finished cleaning.

"You have to be more careful. The molds have to be perfectly clean otherwise when they pour the wax will come out with defects."

"I'll be more careful, I will," I kept on saying and tried harder.

Vaida was also from Romania. Living in the U.S. for five years, she came as a refugee from a German camp. In Romania she was working in a factory that manufactured steel pipes for irrigation. She was born in a small village and became a member of the Socialist Party right out of high school. She was considered to have a 'healthy' background, and was advanced to a quality control position, where she had to randomly inspect the pipes for defects.

As a trusted member of the party she was allowed to attend a conference in Belgium. Over there she shared a room with another woman that was planning to escape. Vaida decided to defect. They both ended in a camp in Germany, and she immigrated to the United States.

"Where are you coming from?" She asked me.

"From a refugee camp in Italy named Latina."

"For how long you've been in the U.S.?"

"For about two weeks," I said.

"If you work hard, this is a good place. You'll get more money and eventually you'll be able to buy gold jewelry for a discount. That's what I do. I keep on saving my money and I buy gold."

The perspective of buying gold was just a fantasy because on twenty dollars per week, it was impossible to save anything. As a matter of fact after the first week of work, I realized that I wasn't earning enough money to live on and already owed the priest about twenty-five dollars, twenty for the hotel on 28th Street, and ten for the hotel on 110th Street.

The priest was insisting that I go to church on Sunday. I felt obliged to go because he helped me out and maybe I needed his help in the future. Arianna didn't go to church. She was managing better on her own.

After one week of work, I had Sunday off and decided to go to church. As I was leaving the church, a man approached me. He was maybe thirty years old, medium high with spiky hair and big ears. He had a good sense of humor and was an engineer working for a prestigious company near Penn Station. His name was Danny.

When I explained to him what I was doing, he became furious and told me to quit immediately. He said that I was being exploited and offered me to stay at his apartment until I found a job that paid a decent salary. I took the opportunity and never went back to my old job, not even to pick up my check.

The following day, Danny came over to my hotel and we loaded all my belongings into his red Ford Mustang that he just bought and was enamored with. We drove to my new residence, a small one bedroom walkup on the sixth floor in Jamaica, Queens. We were sharing the space with a Spanish roommate that just like me, didn't speak any English. His name was Ramos. Ramos didn't talk much and watched cartoons all day. There was no furniture in the apartment and we all slept on the floor. Danny was very frugal, saving all his money to pay for the car. I was getting bored with nothing to do when Danny was at work.

One day we went to a Chinese restaurant on Broadway, in the upper West Side. It was the first time in my life eating Chinese food. I had dumpling soup and fried noodles with chicken and cashews. I was amazed by the taste and the appearance of the food. Danny talked about his job and his ambitious plans for the future. He wanted to buy a house in the suburbs and travel to the Bahamas. I started thinking about what to do next.

Arianna told me that she met Dina on the street, and gave me Dina's phone number. I called her and we decided to have lunch. I was happy to see somebody I knew from Italy. We met at a coffee shop on 42nd Street close to where she lived with her younger boyfriend. Dina told me that she had been approached by an FBI agent offering to give her protection, just in case she might have any problems. I assumed it was because she had been a journalist in Romania and very active politically.

"How come they don't offer me protection?" I asked.

"Here," she said, "take this card, I have another one. If anybody comes after you call him, tell him you know me." I put the card in my pocket. Her hotel was right on 42nd Street near Eight Avenue. I could tell it wasn't a good neighborhood, swarming with pimps, prostitutes and x rated movies.

"Have you ever seen an x rated movie?" I asked.

"Couple of times," she said, "but it was boring and we left in the middle of the movie. There were some perverts in the theatre . . . oh, you don't want to know."

When I arrived back at home, Danny wasn't feeling well. I opened a package of instant soup and put it in a cup of boiling water. He started to drink the hot soup and burned his tongue. He went into a raving rage, throwing the soup on the floor yelling at me.

'You did this on purpose!"

"No," I said, "are you crazy?"

"I am fed up with you! You just sit all day and do nothing."

"I am fed up with you too," I said, "you are the cheapest man I've ever met!"

He left and banged the door. Ramos was curled up in a corner with fear. I called Dina and she immediately asked me to move in with her. They decided to come right away and pick me up. Her boyfriend's name was Radu. He was about thirty years old, and Dina was much older. They lived in a hotel room with a big double bed that occupied the whole space. I was going to sleep on the floor, but for some unknown reason they decided to give me the bed, and they slept on the floor. Dina went to work every morning and Radu and I stayed at the hotel watching TV all day long.

After about a week Dina started to get tired of both of us, and become suspicious and jealous of me being alone with her younger boyfriend during the day. She gave us a week to move out. Radu decided to look for an engineering job advising me to try to do drafting. He gave me a floor plan with electrical symbols, and helped me memorize all of them, explaining some basic theory about electricity and how to draw electrical diagrams.

On Friday morning I washed my hair and dressed in clean clothes, put on some makeup, and we went to an employment agency. They sent me immediately to an interview.

The company was located on Park Avenue South and 28th Street. It was an engineering company designing data systems for different businesses. I was given a test to copy an electrical diagram, and being good at drawing I passed the test and started to work right away.

A young Canadian engineer spoke French and we could communicate. He introduced me to the job, and was there for me to ask questions. Next to the drafting room, there was a large room filled with computers all lined up with a small space in between, enough for a person to squeeze by. They were as tall as a closet. The 'Computer Room' was as cold as a refrigerator. After taking a tour through the company, I told him that I had no money and was given an ultimatum to move out. He arranged with the boss to pay me one week in advance. My salary was $110 per week.

Over the weekend Radu helped move all my belongings into a hotel on Broadway around 82nd Street. The room was immense, with very high ceilings. The single bed on the corner looked like a toy by comparison. Rent was twenty-one dollars per week. I felt rich. The technical drawing class I was complaining about in high school paid off.

After arranging everything in the small dresser I went out on Broadway looking at store windows. Not far from the hotel, I found a small boutique with nice clothes for a very good price. Trying on some outfits, I matched a brown pair of pants with a brown vest and a lavender blouse. I bought the whole outfit for only twenty-one dollars. The casher put everything in a pink shopping bag and handed it to me. It was the first time in my whole life that I was able to buy a whole outfit with my own money.

That evening I decided to celebrate. It was a clear evening. I could see all the way to Columbus Circle. Wearing my new clothes I went back to the Chinese restaurant and ordered a couple of dishes I had never tasted before, savoring each bite. A whole new World was opening before me. On my way back to the hotel I was walking on air, enjoying my first taste of freedom and watching the multitude of people dressed in an endless variety of styles strolling up and down Broadway.

PART TWO

ON THE EDGE OF FAITH

CHAPTER 9

10 YEARS LATER IN NEW YORK

1980. End of summer in New York City. The warm and sticky air felt oppressive. Due to a sluggish economy, I was out of work for a long time living on a skimpy budget, surviving on four dollars a day or less. The few friends left in my life were tired of me complaining about my severe lack of finances. I recall coming home depressed and exhausted, after hours of walking around looking for work and putting out flyers. Those days were followed by endless afternoons sitting at my desk confused, browsing through newspapers and waiting for the phone to ring. I couldn't help but wonder if I will ever find a job. Sometimes the feeling of worthlessness was overwhelming. I would spend most of the day in bed under the covers. Mail was piling up unopened and I felt entangled in a web of negativity, with long sleepless nights and dreary mornings.

One afternoon in the subway station, I passed by a homeless man. He was staring at the crowds. It reminded me of a hunted animal with no place to hide. He looked at me through big weary eyes sunken into his bony face, with the innocence of a child. For a moment, I could feel his pain. "What all those people know that I don't?" He asked me bewildered. I was stunned. Many times I asked myself the same question, and knew what he felt like. I wanted to stop but just kept on walking.

I wondered what happened to that man. The possibility of losing my apartment and living on the streets like him, made me shiver. I never had a clue how people were able to keep it together, be successful and support their families. What did they know that I didn't? Their secret was beyond my grasp and I could never keep up with the rest of the world. I felt just like him, outside society, looking from my imaginary prison cell at a forbidden world, I didn't understand. I was wishing that someone would share their secret with me. Some people would say it was Karma. They believed that we lived innumerable lives, coming back into this world to learn unresolved lessons from the past. If I lived so many lives, and learned so much why couldn't I remember anything? In spite of all that knowledge, I couldn't make a decent living or care for another living being. An old friend used to say: "Pain and suffering are the real evils of this world. Those who can release others from pain and suffering are the real saints."

The perplexed expression of that homeless man persisted into my memory. What brought him to this desperate state? How did he become homeless? No matter what, there was a time when he had a place to live away from the freezing winters and the coldness and cruelty of people. Maybe he had dreams of fame and fortune . . . The hard reality hit him as soon as he became homeless, in a city where if you are down and out, you become invisible. Tears started rolling down my cheeks. People were watching but I didn't care.

While riding the train downtown, that strange encounter lingered in my mind. Maybe that man was an angel showing me I wasn't the only one in distress. When I got off the subway, somebody handed me a flyer about a Spiritual Poetry Workshop to be held the following day, a few doors down the street at a place called 'The Interfaith Center'. Years ago I used to write poetry, but I couldn't anymore. However, I made up my mind to attend the workshop.

The following day I woke up early, selected some poems and walked down to the Village. On St. Marks Place, close to Second Avenue, an inconspicuous door was leading to a long corridor full of graffiti. At the end of it, I arrived at a small courtyard paved with large, uneven slabs of stone and grass growing in between. I paused for a moment in front of a two stories old building trying to decide if I should go in. Just then, a young woman with a long scarf wrapped around her head, opened the door welcoming me with a smile.

"I am looking for a poetry workshop," I said.

"This is it. Please come in, we were just getting ready to start."

I walked in. The room was square with two large windows, a spiral stairway to the second level and some tables scattered around. A few people sitting at a table drinking tea turned around when they heard us coming. The woman went upstairs and I felt a little nervous following her. The space on the upper level was clean, with shiny wooden floors and a carpet in the center. Three men sitting on the floor were facing each other. Hanging on the brick walls numerous small shrines were representing different religions; Christian, Buddhist, Hindu, Muslim and others. One of the shrines caught my attention with the word Gaia written on the background. I went closer to look at this unusual shrine, and asked one of the men about it. He explained that the shrine belonged to the Pagan religion and that Gaia was the name for Earth.

"Pagan," I said, "I thought Pagan meant sinful or savage or something like that."

"No. The Pagan religion is much older than Christianity and some of them worship nature and the Earth as God." He paused for a moment, examining me from head to toe. "Are you here for the workshop? Please join us, we'll wait a few more minutes, maybe someone else might show up."

I sat on the soft carpet, took the poems out of my bag trying to decide which one to read first. A sweet fragrance of incense was permeating the room. A lot of plants were hanging by the stairway. One could see a patch of sky and the twisted branches of an old oak tree through the large skylight above. From behind the clouds, beams of light were reflecting curious patterns on the carpet.

"I am John," the man said, "what is your name?"

"Anna."

"Have you ever been to India?"

"No. I'd like to go, but I can never save enough money."

"You don't need much money to live in India."

"It cost at least fifteen hundred dollars for the round trip."

"It's true," John said, "if you stick around, somehow you might be able to take a trip to India. I am sure of it."

The other men started to get restless. "Let's begin," one of them said, "I don't think anybody else will show up."

"Okay," John said, "let's get started." He began talking about different spiritual scriptures written in poetic form, especially the Sanskrit Indian scriptures. He instructed us to write a poem about our understanding of God. I expected to read and analyze my poems rather than write anything, and felt a little disappointed.

"I can't write a poem just because you ask me to," I said.

"Well, you can try," he was a little annoyed.

The two men started to write. I couldn't come up with anything. The workshop was not at all what I expected, and lasted too long. At the end as I was leaving, I noticed a small wooden musical instrument in a corner of the room. John looked at me.

"This is a harmonium, a musical instrument from India. Would you like to try it?"

"Yes, I would."

"You can come here and practice, mornings are the best. Usually nothing goes on here before lunch. Some of us get together every evening to chant and after that we have a great feast. Why don't you come back tonight?"

"Thank you, maybe, if I'm not busy."

The afternoon seemed long and uneventful. I was restless waiting to go back to the Interfaith Centre that evening. When I arrived the program already started. Some people were sitting in the courtyard. I could see their dark silhouettes projected against the windows. Rhythmical sounds of drums, harmonium and flute were reverberating into the night sky, accompanied by cymbals and many other instruments. A man in a melodious voice singing an ancient Indian chant was creating strange and awesome harmonies. I stood there for a moment, listening. Time disappeared into the ancient ritualistic music, bringing back to life thousands of years of history, right there in the middle of Manhattan.

When I went inside, a man sitting at a table was looking straight at me with penetrating eyes. He was wearing a long brown robe with a hood over his head. When he smiled his face had a radiant glow. At the table next to him, the girl that greeted me earlier at the door was sitting with another young woman. She was wearing a traditional Indian sari. The girl was dressed in a long velvet skirt with an old, embroidered vest. Shiny brown hair was flowing over her shoulders. She had dark, intelligent eyes. Both of them looked at me and smiled.

"Welcome," the man said. "I've seen you here this morning, I am glad you're back. How did you like the workshop?"

"It was fine," I said, trying to be polite.

"I want to introduce you to Blossom and Christina," he pointed to the two girls.

"Hi, I'm Anna," I said.

"Anna, would you like to sit with us? Why don't you all join me for dinner?" He made some room for us at his table, and we all sat around him.

"What's your name?" I asked.

"Nandana Swami," he said.

Blossom brought a round stainless steel tray filled with many different types of Indian foods, placing it in front of him.

"Would you like some juice, Maharaj?"

"Just a little please," he said. "You girls get some plates and bring one for Anna."

They brought me a big plate with all kinds of Indian delicacies. We ate rice with nuts, cauliflower, peas and potatoes with homemade cheese and a special flat Indian bread that tasted light and buttery. The flavors were so artfully combined especially the yellow rice. Blossom brought me another plate full of all kinds of sweets.

"Thank you, but I can't eat any more."

"You must eat," Blossom said, "this is not ordinary food, it was offered to Krishna. It's transcendental."

I could hardly finish and Blossom tried to give me some pudding. I covered my plate laughing.

"No more please, I wish I could eat more, but that's it." Nandana Swami hardly touched his food.

"Why do they call you Maharaj?" I asked him.

"Because I am a Swami, it's a Hindu spiritual order, like being a monk."

"How would you like me to call you?"

"You can call me Nandana Swami or just Maharaj. Some people call me Nanda."

"Maharaj, thank you for the great dinner, best meal I had in a long time."

He nodded, and I found his expression intriguing. His brown eyes were deep and clear. There was a discrepancy between the way he acted—full of animation and emotion—and the aloofness of his eyes.

"Let's go upstairs and chant," he said, and turning toward Blossom, "You stay here and watch the door."

"Yes Maharaj," she nodded shyly looking at his feet.

The Swami went first and we followed him closely up the stairs. The room was packed with people, some of them wearing brown robes, others the usual mélange of clothing typical to the East Village. A pleasant fragrance of Indian incense, sage and sweet grass permeated the air. A man with shaved head and friendly blue eyes, maybe in his mid thirties, started "purifying" us with a smoking bundle of sage and then bowed in front of Maharaj with

111

reverence. He seemed pleased, and patted the man on the shoulder.

The music stopped and Maharaj went to Krishna's Shrine, bowed in front of it, and sat facing us. On the floor, everyone was shuffling and pushing, trying to find a more comfortable position. Maharaj folded his hands in prayer, mumbled something and then looked around, his eyes animated and joyful. His golden-brown skin seemed to be glowing. Dark hair framed a large forehead with perfectly arched eyebrows. His big olive eyes had a compassionate expression. I've never seen such clear eyes. With a sensual mouth and well proportioned body he looked like a Roman statue. Watching him gave me a sense of comfort, a feeling that everything was going to be all right.

At first, he started to eulogize his Guru, other Gurus and sacred places, and then he began to talk about Krishna. He said that Krishna, just "a little boy" was actually the Supreme God Himself taking birth into the world out of compassion for the suffering people of this Earth. The secret reason Krishna came into this world was to experience the company of his beloved devotes, and to perceive the highest human emotion, 'Pure Love of God'. Krishna lived in this world about five thousand years ago. As he was talking, I was mesmerized by his beautiful face illuminated by flickering candles. Something about him filled me with wonder. After a while he said:

"If you are here for the first time, raise your hand." A few hands were up. Looking straight at me he asked: "Anna, why did you come here tonight?"

"I am not sure," I said. "I like to chant, and . . ."

"Welcome, you're in the right place."

A man with long braided hair, holding a flat drum in his hand got up and said:

"My name is Sun Rise. My friend Brian told me about this place. He said that you guys have the best food in New York City." He laughed. "I was just curious, that's why I'm here."

"Welcome to all of you," the swami said. "We have a great feast tonight, but first we will nourish our souls by chanting the name of God."

Everybody started beating the drums, shaking the rattles and banging the cymbals as loud as they could. Christina passed around a basket full of instruments. I took a small pair of cymbals. Nandana Swami started to play the harmonium. Suddenly the whole room was silent. As he was playing, he said:

"We are going to chant the name of Krishna.

Krishna is the most beautiful,

He is the most powerful,

The most intelligent,

Krishna is our only friend."

He began chanting Hare Krishna in a slow tempo. Other instruments joined in one by one. We all started to chant harmonizing our voices in unexpected ways. The tempo was escalating rhythmically. Maharaj was leading us into beautiful melodies. I could see images of pastoral landscapes, rolling like a movie in front of my closed eyes following the music. Sometimes the melody was hard to remember, other times very familiar. My mind was captivated by the repetitive, rhythmical sound, and many thoughts and worries were melting away into the magical music.

A few men began to dance in a circle, others followed and soon everyone was dancing around the room faster and faster, sometimes running, sometimes jumping high, in an ecstatic frenzy that was contagious. It was hot in the room and I was soaked. The dance lasted a long time and ended abruptly. We all sat on the floor and I was in a state of suspension. Maharaj was sitting motionless with his back straight and his head tilted to the right side, almost as if an invisible pillow was holding it. His forehead was full of light. I had the feeling that I already lived this moment before. I closed my eyes. Beautiful images of soft meadows in the moonlight were scrolling in front of me. I could see silhouettes of trees emerging from the blue mist.

Everybody was sitting quietly, watching him. He started reading from a book a few verses in Sanskrit and then translated them in English. He talked for a long time and all I remembered was something about giving up all "material desires" and becoming immersed in worshiping God (Krishna) constantly. After the talk everyone was given a plate of food. Christina brought me another plate and in spite all my efforts to refuse it, I resigned myself to eat again, and to my surprise, the food tasted even better than before. I don't remember talking to anybody in particular and in a short while I left and decided to walk home.

St. Marks Place was as busy as ever. A young girl dressed in black with chains all over was begging for money. She was holding a sweet puppy with floppy ears that was licking her partially shaved head. A man with short hair dyed like a leopard's skin was sitting on the sidewalk next to her. They seemed to be so free . . . I always wanted to be free, with no worries or responsibilities, to be a kid again and never worry about my next meal. I had an intense desire for someone to care for me. I wanted to find a home. The swami's words rang loudly in my ears.

"This is not your home! Your home is in the Spiritual World. You give so much importance to this body which you will have to give up soon. Everything that belongs to the body is temporary . . ."

I started to walk up Fifth Avenue. Suddenly the street was quiet, the atmosphere clear, with a few stars shining in the purple sky. Once in a while I could see a silhouette approaching from faraway. Passing by Barnes & Nobles, I stopped and looked at the new books in the window. Everything was so peaceful. Somebody used to say that the world is always the same but we perceive it as good, bad or indifferent according to our mood. That night the world was great. I was not afraid of anything. The melody that Maharaj chanted was still reverberating in my mind and I found myself singing it out loud. The thought that I was just another crazy person singing on the streets of New York made me smile. What would people think of me? Nobody cared. They were too involved with themselves to even notice. Arriving home, I lit some incense and sat on my meditation pillow for a while, quiet, trying to imprint that wholesome feeling of peace into my memory.

The following day, I slept late and couldn't get it together to make lunch. A vague feeling of guilt was lingering in my consciousness and a punishing voice nagging at me. What was I doing hanging out with the Krishnas? They had such a bad reputation! It was said that they brainwashed people and did all kinds of bad things. On the other hand, everything seemed fine. I wasn't going to turn away from the promise of a new experience, a new life, maybe happiness . . .

Around four o'clock, I got out of bed and decided to walk down to the East Village. Entering the familiar courtyard, I saw the man with shaved head and friendly blue eyes, washing some stainless steel trays and silverware. He was using an old hose and his face lit up with a big smile, when he saw me.

"Hi there," I said, "I'm Anna. What's your name?"

"Ram," he said. "Actually my name is Ramachandra Swami, but everybody calls me Brother Ram."

"Why do you wash the dishes out here?"

"The sink gets clogged. We have to get a new sink. Would you give me a hand?"

"Sure, just tell me what to do."

"Are you sure you don't mind?"

"No I slept the whole day, I need something to do."

"Okay, just dry those trays and put them inside on the counter. How come you slept so late?"

"I don't know maybe I am a little depressed."

"You must get up early and take a cold shower, you'll feel better."

"What time do you get up?"

"We usually get up at four. We all live in a temple in Brooklyn. Every morning we do a mantra meditation for an hour and then we have a nice program with chanting and dancing in front of the Deities. Usually Maharaj gives a lecture. Only after the program, we sit and have breakfast. Maybe sometime you'd like to come to the temple with us."

"Someday I will," I said and started drying the trays with an old rag. "I used to get up early and meditate. It was really good, but now I don't know . . . everything seems so difficult."

The door opened and a young looking girl came out holding a big box full of candles. "Where should I put those?" she asked Ram. "Quickly, I can't hold them any longer."

"Put them anywhere, I don't care," he said.

She just dropped the box in front of the door and turning around on her heels went right back inside. Ram made a long face and picked up the box, moving it away from the door.

"That was Nina," Ram said. "We met her last year at the Rainbow Gathering. She is doing much better now. Nina and her friend Christina roaming around half-naked at the Rainbow, were getting into all kinds of trouble. We brought them back here. You'll meet them, they're good kids."

"I already met Christina last night. She was very sweet to me."

"She can be sweet if she wants to."

"What's a Rainbow Gathering?"

"It's a peace gathering of people from all over the world. We come together once a year in July, every year in a different location. The highlight is the peace meditation on the 4th of July. It's awesome."

"Sounds interesting,"

"We go every year and feed hundreds of people. There are many young kids that end up sleeping in our camp. They feel protected because we don't allow them to do drugs. Many come back to our ashram in West Virginia and some of them turn their lives around."

Nina came out with a big pile of dirty trays. She walked toward us, checking me out without any reservation. She had long blond hair, dark mischievous eyes and looked very healthy, with rosy cheeks. She was a little overweight.

I couldn't help thinking that those girls looked so healthy, probably because they lived most of the time in the country, or maybe it was the effect of living a spiritual life. New Yorkers don't look like that. She was wearing a long, embroidered skirt and a dirty blouse that once was all white. Dumping the trays in front of Ram, she looked directly at me.

"Hi, I'm Nina. Maharaj wants you to come inside and help him with something."

My heart skipped a beat. I followed her inside and didn't expect to see him again so soon. I was excited and a little bit frightened.

"Anna, how nice to see you, did you like the program last night?" He asked.

"I had a great time, thank you. Is there anything I can do?"

He paused for a second, lost in thoughts. "Yes, you can go upstairs and get the room ready for tonight. Nina, please show Anna what to do. It's nice of you to come and help."

Nina went first and I followed.

"Just straighten up the room," she said, and went back downstairs.

It was a mess. I started to pick all the instruments from the floor and put them in a basket by the stairway, and I went downstairs to look for a broom. Maharaj and Nina were gone. Ram was still outside washing dishes.

"Where did they go?" I asked

"To the corner, to preach and hand out some flyers."

"The floors need to be washed," I said. "You have a mop and a bucket of water?"

"Come, I'll show you where we keep them." He gave me a mop and a plastic bucket from under the stairs. I cleaned the floors very well and realized that everything else was dusty. I had to dust and clean the floors again.

When Maharaj and Nina returned, he came upstairs, looked around and smiled.

"Anna, you did a great job." He turned to Brother Ram: "See, the place should always be this clean."

Brother Ram a little embarrassed nodded: "Yes Maharaj."

"Let's go and get the food from the van," Maharaj said. Anna, can you give us a hand?

"Yes, Maharaj," I said.

We went back and forth from the street through the long corridor, carrying the stainless steel trays of food into the dining room. I was very hungry and the food smelled good. Maharaj read my mind.

"If anybody is hungry, just make yourself a plate." I was a little hesitant and Maharaj continued, "Krishna is happy to see his Devotes eat the food that was offered to Him. It's called Prasad, a gift from Krishna." Looking directly at me he said: "Anna, you sit and Nina will make you a plate." He looked at Nina over his shoulder. She was watching him intensely and whispered:

"Yes Maharaj."

I sat at a table and Nina came with two big plates of food and sat in front of me. She started eating in silence watching me when I wasn't looking with her sharp eyes.

"Where is Christina? I asked"

"She had to do something, she'll be here later for the program," Nina said and pulled out of her pocket some prayer beads handing them to me. "This is for you to chant the mantra every morning when you get up and before you go to sleep. Smell it, is sandalwood."

"Oh, I love this fragrance, thank you so much." I put the beads around my neck. They felt light, like a feather.

Nina looked somewhat familiar and I was trying to figure out why. "What does your father do? I asked.

"I don't have a father, he left when I was very young. I don't remember him."

"I am sorry."

"That's okay, I am used to it. I have fewer material attachments and feel freer this way. I can go anywhere and do anything I want.

"How old are you?"

"Twenty-three" she said.

"You look about nineteen. I left home at nineteen and never went back. Never got along that well with my family, I am better off on my own. Actually, I hated my life at home drinking a lot just to numb my feelings. I don't drink anymore, alcohol makes me sick now."

"I am glad you don't drink. No alcohol is one of our principles."

"What are you talking about?"

"We try to follow four principles; no intoxication, no meat eating, no sex and no gambling."

"You cannot have sex, ever?"

"Only if you are married and want to have children. Also, before sex both people must chant the mantra for six hours, to purify themselves."

"You're kidding me!"

"No, this is true. We try to live by the Vedic principles. It's not always easy, people break them quiet often. They must chant for a long time to purify themselves."

"I think I can follow those principles," I said. "I am not planning to have a boyfriend in the near future."

People started to trickle in few at a time, carrying all kinds of drums. Some wearing beaded head bands or feathers braided into their hair. A tall man walked in dressed in native clothes, but he had blond hair pulled back in a pony tail. Everyone seemed to know him. He had a self-assured walk and a friendly smile. He spotted Nina, came over and gave her a hug.

"Hi Nina, nice to see you again, I brought you some sage to try. It's the best!" He handed a plastic bag to Nina, and then looked at me "I don't remember seeing you before. Are you new?"

"I've been here a few times," I said.

"Are you staying for the ceremony?"

"Yes, I am."

"Tiger-Eye is leading this program, a Native American ceremony. Tonight is the Native night," Nina said.

"I had no idea," I said surprised.

Two women came over and Tiger-Eye hugged them at the same time and walked away holding them both.

"How about some tea?" Nina asked.

"This time I'll bring it. What kind of tea you like?"

Nina seemed a little embarrassed.

"Red Zinger and a bit of honey," she said.

I got up to get the tea when Blossom walked in. "Hello, Hare Krishna," Blossom said, "Good to see you here."

"Anna helped us get ready today," Nandana Swami said with a big smile.

"It's been fun, much better than staying home sleeping."

"We're going out to preach," Nandana Swami said. "After the program we can give you a ride home. See you later, Hare Krishna." They went out and I was a little disappointed, hoping to hear him give another lecture.

"Let's go upstairs," Nina said. "Forget about the tea."

Upstairs everyone was seated in a circle. The air was thick with the fragrance of sage and sweet grass. Tiger-Eye was wearing a feathered headband and was carrying a native drum ornate with beautiful designs. He was leading the circle. I looked around the packed room but nobody seemed to be Native American.

An interesting looking girl sat next to Tiger-Eye. She was a big, heavy woman with a pile of feathers in front of her on the floor, laid on a woolen blanket. The feathers were brightly colored and each one had a seashell attached with a red thread. Several pipes carved into various types of stones were arranged in a circle in the center of the blanket.

The woman started to distribute feathers to everyone. I received a red turkey feather. It was a gift for us to cherish. Different colors represented the four directions where we could send our prayers. After that Tiger-Eye said:

"We will dedicate this gathering to our friends and well wishers the animal people. Let's imagine that each of us is a channel for the animal of our choice. Let's give them a voice. Let them speak. We must hear what our friends have to say. Who wants to start?"

A woman got up. "I am an orange cat, please help me! I live in dark box in a laboratory. They fed me poison and burned my stomach and now put needles into my veins and they will kill me as soon as they are finished. I beg you to help me!"

A young man very thin with long curly hair and a funny little hat on top of his head said in a high-pitched voice: "I am a cow and hate you! You just killed my baby. You took him away when he could hardly stand. Now you are stealing my milk that was meant to feed my baby. You keep me and hundreds of others in cubicles so narrow that we cannot even lie down. We have to stand all the time. When my milk will dry out, you'll kill me too. You are the most despicable creatures on this earth!"

Another woman got up. "I am a bird," she said. "I live in a small steel cage. The people that own me love me very much. They play with me; give me toys and more food than I can possibly eat. But I am so lonely. I have nothing to do all day. I don't have a mate, nothing to live for. Life makes no sense to me. I want to fly, to see trees and flowers and gather with other bird friends. Sometimes I think I'll lose my mind. How long is this going to last?" Many people got up and talked and most of us were in tears.

Tiger-Eye finally said: "Let's dedicate this pipe to all our friends that spoke through our voices. Maybe we cannot help much, but every little thing we can do for our friends that are suffering so much is very important. By refusing to contribute to this massacre and abstaining when we can from eating meat or buying the furs and skins that are the result of so much pain, we can make a difference. Saving one life at a time, we can save many lives at the end." Everyone cheered and the pipe started to go around the circle while we were chanting accompanied by a loud drum beat. After the pipe went around people were more cheerful, and Brother Ram invited us all to have a free feast downstairs.

When I went downstairs, Maharaj was seated with some young man talking. Blossom and Christina were helping serve food to everyone.

"Anna," Maharaj said, "why don't you come back to the temple with us tonight? You can stay in the women's ashram and come to the program in the morning. We have a very nice temple. You'll see."

I was just thinking about how much I wanted to go to the temple but I was too shy to ask.

"I'd love to," I said, "I have nothing to do tomorrow anyway."

"Okay, we'll leave after we clean up. Have something to eat, you must be hungry."

Soon everybody was gone except a few people that were coming back to the temple with us. I cleaned up a little and helped carry the empty trays and utensils to the van. Brother Ram and Maharaj sat in the front, and the rest of us piled up in the back. Brother Ram was driving and the van was in a deplorable shape. One of the windows patched with cardboard and duct tape, and the back seats missing. I sat on a pile of coats which probably belonged to the swamis. At every turn the trays were sliding from one side to the other making so much noise that Maharaj had to turn around and anxiously check if everything was all right. Christina was seating next to me.

"Look at the lights," she said in awe.

We were on the Brooklyn Bridge. Millions of lights were illuminating the sky and the whole downtown area looked like a honeycomb. The atmosphere was so clear that you could see every detail.

"It's really something," I said. "You're lucky to see this every night."

"It's my favorite moment," Christina said.

"How about the morning japa? I want to see everybody at five o'clock tomorrow morning in the temple." Maharaj said. There was a moment of silence.

"Japa means repeating the mantra," Blossom explained.

"I know."

"Christina, you make sure that everybody gets up in time," Maharaj said.

"Yes sir!" Christina said and gave him a military salute.

After a few turns the van stopped in front of an old building. The street was empty except for a few people hanging out in front of a bar. Some other buildings looked abandoned.

"Let's empty the van," Maharaj said.

We started unloading the trays, empty containers and utensils into a narrow corridor with old mosaic tiles on the floor. Many tiles were missing. It was very cold and Brother Ram decided to move everything into the kitchen. The small kitchen was warm, well lit and professionally equipped with a big iron stove and a stainless steel counter in the center. Big pots were hanging on top of the counter and lined up on shelves, all kinds of spices and containers neatly labeled. It smelled like Indian spices and incense. Everything was very clean and orderly.

"What a nice kitchen," I said.

"Let's see the temple," Maharaj said, "but the Deities are sleeping now. You can see them tomorrow morning."

The temple was a large square room with high ceilings and wooden beams supporting it. On the walls pictures of Krishna were painted in a very realistic manner. Two brass chandeliers hanging from the ceiling, were giving a dim light. A dark-blue curtain covered the whole back wall with the altar behind it. With benches along the rest of the walls and pillows scattered around the shiny wooden floor, the temple invoked a feeling of authenticity. Piled up on the far corner were numerous musical instruments, a microphone stand and a full bookcase. Christina came out of the kitchen with a tray of sweets, and put it on the floor in front of me.

"Let's have a snack before we go upstairs." She sat next to me.

Everybody disappeared quickly to their rooms. Christina took a cookie from the tray and looked at me with a mysterious smile.

"Next week a swami from India is coming and he'll be here for a while. Can't wait to see him! I think of him as some kind of a saint. He's very compassionate, has a great sense of humor, and leads wonderful chants. I really like him. I want to go to India and stay in his ashram."

"What's his name?"

"Radhakund Swami," she said.

"What does that mean?"

"Radhakund is a sacred lake in India. It is the lake where Radha, Krishna's girlfriend, liked to bathe in the moonlight with her girlfriends, before she went to secretly meet Krishna."

"What a beautiful name. Please, let me know when he comes, I'd like to meet this swami."

Christina was gazing into space and she seemed far away. After a while, she said:

"I'll tell you something, but don't tell anybody."

"Of course," I said, "I hardly know any of those people, anyway."

"Well, I think I am in love with Radhakund Swami. He is a very pure devote and he treats me like a daughter. I want to serve him. It makes me happy. When he stays here in the temple I get to do his laundry. You should see, his clothes smell like sandalwood, and when I hang his shawls to dry, the whole room fills with this incredible fragrance."

"Is he your Guru?" I asked. "Sometimes people fall in love with their gurus."

"No, he's not officially a guru but many people consider him so. He just cannot initiate anybody. He will in the future. I am sure of it, and I'll wait for him to initiate me."

"What about Maharaj?" I said. "I like him very much. At first I thought he was nineteen years old, he looks so young."

"He's about thirty years old but he looks young. He's the president of the temple. When we raise money, he always raises twice the amount and in half the time. People just give him money. It's almost like he hypnotizes them or something. Devotes constantly go to him for advice for one thing or another. He is always very busy." She paused for a while. "I think he likes you, Anna, I can tell . . ." Suddenly we became aware of another presence in the temple. Maharaj was standing by the door, watching us. He said in a sweet voice:

"Time to go to bed girls."

"Good night Maharaj," I said, embarrassed wondering if he heard us.

He waited until we left the temple. As we passed by him, I felt the warmth emanating from his body. He was standing by the door, motionless, like a Gate Keeper to the Gods. He touched my head and said:

"Go to sleep now Girls, tomorrow we have a long day."

The women's ashram was on the fourth floor. We ascended the narrow stairway, entering a small apartment. People were sleeping on the floor. Christina walked in first, tiptoeing around the sleeping bodies. She entered a small room that used to be a walk-in closet, closed the door and lit a candle.

"We can both sleep in this room," she said. "You sleep there and I usually sleep here," she pointed to a pile of pillows and some dirty sheets. Next to 'her bed', a mattress laid on the floor for me, had clean sheets and a red pillowcase.

"Let me show you something," Christina said, opening a cardboard box. She pulled out some old photographs. "This was Maharaj before he became a devotee."

The picture was of a handsome youth with beautiful wavy dark hair covering his shoulders. I did not recognize him for a moment.

"He looks like a God," I said.

Christina said jokingly:

"If I met him then, maybe he'd still have long hair. He was a nineteen years old hippy, searching for God everywhere. About ten years ago when he met the devotees, he knew right away he wanted to dedicate his life to God. He doesn't know I have this picture."

She pulled another picture out of the box. It was a picture of her and Nina, half naked in the midst of a crowd of hippies.

"This is us right before we met the devotees at the Rainbow Gathering.

"You look so happy in this picture," I said.

"I was very unhappy and didn't know what I was looking for, and very self involved. Now, I just want to serve the devotees. It makes me happy."

"Your parents know you live here?"

"Yes, but they don't like it. Is nothing they can do to stop me, I am twenty-four years old."

"You look much younger."

Cristina lay on the "bed" and smiled. "I am so tired, good night, Anna. Put out the candle please, before you go to sleep."

I lay on my mattress for a while watching the shadows made by the candle on the walls. Christina fell asleep right away. Her pillowcase was filthy but her face had a serene glow and looked like an innocent child. With all her possessions piled up in a corner of the room, she seemed to be a true renunciate. That image made a deep impression on me. I put out the candle and the room was in complete darkness. As I was watching the phantasmagoric shapes created in my mind from the absolute blackness in the room, I vividly remembered being in my bed, back in Romania.

CHAPTER 10

1964 ROMANIA—END OF INNOCENSE

It was a cool winter morning. I was in the seventh grade and overslept. My mother rushed in with a strong cup of Turkish coffee. Its bittersweet taste gave me a jolt of energy. My school uniform was on a chair in my room, freshly ironed. It was a simple navy blue dress with a detachable white collar, which I could unbutton and wash separately. I was wearing knee high socks with boots. My camel hair coat was really a spring coat way too big, but it made me look more presentable even if I was freezing. I had to comb my hair back with a white band around my head.

I got dressed as fast as I could and ran downstairs to grab a sandwich. My mother was in the living room waiting for me. She was a short, heavy woman always on a diet and constantly complaining about gaining weight. She often wore a shapeless dress that was covering the whole body. Her hair was salt and pepper, parted on one side. Sometimes, one of her sisters gave her a bad haircut and she would always say that when it grows a little it would look better.

"Anna, are you going to see Lester today? She asked.

"I don't know," I said, "why?"

Suddenly her psychic green eyes opened up and she handed me a pink envelope.

"Another letter?" I asked a little annoyed.

"Yes," she said, "you should give this letter to Lester. Don't forget to read it."

I opened the letter. It was a love poem and my name was on the bottom. After confessing to her that I was a little interested in Lester, she started writing love poems to Lester and had me tell him that I wrote them. He was eighteen years old and my counselor in school. Lester was studying journalism and his father was a well-known writer. My mother insisted that I let her write those love letters to Lester. He was impressed by the 'maturity' and 'sensitivity' of my writing skills. I tried to argue with her, but she was convinced that he would never find the truth. She was encouraging me to have a relationship with him.

Lester was a tall, well-built young man with dark eyes and thick eyelashes. His hair was black and he kept it perfectly combed. He was wearing thick eyeglasses with a thin silver wire frame that made his eyes look even bigger. I took the pink envelope, put it in my school bag and ran out in the cold snowy streets all the way to school, stopping to catch my breath every so often.

Later in the day I gave Lester my letter and he gave me his with a note attached to it. I opened it and to my surprise, he was inviting me to visit that evening. He had a separate room in his parents' house with his own entrance and talked a lot about it. I was curious to see it. It was hard for me to tell if I really liked Lester but somehow I felt I should. I had a sinking feeling about going to his house that evening. He suggested that I don't tell my mother, and instructed me to say that I was going to a party with him and his friends. I lied to my mother and she helped me get dressed for the 'Party'. She was all excited. I wore a pink satin dress and spend a long time in front of the mirror teasing my hair. I penciled my eyes and put a lot of mascara on my eyelashes. I always thought my eyelashes were too short.

I met him at a street corner, close to his home. He was nervous and looked up and down the street to see if anybody was coming before we went in. In a rush to get upstairs he was climbing two steps at a time. I couldn't keep up with him.

"Wait for me," I said.

Putting his fingers on his lips he told me to be quiet. His room was on the third floor and after we entered, he locked the door.

"I don't want my mother to know that I have visitors," he said.

The room was so small that all he could fit in there was a bed, a desk and a chair. Everything was perfectly clean and his papers, arranged in neat piles on the desk. It was an old school desk but he kept it waxed and shiny as well as the big, heavy chair next to it. A bunch of books, were piled up on the chair.

"I am so impressed with your poetry," he said, "one day you're going to be a great poet."

"Thank you," I said embarrassed, "but I don't always write."

"It's understandable, happens to everybody, even to the best writers. Would you like some vodka?"

"Sure," I said. We both lit a cigarette.

"I didn't know you smoked," he said.

"Of course, I do. My girlfriend's brother thought us how. He gave us the strongest non filter cigarettes. He said that if we get used to smoke those, we could smoke anything."

"I only smoke filter cigarettes," he said and laughed. "I like to live a healthy life."

He pulled a bottle of vodka and two glasses from under the bed. He only poured one finger of vodka in each glass. "You should never fill the glass," he said.

I put the glass on my lips and felt the burning sensation of pure alcohol in my mouth and down my throat. It didn't taste like much, except for the strong, burning sensation and the smell of alcohol.

"How do you like it?" He asked.

"Very good," I lied.

He sat on the bed next to me with sweat bubbling on his forehead. "You look so beautiful in this dress," he said, grabbing my legs and stretching them on the bed. "Let me take your dress off. You don't want to wrinkle it."

"Okay," I said and he carefully took off my dress and put it on the chair.

"Would you like more vodka?"

"Just a little more, please."

He filled half the glass and handed it to me. "This is the best vodka," he said. "Somebody gave it to my father as a present. He lay in bed next to me, all dressed, and started to kiss me and squeeze my body with his strong hands. It was hurting but I didn't say anything. The vodka made me a little dizzy. He asked me to touch him. After a while he looked at his watch.

"It's late. I have to take you home." He was a little annoyed. "Why are you so cold? A woman like you should be more passionate."

"I am not cold," I said, putting my dress on.

He made up a story for me to tell my mother. When I arrived home I told her that I danced the whole night and she wanted to know every detail. "I am sleepy," I said, "good night Mother."

I went to the bathroom and washed my body with cold water. We didn't have hot water. In spite of it I felt very dirty and lonely. I sat in my room by the window and looked at the sky. It was the first time I had an overwhelming desire to be somewhere else. I imagined a bridge crossing over the sky, and me walking away from my life, to another place where I would be happy and free.

A few weeks later on a Saturday, my mother went to visit some friends outside the city. She would often spend her weekends with them. They had a small house and a beautiful garden. The house used to be an old shack, which they transformed into a work of art. Every corner was hand painted with flowery designs and they collected the most exquisite woven fabrics and ceramics from the old country. Around the house they planted a lush garden with vegetables, flowers and herbs and on the rest of the property many types of trees. The orange and fig trees had to be covered every winter with blankets and grass cloth to insulate them from the cold.

I told my mother I wasn't feeling well and stayed home. Lester called me and when he heard that my mother was away, decided to come over. I didn't want to see him, but he insisted. He came over sooner than I expected, out of breath and wearing a blue shirt drenched in sweat.

"Hi Anna, it's so hot out there," he said. "How are you?"

"You got here fast," I said. "Would you like some coffee?"

"Yes please, I'll have a cup."

I used a small copper kettle for Turkish coffee and put five teaspoons of coffee, lots of sugar and four cups of water, and stood by the stove to watch it boil. Lester sat on the wooden bench at the kitchen table, watching me with his intense eyes. The coffee began to rise and I waited until the last minute to turn off the flame. I poured the coffee in two large ceramic cups.

"That's a lot of coffee," he said.

"I am used to it. We drink it all the time."

"Do you mind if I take off my shirt?"

"No, why would I mind? It's hot today"

"I miss your letters, you didn't write me in a while."

"I am here," I said, "You don't need any letters." He acted surprised.

"What are you reading?" He asked.

"Nothing," I said, "How about you?"

"Oh, I am reading a book on Darwinism."

"We didn't study Darwinism yet, maybe we will in the ninth grade or so," I said.

"Oh, I forgot you're so young."

"Thanks," I said laughing. "What was Darwin's theory all about?"

"He was a genius and believed that all species evolved from a simple molecule to the complex human beings that we are today. It's fascinating!"

"I guess," I said. "Do you want more sugar?"

"No thanks. Come and sit next to me."

I went to sit on the bench next to him but he grabbed me and sat me on his lap. "Are you sure your mother is not coming home today?"

"Of course I am. Every time she goes to visit her friends, spends the whole weekend with them."

"What do you do all day?" He asked.

"I don't know," I said, "sometimes I go to the lake and swim."

"Let's go and have the coffee in your room."

"It's kind of messy, but okay."

I tried to stand but he was holding me tight. "Let me go," I said.

He loosened his grip and we went upstairs to my room, which was in complete disarray with books and records everywhere and piles of clothes on the floor, I never hung up. What wasn't on the floor was piled up at the bottom of the closet. He looked at my room with displeasure and than checked the door knobs.

"You don't have a lock to your room?"

"No," I said, "my mother doesn't want me to lock my room."

"I have an idea. You've got a key to the attic?"

"Yes, but why do you want to go to the attic?"

"I want to make love to you," he said.

"What? I don't think so!"

"Just a little bit, please, why don't you want to?"

"I don't know . . ."

"Why are you so cold, you don't like me?"

"I do, really," I said.

"Come, let's go!" He said and pulled me close. His body was all hot and sweaty. He dragged me up to the attic and locked the door from the inside. He laid some old blankets on the floor and started undressing me, fast almost ripping off my blouse.

"Take it easy!"

"Yes, yes," he whispered under his breath. With one hand, he was holding me and with the other was taking off my pants. "Your skin feels so good," he said.

It was very hot in the attic and he was more determined than ever. His grip was so strong that I couldn't move. He kept on pressing himself against me and it was painful.

"Just a little bit," he said and stopped for a few seconds. "You complain so much, you should be enjoying it. You're not a real woman."

I felt ashamed and gave in. He was like crazy, breathing heavily, grabbing and squeezing me with all his strength. When he calmed down, he lay next to me.

"I am going to take a shower,' I said. "I feel hot."

"I have to go home," he said "I've got a lot of studying to do. I'll see you later." We got dressed and went downstairs. I walked him to the door. After he left, I collapsed on my bed. That evening, he came back and took me to the attic. He was very violent and hurting me. He kept on saying that I should be more loving. In the next couple of weeks he kept on showing up when I was home alone, repeating the same thing over and over.

One afternoon, my mother was away. Lester came up to my room and was kissing me, took off my clothes, rolled on top of me on the floor, and started violently to have sex with me. Suddenly the door opened. It was my mother. She stood there stone-faced, watching us. Lester couldn't see her. She closed the door and left.

"Stop, stop!" I pushed him away, but he was holding me tight. "My mother opened the door, she'd seen us."

He suddenly stopped with a panicked expression on his face. "What? You told me she was away!"

"She was," I said "but she came back."

"I've got to go!" He got dressed quickly ran out the door.

I felt like sinking into the floor. My mother was gone as well. I took a cold shower and waited for hours. That evening she came back but didn't say a word. She acted like nothing happened, and never mentioned Lester again.

A few weeks later Mother opened the door to my room. It was early in the morning. "What are you doing Annie? I thought you went to school, what happened?"

"I am not feeling well. I am dizzy and noxious."

"Maybe you have a cold." She touched my forehead with her lips to see if I had a fever.

"You don't have a fever," she said. "I'll make you some mint tea. It's good for your stomach."

"I didn't get my period in two weeks. It's that normal?"

She suddenly became pale and stone-faced.

"You have to go to a doctor right away. I hope it's not what I am thinking."

"What are you saying?" I asked.

"I hope that you're not pregnant."

"Oh my God, that cannot be!"

"You've been sleeping with Lester."

"Yes'" I said," He loves me."

"What are you going to do now?" Mother asked.

"I don't know, to be honest I don't think I love him"

"He is such a good man . . ."

"Well, I don't want to have a baby with him. It gives me the creeps."

"That's nonsense! He is a fine man, what's wrong with you?"

"Nothing, you should understand, you hate it when Father touches you."

"Yes, but we are still married," she said in a dignified way.

"Well, I don't want to get married, I don't want to have a baby and I don't want to sleep with Lester anymore!"

"You better think seriously about this," she said.

"I thought about it, I don't love Lester, period!"

"But you told me you loved him."

"I lied to you, because you liked him so much." I started to cry.

"I am going to make an appointment with a doctor for tomorrow." She was very angry. "If you're pregnant you should get an abortion right away."

"Okay," I said. "Leave me alone, now!" She left slamming the door.

I was petrified. I knew that I was pregnant, I could feel it. I was definitely going to have an abortion. I was wondering if it was going to hurt and if I should tell Lester. I didn't want to see him at all. I felt angry with him and my mother. I wished there was a place where I could get away from both of them. I hated living there, with Lester coming by and having sex with me every time he wanted to. Nobody cared about how I felt. I propped a chair against the door and cried for a long time. I pulled the blankets over my head and began touching my body to see what was going on. My breasts were tender and seemed bigger. I spent the whole morning in bed. Mother never came back with the tea. I felt noxious and famished at the same time. I went downstairs. She was on the phone. The kitchen was dirty and full of grease. On top of the stove, there was some fried chicken, which I couldn't even look at. I made a sandwich with butter and some tomato and went back to my room. She was still on the phone. After eating, I felt much better. After blocking the door with the chair, I lied on the bed and fell asleep. My mother's voice woke me up.

"Open the door, Annie!" She yelled from behind the door.

"What do you want? I am sleeping!"

"We need to talk, open immediately!" I opened the door and she stormed into my room.

"I made an appointment with the clinic," she said. "If you're pregnant you will get an abortion right-away. Here, take some money to pay for it and for a cab on the way back. The appointment is at nine tomorrow morning." She was very cold and distant.

"Wake me up at seven thirty."

"I am going out," she said and left.

I put on some music and got under the blankets, thinking about Alexander and how much I was missing him. The idea of having a child with Lester was appalling. I could hardly sleep that night. In the morning she woke me up at seven thirty. I took a cold shower and put on a fancy slip under the dress to make me look older. I tried to talk to my mother but her door was locked.

I went out and slammed the door. The streetcar left me only couple of blocks away from the clinic. I looked at the massive building, constructed right after war, like many other government buildings. I couldn't understand why she didn't come to the clinic. Maybe she was angry because I didn't love Lester. She liked him. She cared about him more than me.

I walked in and a nurse took me to a small room with a wooden consultation table, couple of metal chairs and many shelves full of boxes and bottles. On a big tray on wheels, all kinds of shiny instruments were neatly lined up. The nurse told me to undress and gave me an old flannel gown. I left my slip on but she told me to take everything off. She asked me if I eat anything and I told her that I only had coffee. She had me give her a urine sample in a paper cup, after which I lay on the table and she came with a syringe to take some blood. I turned my head the other way.

"That's it," she said. "We'll do a test and you can wait right here. By the way, how old are you?" I decided to make myself a year older.

"Fourteen," I said. She gave me a long look and left the room. I waited and waited for a long time. Finally she came back and sat on a chair next to me.

"You are pregnant," she said. "Do you want to keep the baby?"

"I can't believe I am pregnant. Are you sure?"

"Yes," she said, "definitely."

"I don't know . . . I am still in high school."

"Do you want to have an abortion?"

"Yes, I mean, yes I think so."

She took my hand. "You are too young to have a baby. I don't know what happened to you but you need to be sure that you don't want the baby."

"I don't want the baby. I didn't know I was going to get pregnant," I said.

"Okay," she said, "you need to pay at the cashier before you go. Do you have any money?"

"I do."

"All right, you need to sign a paper. I'll be right back." She came back with a piece of paper and gave it to me. My hands were trembling.

"Don't be afraid. We do this all the time. It's an easy procedure."

"It's going to hurt?" I asked.

"A little, you'll be all right, don't worry." She grabbed my hand and squeezed it firmly. I started to cry. "You're a young girl, be more careful from now on." She took a small towel and wiped my tears.

"I will definitely be careful," I said.

"Don't worry," she smiled at me, and covered me with a heavy rubber sheet.

The doctor came in. "Hi there," he said. "How are you feeling?"

"Okay."

"I will give you a shot and it'll make you a little dizzy," the doctor said.

He gave me a shot and my heart started to beat faster. My head was swimming and I couldn't think clearly. It felt like I was spinning into space. Everything seemed to be faraway, the noises, the doctors, me. I was there and wasn't at the same time.

"You will feel a pinch," the doctor said.

I could see everything. He took a syringe with a very long needle and I felt a pinch inside my abdomen.

"It's the anesthesia," he said.

I was feeling pain, but it was not unbearable. The procedure lasted for about forty minutes. Something was unusual about the position of the fetus and for that reason the procedure took longer than usual. I felt like I was in a deep tunnel.

"There you are, finished," the doctor said.

The Nurse helped me get up and put my clothes on. She gave me a bottle of antibiotics.

"Take this for ten days," she said. "We want to make sure you don't get an infection. You have to refrain from intercourse for a week."

I put the antibiotics in my purse and paid at the cashier. Being so dizzy, I lost my balance and almost fell on the floor. The Nurse grabbed me and sat me on a chair.

"Sit here for a while. You'll feel better in about an hour."

I was feeling a dull pain inside my abdomen and sat there in a daze for a long time. The Nurse came back. "Is anybody picking you up?" She asked.

"No. I'll take a cab."

She shook her head and helped me down the steps. In front of the clinic, there was a long line of cabs, waiting for customers. She helped me get into the cab and waved goodbye.

"Thank you," I said, "I appreciate your help."

"It's Okay," she said, "rest when you get home."

The ride was bumpy. With each bump I felt a sharp pain in my abdomen. When I arrived home, I gave the cabdriver a good tip. I walked slowly and opened the front door. I was still dizzy. In the living room, my mother and Lester were sitting on two big chairs watching me. Nobody said a word. My mother was looking at me with a stone face and neither of them wanted to help me out. They were afraid to touch me, like I was contagious.

"I am going to lie down," I said and slowly climbed the stairs to my bedroom.

The pain was lessening. I crawled under the blankets and slept for a long time. Nobody came to bother me. I woke up feeling much better, but with a lingering headache, and very hungry. Downstairs, nobody was home. What a relief! The food tasted really good. I took the antibiotic and an aspirin and went back to bed. Pulling the heavy drapes over the windows, I rested my eyes on the bundles of herbs that I collected from the countryside over the summer, hanging above my bed. My intention was to make potions from those herbs and heal people. I took a few leaves of mint and inhaled the fresh, clean fragrance. The opposite wall was full of posters from many beautiful places from around the world. They were given to me by a friend. Her mother worked for the airlines. I wondered if I was ever going to see any of those places.

Every so often, I felt a sharp pain shooting through my abdomen. Nothing made any sense. My mother and Lester did this intentionally? Did they set me up intending to hurt me? I felt so lonely and made a decision to never listen to my mother again. This experience changed me in a profound way. I felt used, manipulated and very angry. I was like a doll in her hands, to do with me whatever she pleased. For her I was just a toy, an inanimate object, without feelings, emotions or a mind of my own. I had a right to do whatever I wanted with my life and my mother and Lester from then on, did not exist anymore. One day I would leave and go faraway, someplace where nobody could find me and where I could be myself.

CHAPTER 11

BROOKLYN TEMPLE

It felt safe realizing that it was all behind me and I was in Cristina's room in Brooklyn far away from my painful past. Gradually I was able to let go of all my problems, falling in and out of a light trance-like sleep where I could see images Maharaj dancing in beatitude with open arms and graceful movements.

A loud knock on the door startled me and I wasn't quite sure if I really slept, thinking that only a few minutes had gone by. My whole body was still buzzing with some strange energy keeping me awake. Christina was already up.

"Stay and sleep, if you want," she said, "I'll come and get you when breakfast is ready."

"I can't sleep. I want to go to the temple."

"The bathroom is over there," she pointed to a shabby door and handed me an old, stained towel. "It's clean," she said, "I just washed it. I have to go now, see you downstairs."

I looked in the mirror and my cheeks were pink and fresh in spite of the lack of sleep. I sprinkled some water on my face and straightened up my clothes. Everybody was gone. I rushed down the steep, wooden stairway and walked into the temple. It was dark. When my eyes started getting used to the darkness I could distinguish silhouettes of people wearing hooded robes, seated on the floor or on benches chanting on their prayer beads. I was trying to concentrate on the mantra but my eyes were searching around the room for Maharaj. I couldn't see him and feeling disappointed I tried to sit very still and focus on chanting.

My mind was agitated and the hour passed slowly. When the meditation was over, Brother Ram went behind the curtains and started blowing a conch shell loudly, creating an even sound which only an expert could. The ringing of many small silver bells made a high pitch sound when the curtain opened. Everybody kneeled on the floor bowing in front of the altar. It was breathtaking; all carved in dark wood, with Radha and Krishna in the form of young children lavishly dressed in magnificent silks and jewelry. Krishna was holding a silver flute in his hand and Radha a basket of roses. The whole altar was full of roses. The Deities looked so real, I had the feeling they were smiling at me, so beautiful and innocent looking.

Christina was holding a basket full of rose petals. Somebody stood up from the bench behind me, took a handful of rose petals and sprinkled them at the feet of the Deities. It was Maharaj. He had been behind me all that time and I didn't have a clue. One by one other devotes followed, sprinkling fresh petals on the altar. Somebody nudged me gently toward the altar. I took a handful of rose petals and put them at Krishna's feet. There was a faint smile on His flawless marble face, and when I turned around Maharaj was looking straight at me. I felt very self-conscious.

A devotee handed him a drum and he started to chant a beautiful hymn. After a while everyone joined in and Maharaj began to dance. We all followed. I was behind him trying to move in the same rhythm. Brother Ram took the drum away and started chanting Hare Krishna in his melodious voice, speeding up the tempo. Maharaj was dancing ecstatically and a group of devotes gathered in a circle around him. He was a wonderful dancer moving gracefully, hardly touching the floor. It was an awesome sight. He danced in the center of the circle. While everybody was clapping hands and chanting, he pulled a young devote inside the circle. He was a short and stocky boy, wearing a long brown robe, spinning around faster and faster until lost balance and almost fell over. Now the whole circle was moving around in a clockwise motion, slowly at first, and then faster and faster. In the center, young devotees were jumping up and down and then everyone was jumping as high as they could. I was surprised how high I was able to jump. I could see above everyone's heads.

All this came to a sudden stop. Maharaj bowed in front of the Deities and we all followed. I could hardly catch my breath. As my forehead touched the floor, my temples were pulsating, ready to explode. I could hear his voice offering obeisance to the Krishna, all the gurus, holy places and great devotees from the past. We all sat on the floor in silence for a few minutes. He started to read from the Bhagavat Gita and some devotes went to the kitchen. Christina asked me to help with breakfast. I was disappointed, and reluctantly went to the kitchen. It was buzzing with activity and I started cutting some vegetables.

Somebody was making pancakes. In the small kitchen at least six people were skillfully avoiding bumping into each other. After the lecture Brother Ram asked me to distribute the big stainless steel trays. I carefully put a tray on the floor in front of each devote. Christina and a few young men served breakfast. It was a feast with pancakes, fruit salad and honey, rice, vegetables, fruit juice and cookies. Maharaj sat next to me.

"Anna, it's nice to see you here. You got up this morning to chant with us and helped in the kitchen. I am proud of you!"

"I am really sorry I missed your lecture," I said.

"You did devotional service. Nothing is more ecstatic than serving the devotees. Besides, I don't know what I am talking about anyway."

"Maharaj, the lecture you gave at the Interfaith Center was great."

"Come here more often, you'll hear a lot of good lectures. What are you doing later?"

"I don't know, maybe look for some work."

"There is plenty of work right here. You can help the devotees cook dinner for the Center."

"I have to go home and feed my cats," I said, "I'll come back later."

"Come tonight to the Center. We need somebody to serve dinner and clean up a little after everybody leaves. It's a job. You'll get paid. We can pay you ten dollars an hour."

"Thank you Maharaj, I don't know what to say," I felt like crying and put my head down, trying to swallow my tears and avoid making a scene. Maharaj took an Indian candy ball from his tray and gave it to me.

"Anna, remember this is your home. You're always welcome here!" He patted me on the head on his way out.

"We'll see you at five o'clock at the center. Stay here for a while. You don't have to go."

I didn't want to leave. With the exception of my cats, I had no reason to go back to my apartment. I wondered about how many of the devotees left their families, jobs and friends to follow this spiritual path in search of God. I was thinking about letting go of all material things and becoming a devotee. I wanted to be free from worries, money, career, work, and the rest. I thought "spiritual life" meant to give up all those things and spend the rest of my life praying, meditating and thinking about God. Cristina wanted to know about my plans for the day.

"I think I'll go upstairs and rest," she said, "you can take a nap before you leave. We're going to a concert in the afternoon to raise some money. You can come with us if you want."

"Maybe, but I need to go home and feed the cats. Maharaj asked me to help clean and serve dinner at the Interfaith Center and I have to be there at five. I better go home."

"You should come and keep some of the money for yourself."

"I don't know how to beg for money, I am not sure I can do that."

"Just try to make them laugh. Tell them a joke and hand them one of these stickers. If they take it, ask for a humble donation. It's easy. Some give a lot of money but most people only give a few dollars." The idea of begging for money was appalling to me.

"I don't know any jokes," I said. "As a matter of fact I hate jokes."

"Come on, nobody hates jokes, It's easy. You just learn a few lines, it shouldn't be that hard."

"I don't think I am good at this, really." Cristina was losing her patience.

"All right, I'll see you upstairs," she said.

"Wait, I am coming with you." We went upstairs and I lay on the mattress in the little room.

"Maharaj told me that you can always come and stay here," Cristina said.

"I really appreciate that, thanks. He's so nice to me."

"He really cares for you. He wants to take you to Krishna."

My eyes were closing and I finally fell into a deep sleep. When I woke up Cristina was gone. I looked around the small apartment in disarray, and wondered how I ended up in that old building in the middle of Brooklyn. Overcome by a sense of urgency I rushed down the steps to the street. The subway was a few blocks away. I had the uncomfortable feeling that everybody was watching me. After changing two trains I finally arrived back to my apartment in Manhattan.

The cats were waiting by the door and everything was quiet. Post box was full and the pile of bills was getting bigger every day. I shoved them in a plastic bag under the table. The terror I used to feel every time I picked up my mail was gone. I was a changed person and didn't care anymore. All I cared was to see Maharaj again. Every time he gazed at me, a wave of warmth filled my chest, melting away all negative emotions. I was intrigued. Who was this mysterious person?

CHAPTER 12

RADAKUND SWAMI

Two weeks went by very fast. I was spending every evening at the Interfaith Center, cleaning or washing dishes. Sometimes I handed out flyers on Second Avenue and often I slept at the temple in Brooklyn. Maharaj took me under his wing. I was chanting every day and without any effort, everything in my life was working out in miraculous ways.

One morning Cristina called me all excited. Radakund Swami was arriving from India and she wanted me to attend the program at the Interfaith Center. He was going to give a lecture that evening. Her excitement was contagious.

Somebody I knew asked me to work at Bloomingdales that day, selling cosmetics. One of the sales girls was sick and they couldn't find a replacement. I was going to earn $100 for the day, more money than I have ever earned in one day. After digging deep into my closet, I found a white silk blouse and a black pair of pants. I wore some red lipstick and a fake string of pearls. On my way to Bloomingdales, I stopped for a cup of tea.

When I arrived, Lexington Avenue was swarming with people. Many tourists moving in groups undecided where to go, were obstructing the traffic. It was driving me crazy. I had to push my way through the crowds and some people were giving me dirty looks. The American tourists were wearing casual clothing, mostly jeans. The Europeans were wearing fancy clothing and they all had neat haircuts, very well groomed indeed. I finally made it through the crowds inside Bloomingdales, to the cosmetic department.

Each famous cosmetic brand had a small isle where they displayed their products. One or two salesladies that looked like fashion models were stationed behind each counter. Most of them had impeccable makeup. I glanced in a few of the countless mirrors and my looks needed a little polishing. My hair was already messy and the makeup hardly visible, I had bags under my eyes and my posture was bent forward. I straightened my back and ran my fingers through my hair.

When I turned around, my friend Estella was waving at me. She was at the Elisabeth Arden counter and looked really good. I wouldn't have recognized her.

"Hi, Anna," she said. "I was afraid you wouldn't show up, I am so glad you came! You look great. I'll put a little makeup on you and we'll do something with your hair in a second, but now I need to go to the bathroom. I'll be right back. If anybody comes to the counter just keep them busy till I get back."

Suddenly, from behind the counter I could see the huge room with people rushing everywhere. It was intimidating to see groups of people advancing toward me. I was hoping that they would just walk by me. A lady stopped and looked at some cologne. I smiled at her and she smiled back and then left. Estella returned running.

"What did that lady want?" she asked.

"Nothing," I said, "she just tried on the perfume."

"And you didn't say anything?"

"No. What was I going to say?"

"Listen," she said, "I engage them by saying that I also use the same fragrance. It depends from person to person. Sometimes I say 'You made a perfect choice', or you can say whatever you want to make them buy something."

"I don't know . . . I've never done this kind of job before."

"Don't worry, you're doing just fine."

She waved to a woman behind the Revlon counter. "Go over there," she told me. "Her name is Linda. She is a friend of mine and she'll do your makeup for free."

I had to find my way carefully through the crowds, making sure that I don't bump into anyone. It felt like being in Grand Central Station.

"Hello Linda," I said, "my friend Estella said you might be able to help me with the makeup. I am here only for today or maybe tomorrow. What a busy place this is!"

"Come here," Linda said. "When I'm done with your makeup you won't recognize yourself. You have beautiful eyes and all you need is a little touch up. Just sit on that chair. I'll be right with you."

I sat on a tall chair and Linda brought a makeup case filled with all kinds of cosmetics.

"Close your eyes," she said. "You mind if I put your hair up? It'll look better!"

"I don't mind. Please do whatever you think is best. You're the expert."

I had to admit it felt better than being in a dentist's chair. Some customers interrupted her several times. They all left with a little complementary makeup case after buying something from her. She was a good saleslady. Revlon was less expensive than Elisabeth Arden and I guess people were trying to save money. When she finished, she gave me a mirror. I couldn't recognize myself. She really did a great job. Some people were watching the whole show. I never knew I could look so good.

"How do you like it?"

"I love it! You're a real artist," I said, "thank you so much."

"Here," she said handing me a bag full of cosmetics. "This is for you, all for twenty-five dollars. The real value is over two hundred. It's a promotional gift that we sometimes give away. Good luck to you!"

I couldn't say no. The last thing I needed to buy with my money was makeup, but I gave her the twenty-five dollars and thanked her for the great makeup job. On my way back, I noticed people looking at me. It made me feel like a million bucks. I stopped in front of Estella's booth.

"Oh, my God," she said, "I didn't know it was you . . . You look so great, Anna! She sold you some makeup, the little witch. You didn't have to buy anything. The makeup job is free. She gets paid to do it."

"I couldn't say no, after she worked so hard."

"Let's see what she gave you . . ." she carefully looked through my makeup, "how much did she charge you for all this?"

"Twenty five dollars," I said.

"Not bad, she gave you a lot of stuff, but most of them are free samples. I guess is okay. Don't buy anything anymore! You don't want to spend all your money before you earn it."

"I have no intention of buying anything. This will last me for years. How are things going?"

Estella made a long face: "It's very slow today, I don't know why?"

We sat around the counter the whole morning. A few people stopped by. Estella made some sales and I didn't sell anything.

"Are we getting a lunch break?" I asked.

"Yes," she said, "somebody will cover for us for forty-five minutes at one o'clock. We can both go for a cup of coffee and a sandwich around the corner. I'll buy you lunch, how about that?"

"That's very nice Estella, thank you, I owe you one."

We went to a coffee shop on 58th Street. The waitress seemed to know Estella and she took our order immediately.

"The business is kind of slow today," I said.

"Yes," Estella said, "most of the money I make is from commissions. When I don't sell, I hardly make anything, but when things go well I make a lot of money. Soon I am going to buy an apartment in New Jersey, right across the river. How are you doing? I haven't seen you in a while. You look good," she said.

"I am well," I said. "I am going to a program with this great swami. He's going to speak tonight in the Village. People say he is a true saint. I've heard that he's is really amazing! Since this morning, the mantra they all chant is constantly going through my head. I don't seem to be able to stop it."

"Really," Estella said, "when does the program start?"

"About eight or so tonight. You know, Indian time."

"I am going with you," she suddenly decided.

"You're kidding, how about your boyfriend, you're bringing him with you?"

"I am upset with him," Estella said. "He's so cold to me. I can't take it anymore. I am going with you. I want to meet a guru."

"Okay," I said, "we can go right after work. I know they'll have a great feast in his honor after the program."

After work, we took a cab to rush downtown. The traffic down Second Avenue was bad. It took us about one hour to get to the East Village. Estella handed me a hundred dollars for the day's work. It was the easiest hundred dollars I've ever earned. I literally did nothing the whole day, didn't sale anything.

When we arrived the place was packed with lots of Indian people, mostly men but some women and children as well. Maharaj greeted us and took us to meet Radakund Swami; a small boyish looking man, dressed in traditional Indian clothing. He was American but had a little bit of an Indian accent and a contagious smile. His face looked very young and when he smiled, his small intelligent eyes would become even smaller.

"Hare Krishna, I am happy to see you here," he said looking directly at Estella with such familiarity, that for a moment I thought he already knew her. "Please, make room over there for the girls to sit close to me," he told Maharaj.

Maharaj smiled. Some devotees moved out of the way and Estella and I sat on the floor right in front of Radakund Swami. When I looked at Estella, she had tears in her eyes.

"Do you know him?" I asked.

"No," she said, "I don't but it feels like I do."

Radakund Swami was watching her with a smile in his mischievous eyes. She started sobbing. I handed her some napkins. All the Indians were looking at us. I felt uncomfortable, turned around and smiled at them. Radakund Swami handed her a sugar candy. She started eating it, looked at me and both of us burst into laughter.

"There is nothing to cry about," Radakund Swami said to her.

In the meantime, many musicians gathered around him. The room became silent. He closed his eyes and started to recite some mantras. His voice was strong and melodious. His pronunciation of Sanskrit was perfect. At least that's how it seemed to me. He began to chant and everyone was enlivened by his music. He had a beautiful voice and was able to reach very high notes with an ample volume as well. One couldn't help but be happy in his presence. All worries and problems disappeared in his proximity.

Cristina was running around making sure that everything was in order with the guests. She was ecstatic to see Radakund Swami. She whispered in my ear.

"Come to the temple tonight!"

"Yes," I said "definitely."

Radakund Swami made everybody happy. I admired him a lot but I still liked Maharaj better. I felt a little intimidated by him. At a certain point, he stood up, gave the drum to Brother Ram and started to dance. He motioned to Maharaj to join him. They both began to dance and it was hard to tell which one was more graceful. The devotees were going crazy and soon everyone was dancing and jumping out of control. It reminded me of a wild tribal dance. People always danced, but in primitive societies, dance was part of a ritual. It had a purpose and a meaning. Maharaj used to say 'Everything you do, do it for Krishna.' The intent was just as important as the action. 'Offer everything to Krishna,' meant to constantly live in the awareness of God. Only then the meaning of life would unfold in a harmonious way. Many people thought they should give up all worldly possessions, but that wasn't always necessary. After the dance Radakund Swami began to talk about faith.

"How many people are questioning the meaning of their existence? There is a point in life when everyone asked this question at least once. Faith must always come first; only then, the truth begins to unfold. Faith is the action that propels us into the universe of truth. Faith turns the pages. The book of our life would otherwise be closed. Faith is alchemy. Faith and intent change reality. They actually make reality. We always want to see the Miracle first. Only then we say "I will have faith". But Faith is that which makes the Miracle possible . . ." Radakund Swami was so happy. His state was contagious. He had enough Faith for all of us.

The program lasted late into the night followed by a fabulous feast prepared by the devotees with lots of love. One could feel it. What a great life, always dancing, chanting and feasting! I could live like that forever, I thought . . .

After the program, we squeezed into the shabby van called 'Thunder'. It was Brother Ram's favorite vehicle. Ram and Radakund Swami sat in the front and Maharaj with us in the back. I was very close to him and couldn't help but watch his beautiful face in the dark. Radakund Swami turned around and looked at us, smiling.

"Are you all coming back to the temple?"

"Yes Swamiji," we all said.

"How do you like the Brooklyn Temple?" He asked me.

"I like it all right. It's a great spiritual escape in the middle of Brooklyn. I've been spending a lot of time at the temple. Ask Christina!"

"It's an escape in the middle of Hell," he said. We all laughed. "Is that so, Christina," he continued, "are you taking good care of Anna?"

"Yes, Swamiji, Anna stays in my room whenever she wants too. I made a bed for her. She helps a lot in the kitchen."

"Anna, you should see the temple in West Virginia," Radakund Swami said, "the real spiritual world!"

"Anna is coming with us next time," Maharaj said.

"Come soon," Radakund Swami said, "I will be there for a while."

"Where are you going after that, Swamiji?" I asked.

"I am going back to my little ashram in Bombay. We have an orphanage there. The children want me to go back soon. They miss me."

"I would like to come to India," I said. "I want to study Ayurveda. Are there any good schools in Bombay?"

Radakund Swami gave me an incredulous look. "Someday you might come to India, but now you should stay here in America. This is the best place for you. Maharaj will take good care of you."

"Anna likes to cook," Maharaj said.

Radakund Swami's face lit up with a smile and he asked: "What can you cook?"

"I don't know," I said, "vegetarian. I took a course in Macrobiotic cooking but I would like to learn how to cook Indian."

"Very well, we can teach you how to cook the best Indian food. Come to West Virginia, you can cook for the devotees. Plenty of them can teach you all kinds of great

Indian dishes. We have a tradition; every Sunday we give a free feast for all the local people from the nearby towns. Many devotees join in to cook their favorite dishes." He paused for a while . . . "What's so great about this hellish city, anyway? What keeps you here?"

"Nothing, Swamiji, I can barely make a living. I do all kinds of jobs, clean apartments, paint houses, take care of animals, whatever job I can get. It's hard to find work. The job market is very bad now."

"Krishna doesn't care about the job market," Radakund Swami said, "He employs everyone. We all work for Him."

"Are you a Guru?" I asked him.

"I am not a Guru," he said, "I am just a worthless devotee serving my Guru."

"Who is your Guru?" He looked at me surprised.

"His name is Pandava Swami," he said, giving me a long glance with his sharp, intelligent eyes. There was some anxiety in his voice.

"Where is he?" I asked.

Radakund Swami turned his head and looked at me with a mischievous smile. Christina pulled my sleeve and whispered:

"Shish! Be quiet, I'll talk to you later about this."

We drove in silence for a few minutes and Maharaj said:

"Let's all chant the Mantra for the rest of the way."

They all started to chant Hare Krishna loudly. I joined in the chant but the question was still in my mind, so I whispered to Christina:

"Where is the Guru?"

"He is in jail," she said. The others couldn't hear us.

"What, but why?"

"For murder," she said and pressed her index finger against her lips.

A chill went down my spine. I figured the wise thing to do was to say nothing. I started chanting loudly to cover up my surprise and astonishment. Couldn't wait to arrive to the temple and ask Christina about it. All my enthusiasm had vanished in a few seconds.

I looked out the window. It was a cold, dark night. The heater was broken in the van and we were shivering. From the bridge I could hardly see anything. Thick gray fog was rising above the river obscuring the city lights. Brother Ram made a few abrupt turns and in a short while we stopped in front of the temple. The swamis went upstairs. They had an apartment which belonged to the guru and they also used it when the guru was away. I always wanted to see what the apartment looked like. Christina would never let me see it. Brother Ram remained behind and helped us unload the empty food containers. Maharaj ignored us altogether. We went upstairs to Christina's little room.

"Anna, I am making a cup of tea. Would you like some?"

"Yes, thanks. Christina, are you serious? Is he in jail for murder?"

"Yes, but nobody is supposed to talk about it. They say he is innocent. The story is that the people involved were some drug addicts and the murder happened over a drug dispute. He was set up and charged with many little things. I think that he'll go to jail for a long time. The word is they'll let him stay at the ashram under house arrest until the trial, for a great sum of money the devotees are trying to rise."

"That's unbelievable! Aren't you afraid around here?"

"No," Christina said, "Krishna is watching over me. The devotees helped me a lot. They really help people, all kinds of people. All kinds of people are always welcome here no matter what their situation. Many are homeless, poor or in distress. When nobody wants to have anything to do with them, the devotees give them food, a decent place to sleep and most of all give them God. Some devotees are well educated, scientists, artists, you name it. At one time or another they become disillusioned with society where most people are utterly self-involved and egotistic. Pandava Swami offered them an alternative, a different kind of society where people can devote every moment to Krishna and be relieved from the burden of living in the world. This opportunity is very rare."

"I wonder why people are so selfish," I said.

"In the Vedas," Christina said, "the time we live in is called Kali Yuga, the most evil time in human history and the worst is still to come. There will be a time when children will turn against their parents and kill them and also parents will turn against children. When people will eat human flesh and will execute anybody that believes in God. Religion will be banned. It is also called the Iron Age. It will be almost impossible for people to turn to God. This lineage that comes directly from Krishna is the only religion that will survive and it will become completely underground. It will be kept in great secrecy. It's happening already. The signs are here . . . You know that some local people from a town nearby attacked the temple in West Virginia? They came with shotguns, entered the temple, killed one person and injured a few others. After that, they went to the statues of Radha and Krishna and smashed them with hammers. The statues fell to the ground with such an extraordinary sound that the demons terrified run away. They hate us because we love Krishna. They are envious."

"Christina how horrible, it scares the daylights out of me. I need to think about all this. I'll probably sleep at my apartment tonight," I said.

"Now you're frightened. That's silly, all this happened years ago. Things have changed since then. It's a very safe place now."

"Did you ever meet Pandava Swami?"

"Yes, I met him before he got arrested. I don't like him and he's got this dog, a big German Sheppard trained to defend him. The dog will attack anybody that gets too close. It's really weird. He takes the dog everywhere, even to the temple when people line up to see him after the program."

We finished the tea and some cookies she brought from the kitchen. I was tired and Christina begged me to stay. They were cooking a feast in the morning for Radakund Swami and she needed me to do the food shopping in the morning. I decided to stay. I couldn't see myself schlepping all the way to Manhattan that night.

"Let's chant before we go to sleep. I have to finish chanting my rounds," Christina said.

She started to chant softly, whispering the name of Krishna with her eyes closed. She looked peaceful with the candle illuminating her face, like a Madonna. I took my beads out and tried to chant but wasn't able to concentrate. I kept on thinking about Pandava Swami and wondered how much of that story was true . . .

"It's time to get up, Anna!" It was Nina. I couldn't believe it was already morning. It seemed as if I only slept for five minutes. I was exhausted.

"I need to sleep some more," I said.

"No. You have to get up now. We need to cook breakfast for Radakund Swami. He said he wants you to cook for him."

"Gee, I don't know what to cook."

"He said he trusts you're a good cook. He never asked me to cook," Nina said.

"All right let's go," I said sliding out of my sleeping bag.

It was very cold in the room. I took a quick shower that only got my body a little wet. After the shower still shivering, I asked Nina: "Do you have any idea what he likes to eat?"

"He gets sic a lot. He always has a cold or a cough. He's not used to the cold weather in New York. I think he's on some kind of diet."

"I see . . . how about some steamed broccoli, almonds and scrambled tofu and some sautéed carrots with lemon, the way my mother used to make when I was a kid."

"Sounds all right, I guess," Nina said. "I personally hate diets. The food has no taste, but it's up to you."

"Would you help me get the vegetables from the cooler?"

"I am sorry, I can't," she said and left in a hurry.

I went down a narrow, dimly lit stairway. The basement was divided into small rooms by curtains hanging from the ceiling. A few devotees were living there on top of stacked up old chairs, couches, pots and piles of clothing. They definitely showed a high level of renunciation and very little care about the surrounding environment. I had to walk through a long, dark room. In one of the corners, an old metal shower was standing on top of a makeshift brick platform. That shower, belonging to the basement devotees was separated from the rest of the room by old sheets hanging from the ceiling. The large walk-in cooler was at the other end of the long and narrow room. I feared that somebody would lock me inside the cooler by mistake. I made a few more trips and carried everything upstairs. Some devotees were already in the kitchen. We cooked up a storm, ending up with a real feast for breakfast.

Radakund and Maharaj were having breakfast upstairs in their apartment. The rest of us sat in a circle, on the temple's floor. The devotees were very easy to please. They would eat just about anything I cooked and they were always grateful for the meal.

Maharaj came downstairs to talk to some devotees. Some of them were planning a trip to West Virginia. Something came up and they decided to leave next day. I overheard something about the Guru being released on bail. At some point Maharaj turned to Nina.

"You are going to West Virginia tomorrow morning with Radakund Swami. Pack all your stuff!"

"For how long?" Nina's face lit up.

"I don't know," he said, "take everything."

"Yes Maharaj," Nina said, "I better start packing."

"You'll ride with some Indian devotees. They'll pick you up tomorrow morning." Nina gave Maharaj a seductive look and graciously left the temple.

"Are you leaving tomorrow as well?" I asked him.

"No, I have to stay here for the Interfaith Center, I hope to go soon. You must come with us next time," he said.

"I can leave anytime. I am not that hard to replace, we can always find someone to clean at the center."

"Your service is important," he said, "just as important as Brother Ram's or any devotee's. The love that you put into your service counts, that's what Krishna sees." He looked so happy. I knew he was missing his Guru and couldn't wait to see him again.

After breakfast, I couldn't go upstairs. They were having a meeting in our apartment. Only a few devotees were invited to participate. I was feeling exhausted and did not have the energy to go back to my apartment. I went behind the altar to a little room where the offerings for Krishna were being prepared. The food offerings were transferred into silver cups and trays before being taken to the altar. There was a trap door in the ceiling, hardly noticeable. I climbed a vertical ladder to a small room only about four feet high. Krishna's clothes were kept there. The hideaway reminded me of a tree house. Being close to the kitchen, it was always warm. Every time I needed a break from the world, I went up to that little room, a trip to Krishna's planet. It was the safest place in the whole world. I lay on the floor, closed my eyes and began drifting away on a white cloud.

Suddenly it started to get dark. There was a bluish light permeating everything. I found myself transported to a grove in the woods. There was a lake nearby, as well as many ponds everywhere with water lilies and lotuses rising into the air on long stems. The fog was drifting away uncovering patches of flowers on the silvery water. After a while, they would disappear again swallowed by the blue light. A humming sound was emanating from everything. Each flower had a different sound. There was no Moon or Stars. The bluish light was coming from the cloud. All objects were illuminated from inside. Several girls were sleeping next to me. They were very young, wearing silk dresses decorated with golden ornaments, garnished with pearls and precious stones.

A loud conch shell sound woke me up from the reverie. The blue fog began to lift and soon I was back in Krishna's attic. Brother Ram was blowing the conch shell for the twelve o'clock worship. I decided to rest for another hour until lunch. Only a few devotees showed up for lunch. They were busy getting ready for the trip.

After lunch, I went back to my apartment debating if I should keep on going to the Interfaith Center. Sometime it was too much for me. I didn't want to blindly surrender everything, give up my life in New York, my apartment and move in with the Krishnas. If I joined them, I wasn't sure I could follow the instructions given by senior devotees. The guru in jail for some crimes that nobody was willing to talk about, was a big problem for me. On the other hand, Nandana Swami and all the devotees gave me so much, fed me when I had no money, provided me with a place to sleep and a job. Above all, they helped me recover from a long period of depression and hopelessness that lasted for several years. I was in a bind, not able to decide what to do.

That night I had a significant dream. I was walking on a dusty road and arrived at an intersection. In the middle of it, a statue of Krishna was standing on a marble pedestal. The statue represented Him as a young child, emanating a shimmering blue light. I was pondering which way to go.

One road was going to the left, the other to the right. Suddenly I heard a woman desperately screaming for help. The sound was coming from down the road on the right side. I decided not to go in that direction and began to walk on the other road. At that moment, two young men came running toward me and grabbed both my hands. One of them was only about eight years old, and the other was a youth about eighteen years of age. They looked amazingly similar and both had brilliant purple eyes like amethyst. They firmly held my hands and guided me to safety.

When I woke up from that dream, it was easy to make up my mind. It became clear that Krishna came into my life to divert me from a road full of danger. For the next two weeks, I spent all my time at the Interfaith Center. There was plenty to do since most of the devotees were gone. One evening I received a message from Maharaj that he was going to West Virginia the following morning. They were planning to depart as early as possible. It didn't give me a lot of time to prepare. I packed as much stuff as I could into a duffle bag and into my backpack and left the key with my neighbor to feed the cats while I was away. I had no idea how long I will be staying. The duffle bag was so heavy that I had to drag it from time to time, and the fabric started to rip on the bottom. I carried it up and down the subway steps and almost decided to turn around and go back home. After a grueling trip, I finally made it to the temple and spent the whole evening talking to Christina. I told her about my dream and she reassured me that I made the right decision. We were up late, talking about the ways of Karma too complex for us to understand.

"You never know what's around the corner," she said.

I was too excited at the prospect of traveling with Maharaj and couldn't sleep at all. I spent the whole night tossing, turning, and thinking about the whole situation with the Guru in West Virginia.

CHAPTER 13

GOING WEST

The ringing of a bell and a loud knock at the door woke me up. I heard Ram's voice from the hallway.

"Four thirty, time to get up girls! You slept late this morning. Anna you're leaving right after the program. Bring everything downstairs."

"Yes Maharaj, I'll be right down."

The room was completely dark and my sleeping bag felt warm and comfortable. I didn't want to get up and Christina was still sleeping. Dragging myself into the bathroom, I stood in front of the mirror. My face looked pale and tired. It was cold in the room and when I turned the shower on, the mirror started to get fogy and my image slowly disappeared. I forced myself to step into the bathtub. A layer of dust was covering the window seal. Up in the corner right above the shower, a minuscule spider waved its intricate house.

Outside everything was frozen and the tree trunks were covered with a thin, glossy layer of ice. The back yard looked immaculate under the fresh snow. A reddish aura was enveloping the moon, sign of a very cold day. After the shower I dressed warm, wearing a few layers of clothes and a clean brown robe on top.

"Christina, are you up yet? I am going downstairs."

"I'll be down in a minute," she said.

In the hallway the dim light was drawing shadow pictures on the walls over the chipped paint and the deep cracks that followed the stairway all the way down to the ground level. I rushed into the kitchen and Blossom was there getting breakfast ready for Krishna. She looked at me startled.

"What are you doing here Anna? I thought you already left."

"I want to take some food for the road."

"Hurry," she said, "they want to get going as soon as possible to avoid the morning rush hour."

"I'll be ready in a minute."

I took some vegetables from the cooler, cheese, butter and bought a bunch of hot bagels from a nearby bakery. On my way back, passing by the vegetable store I noticed some huge, ripe avocados. I bought some using my own money. It was a luxury but I didn't care. Back to the ashram I put everything in a box and took it to the car.

The sky had a pink glow. Birds were chanting their morning prayers and a few silhouettes of people were digging their way through the fresh snow. My big duffel bag was so heavy that I could hardly carry it. Brother Ram was watching me.

"You've got new boots," he said.

"They're not new. I bought them at a thrift shop around here for five dollars. I figured they might come in handy in West Virginia."

"It snows a lot over there," he said. "Come back soon, we'll miss you!"

I could tell he was upset to see me go. On the other hand, I was ecstatic to spend eight hours in the car with Maharaj. I put the bag and my backpack in the trunk and the box of food on the seat. Sunrise sat next to me and Brian in the front. We waited for Maharaj for a long time. He finally arrived running and dragging his feet in his Chinese brown slippers. This time instead of the usual brown robe, he was dressed in a traditional saffron Indian robe. When he got in a subtle fragrance of Sandal Wood permeated the whole car.

"We lose some, we gain some," he said to Brother Ram. Then he added, "I want you to chant Hare Krishna until we get out of the city. No talking!"

"Yep, let's chase away all these evil spirits," Brian said." Look, there is one right over there."

"Brian, shut up and chant," Maharaj said.

We all started repeating the mantra while Maharaj was driving. The chant was making me sleepy and I started dosing off. Occasionally I would wake up and look out the window. We were somewhere in New Jersey, a monotonous drive through endless fast food joints, furniture stores and malls. Brian and Sunrise were soundly asleep. I closed my eyes and drifted away.

Next time I opened my eyes we were driving through the hills of Pennsylvania. Patches of pines were adding some color to the white landscape. The deep blue sky opened wide above us with strangely shaped white clouds sailing through in slow motion. Beams of light were filtered through the clouds. Touching the grounds they were forming vast patterns, a huge curtain of light stretching over the sky.

"When I was a child," Maharaj said, "I thought God talked to us through those beams of light."

"Maybe He does," I said.

"I was eight or nine years old," he continued, "my parents took me on a trip to Disney Land. On the way there, I was watching the clouds rolling in the sky, just like today. All of a sudden the light became so bright that was hurting my eyes. It covered the whole sky. The whole world seemed to be on fire. I became frightened and closed my eyes. When I opened them the light was gone. I told my mother about it but she didn't see anything unusual. She told me I was imagining it, but I knew that God was speaking to me directly. Maybe that was the moment when I decided to look for Him for the rest of my life."

"Jay Maharaj," Brian said. "I must have been six or seven years old when I became very sick with a high fever. The doctors didn't know what was wrong. That night a strange noise woke me up. It sounded like the ringing of bells. I saw a being of light, shimmering and pulsating next to my bed. He stretched his arms and gently touched my chest. 'Brian, you are healed,' he said. 'I will see you again,' and slowly vanished. I fell into a deep sleep. Next day the illness was gone. I went to the kitchen and when my mother saw me, she was shocked as if she'd seen a ghost. She checked my temperature and realized that I was okay. I never told her about my beautiful Angel. I still remember his face. I know I'll see him again."

"You guys are weird," Sunrise said and laughed. "No, you're all right. What if I tell you that I've seen a mermaid?"

"Get out of here," Brian said.

"It's true, it happened when I was surfing in San Diego. I fell and hurt my head on the surfboard. It was a windy day with huge waves, twirling me around like leaf. I swallowed a lot of water and lost my sense of direction.

Suddenly this beautiful woman appeared out of nowhere. She was necked and I think she had a fish tail. She smiled telling me to follow her. I desperately tried to swim towards her and I lost consciousness. When I came to, I was lying on the beach with a circle of people around me. They all began cheering. My head was bleeding with a big cut close to the temple. I wanted to get up but I couldn't move at all. I was taken to the emergency room where they gave me lots of painkillers. I got high for the next five days.

"What color was her tail?" Brian asked.

"I don't know man, I think it was blue."

"You didn't ask her for her phone number?"

"Get out of here," Brian said, "I swear this is a true story."

We stopped at a truck stop and changed places. Now Brian was driving. Maharaj moved next to me and Sunrise moved in front next to Brian.

"Anybody wants to eat?" I asked.

"Yeh," they all said.

"How about a bagel with cheese and avocado?"

"I don't like avocado," Brian said.

"I'll make a cheese sandwich for you with some radishes and tomatoes."

"I want radishes and tomatoes too," Sunrise said.

"Everybody gets radishes and tomatoes," I said and started the make the sandwiches.

"I would give anything for a cup of coffee," Sunrise said.

"No coffee," Maharaj said. "You can have milk or herbal tea."

"I'll have milk," Sunrise said.

"Me too," I said.

Maharaj went to the little store by the truck stop to buy milk. The sandwiches were ready. We all received a small carton of milk. I was famished and the bagel never tasted so good.

"I'll rest for a while," Maharaj said, "Brian let me know when we get close to Pittsburgh. We're going to a program held by some Indian devotes at their home, near Pittsburgh. They are old devotes and they donated lots of money to the temple."

"I love those programs. Anna, have you ever been to one? Brian asked.

"No. Not really."

"Oh, there is so much food, and the chanting is great."

"Will you give a talk Maharaj?" I asked him.

"Yes, I must. I hope that Krishna lets me speak about His past times."

"I'm going to tape your speech."

"Anna, you shouldn't do that. I never know what I am talking about." He looked at Brian. "Let's get going, we must be there by four or five the latest." He stretched his legs, leaning back and covered his whole body with a big woolen shawl. "Don't wake me up Anna," he said.

"Even if you try you couldn't wake him up," Brian laughed. "Is scary, man, sometimes I think he's dead. I have to check his breath."

I was watching Maharaj from the corner of my eye. He fell into a deep sleep. I was afraid to move, not to disturb him. I closed my eyes and relished that perfect moment, where time and place were in complete harmony. A moment in my life where there was nothing more to desire.

After a while I realized that my body was all contracted. I was so nervous to be seating near him that I froze in the same position for the longest time. I decided to relax. My eyelids were getting so heavy that I had to force myself to keep them open. In the middle of a dream, I heard Brian saying.

"Maharaj, we're getting close to Pittsburgh!" Maharaj opened his eyes.

"Let me drive," he said, "you don't know the way." They changed places. Brian collapsed on the seat next to me.

"It's my turn to sleep," he said.

"We'll be there in a few minutes," Maharaj said, but Brian was already asleep.

Soon we stopped in front of a big house somewhere near Pittsburgh. It was a huge new house that looked like a mansion, with many cars parked in the back yard. The owner was an Indian doctor and his family. We got out of the car and they went inside the house. I stretched and my back was stiff after so many hours in the car. A woman dressed in a purple silk saree, embroidered with golden designs came to welcome me.

"Mother," she said, "please come in the house, you must be hungry. Come to the kitchen with me."

"Thank you," I said. "We are a little late, I am sorry."

"It's okay," she said. "We have a surprise. Gaura Chandra Swami is here."

"I don't know him."

"Oh, Mother he is one of the most ecstatic devotes. We are very honored by his presence. He travels around all the time and lives in his car. He is one of the most renounced devote I know."

"I guess we are lucky," I said.

A large semicircular room with vaulted ceilings and marble floors was full of people, sitting on the floor. On a golden platform, Radha and Krishna Deities were standing tall, dressed in the most exquisite silk clothing. Two enormous vases of roses of many colors were skillfully arranged on either side of the Deities.

I followed the lady to the kitchen. She was small with a skinny body and her face was brownish-gray. She did not look healthy and she seemed tired.

"Are you from the New York Temple?" she asked.

"Yes Mother, but I don't live in the temple all the time. I still have my own apartment."

"I see," she said and I could tell that her respect for me dropped a few degrees.

"Are you married?"

"No, I live by myself. Occasionally I have a roommate. You know, it helps pay the rent."

She didn't say anything but her respect for me now, reached a new bottom. Not only that I wasn't married but I was poor as well. Luckily she got over her disappointment soon and stuffed a good size plate with food for me.

"Here," she said, "you must be hungry it's a long ride from New York. What's your name mother?"

"Anna." I said.

"Anna, you can sit here." She placed the plate on a huge table in the enormous kitchen.

"Thank you, Hare Krishna," I said.

"Maharaj must be hungry too. I'll make him a nice plate." She opened a cabinet, pulled out a golden tray and filled with food.

"Mother what's your name?" I asked.

"Vishaka."

"Vishaka, what a beautiful name, are you initiated?"

"No, but Gaura Chandra Swami gave me this name until I'll be initiated. He's going to give a lecture tonight."

"I was under the impression that Maharaj was going to speak," I said.

"He was supposed to, but now that we are blessed with Gaura Chandra Swami's presence, we asked His Holiness to speak."

"Oh, okay," I said disappointed after looking forward the whole trip to hear Maharaj. I was savoring the delicious food. "Mother Vishaka," I said, "it tastes so good, I never tasted such a good food."

Her face lit up. She straightened her back and with a very feminine gesture rearranged part of her saree that was elegantly covering her shiny black hair.

"Some of our friends own the best Indian Restaurant in Pittsburgh. They cooked the feast for us. Now I have to take the plate to Maharaj," she said. "After you eat, please come and join us. You mustn't miss Gaura Chandra Swami's lecture. Devotees like him are very rare, you'll see." Giving me a big mysterious smile she left the kitchen. I thought she got over the fact that I was a nobody.

I took my time savoring the subtle tastes melting in my month. What a great life, certainly feasting was a big part of it. I could see through the doorway into the large room. Most of the women were Indian. They were dressed in colorful sarees, wearing gold earrings and necklaces made from a deep yellow-orange type of gold that I rarely see Americans wear. They must have a lot of gold in India. I have never seen an Indian wearing 14k gold.

Close to the Krishna's statue a tall, thin man was seated on a big orange pillow facing everybody. He was talking to a group of devotees piled up on top of each other trying to get close to him. That man was Gaura Chandra Swami. He was moving slowly and graciously. Maharaj was seated next to him. His golden plate full of food was on the floor untouched. Both were surrounded by devotes. Some of them were still eating. An Indian man was playing the harmonium and singing some Krishna chants. Incense and candles were burning everywhere and suddenly the whole room became quiet. Gaura Chandra Swami with eyes closed, seating motionless was holding a thick book in his lap. A young devotee brought a harmonium placing it in front of him, an unusual harmonium that looked like a suitcase with a handle, bigger than most.

I sat on the floor in the back of the room. My eyelids were getting heavy and I closed my eyes for a second. He started to sing in a deep voice reverberating in the big room with sounds so in tune with the instrument that sometimes was hard to differentiate between the two. There was something sad in his voice; sadness about living in this world where nothing was what it seemed, where hopes and desires remained unfulfilled and dreams of happiness rarely materialized. A loveless world! Even those Indians that seemed to have it together, deep inside knew the loneliness of this world. That's why they liked Gaura Chandra Swami so much. He was making them face the truth about life. In the middle of this gathering, with all those people worshiping Krishna life seemed less lonely.

He began talking about the conditions on Earth before the birth of Lord Chaitania. After Lord Krishna left this world five thousand years ago, the Earth plunged into a period of decline called 'Kali Yuga, The Age of Iron', the densest of all. In Kali Yuga, the soul was to be imprisoned by the predominance of greed, anger, lust, fear and dishonesty. People in Kali Yuga were blind to the truth of their own souls, not able to distinguish between good and evil. Suffering was to become a way of life and happiness almost nonexistent. People forgot what true love was. The soul would dry up like a young plant in a drought.

This time, the most degraded in history, was to become bearable when Lord Krishna decided to come back to this world in the form of Lord Chaitania. His purpose was to care like a loving gardener for these dried up souls and sprinkle them with the pure water of love. In that way, they could once again blossom and humanity fulfill its destiny. This transformation was a very long and delicate process in which human beings were given free will to choose their destiny. Now, we are in the middle of this powerful process of transformation. The whole Earth is preparing for a new era.

In this transition time, the forces of darkness are very strong. They are trying to delude us into believing their lies and falsity. Their only goal is to destroy our fragile souls, denying them the sweet nourishment of love of God, the source of all forms of love. If the source was to dry up, the light of the whole world would begin to diminish, and eventually any form of love would turn into hate, indifference and numbness. All living entities, knowingly or unknowingly are engaged on a journey toward becoming whole, full of love and joy and becoming aware of their divine nature.

Lord Chaitania took birth five hundred years ago in a small village in India. His mission was to distribute to all living entities the healing potion of love of God in the form of sound; the chanting of the Name of God. He used to beg people to chant in order to deliver them from the clutches of Kali Yuga.

"You can see the signs of Kali Yuga everywhere," he said, "you can see how greed is presiding over the suffering nations, and people are living a meaningless existence ravaged by desires, poverty and depression. You can see the light of wisdom replaced by corruption, but you also can see the seeds of change. The truth and knowledge once held secret by powerful dictators and organized religion, is bursting out, free, for everybody to access. There are more people searching for an answer today, than any other time in history . . . Just chant the name of God, out loud, to cover the world with this sacred vibration that will protect us from destruction."

Everybody began to chant. Gaura Chandra Swami kept his head down, playing the harmonium. He looked familiar, maybe from a different lifetime. People were saying that he lived most of the time in the Spiritual World and was an old disciple of Lord Chaitania. Somehow Gaura Chandra Swami was able to bridge the time barrier and go back and forth between now and five hundred years ago in Lord Caitania's time.

After the lecture, Vishaka came to me completely transformed. Her eyes were bright and full of life.

"Mother Anna," she said, "come, I want to introduce you to Gaura Chandra Swami. You are lucky to meet him, very lucky!"

I followed her through the mass of people. They were all pushing each other but didn't seem to bother them much. We arrived in front of him and I kneeled on the marble floor facing him. Few women were lined up before me. They were talking to him, telling him everything about their lives and their families etc. They were going on and on. I was restless and impressed by his patience while listening to all that nonsense. Finally the two women moved away and I advanced, kneeling right in front of him. He kept his head down and closed his eyes. I closed my eyes and felt transported into a private world where I could be alone with him. It was a meeting of the souls in silence. When I opened my eyes, he was looking down at the floor.

"Mother I am glad you came to see me," he said.

"Thank you, Gaura Chandra Swami," I said, "I'm on my way to the ashram in West Virginia."

He acted surprised. "I will be there too," he said, "I don't know when."

"Gaura Chandra Swami," I said, "it was the best lecture I've ever heard."

There was sadness in his face, "I am just a servant of Lord Chaitania," he said in a whisper. "I will see you again."

I bowed to him and left. Maharaj was watching me, smiling. Soon Brian came to tell me that we had to leave because Maharaj was restless and wanted to get back to the ashram as soon as possible. I said goodbye to Vishaka and went to the car. Maharaj was in the driver's seat. He turned around and said: "Hang on to your seats, we're going to fly!"

Darkness descended fast over the hills of West Virginia leaving a pink border around the mountains' tops. The road became very narrow, winding through the steep hills with sharp turns that made me hold my breath. I could barely distinguish some trees by the side of the road. Everything else was black. Maharaj was driving so fast, that with each turn I expected the car to take off, flying over the side of the road into darkness.

"Here we are," Brian said, but I couldn't see anything.

Soon a plateau appeared in front of us. A blanket of snow covered the ground. In spite of the darkness, the snow was glowing against the black sky.

"See the Golden Temple over there, on the right."

All I could see were the silhouettes of some buildings and soon the car came to an abrupt halt.

"Hare Krishna," Maharaj said. "Anna, come to the office with me, and Brian you take Sunrise to the temple and get a room for both of you."

"You're the fastest driver I've ever met," I said.

"We made good time."

I took my bags out of the car and followed Maharaj through the snow, trying to step into his footmarks. The bags were so heavy, that I had to stop and catch my breath. He disappeared into the night. I followed his steps that lead to a big wooden building, all enveloped in darkness.

"Over here Anna," I heard his voice. I followed the voice to a door that opened into a long corridor with rooms lined up on both sides. We walked into a small room dimly lit by two candles and a gas lamp. A man with black hair and a beard was seated behind the desk.

"Hare Krishna, Maharaj," he said.

"Hare," Maharaj answered. "Anna, this is Baladev Swami. He is in charge with the gests around here. He'll take you to your room and if you need anything, he is the person to ask.

"Maharaj," Baladev Swami said, "I saved some 'Prasad' (food) for you and the gests. You must be hungry."

"No thanks," Maharaj said, "It's too late for me to eat but give it to the gests. I am sure they'll enjoy it."

"Sit down, Anna," Baladev Swami said. "Please fill out this form."

One of the questions was 'Why I came to the ashram?' I was not sure what to say, so I left it blank. He looked over the papers.

"Very well," he said, "You must know that we practice four spiritual principles around here: No illicit sex, no intoxication, no meat eating and no gambling."

"I can do that," I said, "I don't take drugs or gamble and I eat only vegetarian food. As well as the other one, I am single and I am not looking for a boyfriend right now."

"The Material World is very powerful." He laughed. "It's almost impossible to refrain from sense gratification without Krishna's help. That's why you need to chant as much as you can and constantly engage in service. Krishna loves his devotes more than anything else, so by serving them, you please Krishna the most."

"Yes Baladev Swami," I said.

"Here, you have something to eat," Baladev Swami uncovered a tray filled with all kinds of delicacies. I was famished and gabled everything up. Afterwards I thanked Krishna for the delicious feast.

"The food tasted so good . . . the best. Thank you for being so kind," I said.

"That's because it was offered to Krishna, it's all by His Grace." He smiled, pleased with me. "It's getting late, we have to go now. I'll take you to your room."

I followed him through a narrow stairway to the second floor. He opened a door to one of the many rooms lined up on one side of the corridor.

"This is the women's ashram," he said. "You can stay here tonight, but tomorrow you have to move to another room. You must share a room with Nina."

"Thank you Baladev Swami, by the way, when does the morning program begin?"

"You should be in the temple by four o'clock. Everybody repeats the mantra for an hour before the program. One of the mothers will wake you up; she'll tell you what to do."

"All right," I said, "thank you for everything."

"Hari Boll," he said disappearing down the dark hallway.

The large room covered with brown wood paneling, was empty, except for a small foam mattress on the floor. It was cold so I opened my sleeping bag and crawled inside shivering. It took some time to warm up. Being tired I fell into a deep sleep.

The sound of a bell woke me up. It was still dark. Soon somebody knocked on the door. It was Nina.

"Hari Boll, Anna, let me show you where the shower is. You have to take a shower before you go down to the temple. We only have cold water in the morning but it's not really that cold."

She took me to the bathroom. The showers were dingy, some shower curtains falling apart and some were missing. Spider webs were hanging from the ceiling. I took a two minutes shower and dressed as fast as I could. Nina wasn't very friendly. We had some competition going. The corridor leading to the stairway was dusty and some doors broken. It looked like an abandoned building.

I managed to make it downstairs finding my way slowly in the dark. The temple, covered with wooden paneling, had three large altars and many rows of heavy chairs with elaborate carvings, reminding me of a medieval, Italian church. The altars guarded by iron fences and heavy locks, looked like big cages. It was odd that the Guru himself was going behind bars just like the Deities. All devotes were chanting the Hare Krishna Mantra on their prayer beads. Some were whispering and some were chanting in a loud voice, some fast and some very slow, each in its own tempo making a buzzing sound. They were all clad in brown robes with hoods pulled over their heads. I sat on the floor near the altar, and started to repeat the mantra.

Soon I fell into a deep meditative state and saw a vast battlefield. It was an enormous valley full of warriors. They were wearing shields and heavy armors on their bodies. At a certain point only a few yards in front of me, Maharaj was riding a white horse. He was dressed in armor, carrying the most exquisite shield studded with rubies and diamonds. His body was emanating a golden effulgence. I was so happy to recognize him from the multitude of warriors. The vision started fading away into a white fog and somebody tapped me on the shoulder. It was Maharaj.

"Wake up Anna, repeat the mantra," he said.

When I opened my eyes, the lights of dozens of candles were illuminating the altar and the statues of Radha and Krishna were much bigger than the Deities we had in New York. Suddenly the statues began spinning faster and faster. The whole altar was spinning around at an amazing speed. I could see vibrating circles of light of dazzling effulgence. I closed my eyes but it did not make any difference. The whole room was turning at an unfathomable speed. I could not move. This vision lasted for what seemed to be a very long time. Then the effulgent circles started fading away, sinking into the depths of my consciousness. Soon everything was back to normal.

Later on, the same vision appeared to me out of nowhere, at different times in my life on many occasions. It became an omen. Whatever I was thinking or experiencing at the time when this vision appeared was always the truth.

After the program, Nina came running and asked me to follow her. She told me that Pandava Swami was back from jail under house arrest. Some devotes were going to his house for darshan (visit) and it was a good opportunity for me to meet him. I went along, six or seven of us squeezed into the back of a big van. The sun was hiding behind the mountains and the sky was covered with heavy clouds. It was still dark. With the roads frozen, it was hard to drive.

We arrived at the foot of an abrupt hill, and left all the cars at the bottom. The road up heal was steep and icy. We got off the van, and began climbing with great difficulty. The Guru's house was all the way on top. To my surprise, it was a small house with tinny rooms. The little room at the entrance had two couches facing the door. Radakund and Maharaj were sitting on one of the couches sinking into the soft pillows. Many Swamis were waiting in that room. I had no desire to meet the Guru and sat on the floor in front of Radakund Swami. He looked at me smiling.

"Anna, you're here, I am glad to see you."

All eyes turned toward me. I felt embarrassed, folded my hands and saluted him in the Indian manner. He handed me a cup of vegetable juice.

"Here," he said, "it's leftover from Pandava Swami, very auspicious."

I didn't want to drink after him but I took the cup anyway.

"Thank you Swamiji, he really drinks vegetable juice in the morning?"

"Yes, he is on a row food diet for his health."

I took a sip and the juice tasted terrible. Radakund Swami saw me squint my eyes and laughed.

"Very few devotes enjoy this juice, but is good for you."

Maharaj asked me to follow him. We went into another small room. The walls were full of books and Pandava Swami was sitting on a chair, with the big dog at his feet. The dog would not let anybody touch him. When someone tried to stretch his hand out toward the Guru, the dog would wrinkle his nose, showing a beautiful pair of strong white teeth that would discourage even the mightiest devotes to get too close.

Everybody was seated on the floor so tightly packed that you couldn't drop a pin. I sat with my knees close to my chest. Pandava Swami was not what I expected. He had a long white beard and white hair that made him look like a Russian Patriarch. A pair or wide blue eyes were fearfully scrutinizing the room. He had a rather blank look on his face and a very large robe that was covering his small, strange body. His back was hunched. A large stomach was protruding through his robes. He appeared to be a frightened person.

I was trying to figure what was so special about him that made all those devotes dedicate all their lives to his cause. All I could see was a small man that hardly spoke a few words, behind his huge dog that was ready to rip apart anyone that got too close. Later I found that his health was quiet shaky. He had been the victim of a strange accident; was attacked by some ex devotes that had a grudge against him. They wanted to kill him and hit him on the back of his head with a steel pipe breaking his skull. He fell unconscious in a pull pool of blood and everybody thought him dead. He ended up in intensive care for a few weeks. The doctors gave him a bad prognosis. They said he would never be able to walk or talk again but a miracle happened and he started to recover. Since then, he was in and out of hospitals. Now he could walk with a cane. When he saw Maharaj, his eyes lit up.

"You finally arrived, I was waiting for you. Come to see me later. I want you to move back here. I need you here; there is a lot to do."

"Yes Pandava Swami," Maharaj mumbled. "This is Anna, she's a new devote and came with us from New York. She helps with the Interfaith Center."

"Okay," Pandava said giving me a distrustful look.

After a few minutes he dismissed us with a shake of his hand. Maharaj was excited.

"How did you like Pandava Swami?"

"I don't know, maybe I need to know him better."

He seemed so happy around his Guru. When we went back to the living room, Radakund Swami was gone.

Outside was broad daylight and finally I could see the surroundings. The road was winding around gentle hills. Badly kept houses appeared to be far apart from each other, some of them abandoned. On the way back to the temple we passed by the "Palace of Gold". It was an elaborate construction with gold plated towers. I couldn't decide if I liked it or not, maybe too gaudy for my taste. Soon we arrived in front of the temple.

"Anna what are you doing today?" Maharaj asked.

"I don't know Maharaj . . . there is a lot to do around here. The women's ashram needs a good cleaning."

"It's a perfect job for you. The hallways get quiet dirty. Raccoons come at night and knock over the garbage cans. They make such a mess. Devotes are too busy, they don't have time to clean."

"Yeh right," Brian said, "they're just lazy."

"You help her clean," Maharaj said a little annoyed.

"Maharaj," I said, "we'll get the place super clean. Is that so Brian?"

Brian made a sour face. "I don't want to go to the women's ashram!"

"Don't worry, they don't bite," Maharaj said, "besides there is hardly anyone there during the day. We all work around here."

"Anna," Brian said, "you go first. I don't want to see any naked women. It'll disturb my peace."

"Since when you became such a puritan?" I asked.

"Let's get to work," Maharaj said, "I'll see you at lunch."

"Hari Boll," we said and went upstairs to the women's ashram. Everybody was gone. At the end of the hallway we found some garbage cans kicked over and garbage spilled all over the floor. We looked everywhere for a broom and some garbage bags but we couldn't find anything.

"Let's go to the temple, maybe we can find a broom around there," I suggested. The temple was empty. The whole place was deserted. We went to the back of the temple. There was a door leading to the kitchen. Behind the kitchen, we found a shack full of junk, with bags full of old clothes, books and all kind of things piled up on the floor. We emptied some bags and put them aside.

"Hey! Look at this sweater," Brian said, "isn't it nice? I'm gonna take it. I'm freezing."

It was a nice sweater. We started digging through the pile of clothes. I found a pair of prayer beads and a red, woolen shawl, embroidered with beautiful flowers. We took the empty bags the shawl and some old sheets. Outside, near the kitchen we found a bucket filled with frozen water. I took the bucket to the women's bathrooms and put it in the shower to defreeze it. The water was barely warm. It took forever. We shredded the sheets and began washing the floors with the rags and some soap that I found in the showers. We had to change the water often because the floors were so dirty. We cleaned about half of the hallway on our knees and then Brian stood up.

"This is crazy," he said, "let's do this." He stepped on top of some rags and began dancing around, dragging his feet and twisting his body. "See? It's much faster," he said, "I'll do the floors and you give me fresh rags and change the water."

"It's a deal," I said.

The floors started to look better but there was still a dingy feeling in there. We were almost finished, when a devote came by.

"Hari boll, what are you guys doing here? It's lunch time," she said. "My, this is so clean, too bad it's not going to last too long. Come with me, I'll show you to the dining hall."

"Let's go," Brian said.

We put the rags into the bucket, hid it in one of the empty rooms, and followed the woman to the dining hall. It was a spacious room with two rows of long tables and benches on either side. Many devotes where seated next to each other, most of them wearing brown robes, some with the hoods over their heads. They looked like Capuchin monks in a medieval monastery. The food was served in big pots lined up on a table, with no plates or utensils. Some of the people were using their hands "Indian Style" to eat, but most brought their own. We used paper plates which were kept in the office, for gests only. The lunch was simple and healthy. Soup and salad, Indian bread called Chapattis and a bowl of lentils cooked with vegetables.

After lunch, Brian took me on a tour of the surroundings. We descended a steep hill to a road entering a wooded area.

"Let's go that way," Brian said.

The road was narrow, going downhill winding its way to a pristine river. On the side of the road we discovered a small cemetery with some old stone crosses. We were surprised, and didn't think that people ever died in that place.

"I want to go in," I said to Brian.

We walked in. Our footprints were left in the fresh snow. The cemetery was peaceful and quiet, with a feeling of lightness in the atmosphere. Whatever we expected to find wasn't there. The people buried under the snow, were long gone. Only nature, recycling itself remained. Brian had the same thought.

"I bet there are no ghosts here, they all went to Krishna. You know, I used to be afraid of cemeteries bur now my fear is all gone. There is nothing to be afraid of. Anyway, I have to admit it feels good to be alive, look, we can walk and move. That's something, isn't it?"

"I hope you can do more than that."

"You know what I mean; it's better than being a tree or something."

"Yes, but the trees live much longer than we do."

"Not necessarily, if we keep on cutting them off."

"Brian, what good have we, humans, done for this planet?"

"I don't know. Pollute a few rivers and kill some trees, actually a lot of trees, not to mention the animals. I don't know Anna, I never thought about it. There must be something but I can't think of anything right now. Just can't. You tell me!"

"I think we'll make good compost," I said, "but other than that I don't know . . . Seriously now Brian, do you think we were created in a laboratory by God and His staff of scientists?"

"I am afraid so, but we lost the troubleshooting manual," Brian said.

"We didn't. What about the Baghavat Gita and other ancient texts like Ayurveda?"

"The knowledge is not in books," Brian said.

"It's not in books . . ." I echoed him.

"Hey, I have an idea," he said, "let's come back here tonight and meditate on this to get an answer, like you know some of the Ancients used to meditate in cemeteries."

"I don't know, maybe," I said. "I am starting to get cold. Let's get back to the temple."

"Let's go."

The road uphill seemed longer. When we arrived on top I was exhausted. Brian was in a great physical shape. He was always working out.

"Anna, you're out of shape, you need to do some yoga."

"I know, please don't rub it in."

At the temple, we ran into Maharaj.

"Hari Boll," he said. "Brian I was looking for you all over the place. I need you to help clean the men's ashram."

"Maharaj, we just took a walk by the cemetery."

"The cemetery, what were you doing there?" he said surprised.

"We were trying to meditate on the transitory state of all existence," I said.

"You'll be better off thinking about Krishna," he looked into my eyes intensely. "Anna I want you to clean the guest rooms downstairs. A few Indian guests are coming tonight. We must get the rooms ready."

"Yes Maharaj," I said, "but I need a broom, some detergent and some rags."

"I'll show you," he said, "we keep all the supplies locked up in the library. Otherwise, everything disappears quickly around here. Everybody takes whatever they want. They never ask."

We went to the back of the temple and Maharaj unlocked the door leading to the library; a couple of small rooms full of books from many different religions and in the corner, a closet full of all kinds of supplies.

"Here, it's all yours," he said. "I have to go now, Brian, grab what you need and lock the door behind you. Give me the keys later." After Maharaj left, Brian was angry.

"Why did you have to come back to the temple? Look, we both have to spend the afternoon cleaning again, I am tired."

"Me too . . . I didn't sleep well last night. It was too cold in my room."

"Yes man," he said, "it's so cold everywhere, I can never warm up."

"Look at the books, fascinating!"

Brian pulled a book from the shelves. It was an old book bonded in leather, embossed with flowery designs.

"Look at this one; 'The Code of Discipline for the Sanyasi Order'. Isn't that kind of a monk? Oh, I need to read this! I was thinking about becoming a monk."

"Don't make me laugh, You're not Sanyasi material."

"That's a mean thing to say, Anna! I am taking the book with me."

"Don't forget to return it, stealing from Krishna's Library, I am sure, would be a very bad thing. You'll burn in Hell forever." Brian took the book and we went on our separate ways.

The guest rooms looked very much like a country inn, with flowery bed spreads and curtains that didn't match. They were neat but very dusty. I cleaned everything thoroughly. At some point I heard a bell ringing and went outside to see what was happening. It was seven o'clock already and the evening program started. Very few devotes came to the temple. After the program Nina approached me.

"Go get your things! You'll stay in my room. That's what Baladev Swami wants." She wasn't too thrilled about it.

I went to the office to get my belongings and followed Nina upstairs through the dark corridor into the women's ashram. She walked very fast.

"Come on, hurry up," she said, "I've got to go to sleep!"

She stopped in front of a door with a big lock and opened it with a key that she was keeping around her neck. The rooms were all identical, but she decorated it with lots of pictures of Krishna and Maharaj. She had some long Indian scarves hanging on the walls and window. A big piece of fabric with flowery designs covered her wooden bed made from two by fours with a piece of plywood on top. Her belongings were on the floor organized in neat piles.

"You can sleep there," she said, pointing to the floor right by the door.

The room was freezing. I put my sleeping bag on top of the yoga mat and crawled inside with all my clothes on. She turned off the light and soon was gently snoring. An icy draft was coming from under the door. My body was fighting to stay warm and my mind racing. I felt disappointed and humiliated wondering what was I doing there and missing my warm bed in New York. I decided to get up and go for a walk around the temple. The wind was creating a sad hauling sound shaking the windows. I could hear the icy snow hitting the glass with the force of thousand small pebbles. Quietly I grabbed my jacket, booths and a flashlight and slipped out of the room.

The whole temple was steeped into darkness. The only sign of life was the ghastly moaning of the wind. Careful not to make any noise, I made it to the front door. There was snow accumulated in front of it and after pushing hard, I cracked it open just enough to squeeze out. Snow was flying everywhere. I couldn't see more than a couple of feet in front of me. Sometimes the wind would slow down creating an opening into the curtain of snow for a few moments, allowing me to see the hill. On top of it, a majestic statue was overlooking the whole valley, reminding me of a Buddha from Thailand or India. I started to climb uphill, sinking up to my knee into the fresh snow. It was further than I expected.

When I arrived on top, the wind was even more ferocious. It almost swiped me off my feet a few times. I walked toward the statue and found a niche into the wall to protect me from the wind. I sat on a pile of snow and watched the violent storm that perfectly described the unrest inside me. I concentrated in generating enough heat to keep my body from freezing. I remembered that yogis in the Himalayas were meditating in the snow, drying wet sheets on their naked bodies. I wondered how they did it.

Becoming still I tried not to think about anything. The mind consumes a tremendous amount of energy. Now I was less agitated and started to feel sleepy. That was dangerous. It was time to go back to the temple.

The snow and the wind were hitting my face and it was hard to breathe. Often I had to turn around and walk backwards. The soft snow was accumulating fast. I quietly slipped back into Nina's room. She was heavily asleep and I crawled into my sleeping bag. It felt warmer inside the bag, and was able to distance myself from the whole situation falling asleep.

CHAPTER 14

GAURANGA

Around 3:30 in the morning, Nina woke up and told me to take all my things out of the room during the day.

"Where am I going to put all this stuff?" I was annoyed.

"You can leave the bags in the office," she said.

"You must take a shower before you go," she said.

"I'll take one later on, is too cold now."

She looked at me with disdain. I stuffed the slipping bag into my backpack, gathered all my things and dragged everything out, slamming the door behind. There were many empty rooms on the floor. It made no sense sharing a room with her. Everything was still dark. I left all my belongings behind the door in one of the empty rooms and found my way to the temple.

Inside, the air was warm and smelled like sweet incense. Felt good to warm up a little after such a dreadful night. I chanted for a long time immersed in the peaceful vibrations, when a woman dressed in a colorful saree asked me to follow her to the kitchen, behind the temple. It was a small building. The doors did not quiet close and occasionally a chilling wind would swipe through the entire room. Layers of grease and dust on the walls gave the whole kitchen a tint of gray. The floors were slippery and all the drains clogged. I was impressed with the size of the cooking pots.

"Anna, my name is Yeshoda. Maharaj asked me to show you the kitchen."

"It's cold in here," I said.

"Yes, but it'll warm up when we start cooking. You can help me with lunch. We expect about 40 people altogether."

"I never cooked for so many people."

"You'll do just fine, you help them cook at the temple in New York."

"Yes a little bit."

"Don't worry," she said, "Krishna will help you." It was so cold that I was ready to go back to New York to my warm apartment.

"What are we cooking?" I asked.

"Pandava Swami wants everybody to eat light. He also wants us to become a self-sufficient community so we have to use whatever we have around here. He doesn't like to buy food. During the summer we preserve vegetables from the garden. We also have dried corn, lentils and a big barrel of wheat, as well as lots of carrots in the cooler. We need to use the carrots because they are going bad."

"We can make carrot soup," I said. "Also we can make lentils with cracked wheat and carrot salad."

"Good idea."

"Yeshoda, I need to go and get my jacket. I'll be right back."

"Make sure you come back, I can't do this alone."

I ran to the temple. It was empty except for Sunrise and Brian seated near the altar, playing the harmonium and tamboura. They were making some unusual music, some unusual sounds rather.

"Hey Anna," Sunrise yelled from across the temple, "come and join us, this is great!"

I sat next to Brian. "I can't stay long, I have to cook lunch. It's quite a challenge."

"Do you need some help?" Sunrise asked. "We want to help, we want to serve Krishna."

"Speak for yourself." Brian said, "just kidding, let's go and cook."

"Great. I need some help and I'm not feeling well, coming down with a cold or something. I wish I was back in New York."

"I kind of want to go back too," Brian said, "I am burned out. Yesterday, after we cleaned the hallway, Maharaj had us clean the whole men's ashram, the floors and all. My back is killing me."

"Come on both of you, I like it here. I hate New York," Sunrise said.

"No," Brian said, "I really want to go back. Anna, there is a devote going to New York with a van full of candles. His name is Gauranga. He is leaving this afternoon. I think I'll go back with him. If you want, you can come with us."

"Come on man, what's the matter with you two? We just got here."

"Where can I find Gauranga? I asked Brian.

"He leaves in a tipi up the hill."

"A tipi in the winter?"

"It's a great tipi. He built it himself. It has a potbelly stove in the center that keeps it nice and toasty. He's writing a book and spends most of the time in the tipi, writing."

"How exciting," I said.

"He is from England and his Guru died in a horrible way," Brian said.

"What happened?"

"His Guru had a devote that wanted to be initiated but was doing a lot of drugs, so the Guru didn't want to initiate him. He became obsessed with it and one day lost his mind, took a kitchen knife and cut the Guru's head off. Gauranga was very disturbed by this whole thing. He left England and went to live in different ashrams around the World. He's been living here for couple of years. He's doing much better now but is a little bit of an outsider. He doesn't want to surrender to Pandava Swami. He stays faithful to his Guru."

"Wow, what a story," I said. "You guys meet me at the kitchen I'll go find Gauranga."

Outside, the brightness of the snow blinded me for a few seconds. At the end of the plateau, two giant statues were presiding over the lake, majestically stretching their arms toward the sky. I followed a narrow trail uphill. Looking back from up there the valley opened wide, all white with mellow hills disappearing at the horizon. The temple and the houses surrounding it looked like matchboxes in the snow and that whole world with its joys and sorrows seemed more distant. The immensity of the sky was gently embracing the earth bellow. There I was, facing the Great Unknown alone, all aware of my insignificant existence.

Suddenly I began to perceive another presence, and when I turned around, a tall young man clad in a brown robe with a blanket wrapped around his head was standing there watching the sky.

"Hare Krishna, Mother," he said.

"Hari Boll. Are you Gauranga?"

"Yes," he said, "you must be new around here."

"I arrived couple of days ago from New York. Brian told me you're going back today."

"I am leaving after lunch. Mother, you want to go back with us?"

"Yes please, I need to go back as soon as possible."

"It's not easy to live here," he smiled. "You need a strong desire to be with Krishna. What's your name, Mother?"

"Anna."

"Anna, look at these surroundings, everything is so peaceful around here. I like being above the clouds. The World loosens its grip on my mind up here." He paused for a moment. "Would you like to come in for a cup of tea?"

"I'd love to."

The tipi was a circular construction, like a tent, covered with blankets of different colors. There was a chimney in the centre with gray-whitish smoke rising toward the sky, thinning out and then disappearing in space. The room was larger than expected. There was water boiling on a potbelly stove. Brown paper bags filled with herbs were neatly lined up on the shelves. He put some herbs in a teapot, covering it with a towel.

"Have a seat, Anna," he said.

The walls were made from a thick canvas with many drawings and paintings hanging with safety pins. They were landscapes of the surrounding hills in winter, summer, different times of the day and all kinds of weather.

"Are those yours?" I asked.

"Yes Mother, I like to draw the hills over and over. When I draw, I become one with the landscape. It makes me feel alive."

"Beautiful drawings, you're lucky to be here so close to nature."

He had a faint smile. "Beauty is everywhere. If you try to see God in everything, you'll see the beauty in all." He poured the tea using a bamboo strainer in two ceramic cups of unusual shapes and colorful designs. An entire shelf was full of these cups.

"My ex girlfriend made these cups. She left them here when she went away."

"Where did she go?" I asked.

"She was too young and full of life! She wanted to live in the world and went back to London."

"Are you from London?"

"Yes," he said, "but now I live here. I don't think I'll ever go back to London."

"Do you miss her?"

"No," he said, "I only miss Krishna."

The tea was exquisite. It was a mixture of mint and something else I could not recognize.

"What did you put in the tea? It tastes great!"

"Mint, sandalwood and some rose petals. We have one of the best rose gardens in West Virginia. When the roses start wilting, I take the leaves, dry them and they last the whole winter. I even have a lot left. Would you like some to take home with you?" I nodded, and he took one of the paper bags, carefully folding the top a few times and gave it to me.

"Here, this is for you. Remember Krishna when you drink it."

"Thank you Gauranga, I'll will." Gauranga pulled his hood down. His golden hair was covering his shoulders.

"You and Brian, meet me in the dining hall around one o'clock and be all packed. I am planning to leave right after lunch."

"Okay, I have to go back to the kitchen now, we're helping with lunch."

"Are you a good cook?"

"I love to cook. It's very relaxing and creative. Thank you for everything Gauranga, I must go now."

"Hare Krishna," he said.

I started to walk down hill at a slow pace, watching the temple getting bigger with each step. The world I left in the valley was pulling me back into its complexity. Back in the kitchen Brian, Sunrise and a few others were chopping vegetables. The kitchen was buzzing with activity. Maharaj walked in holding a box full of eggplants. My heart skipped a beat and I felt guilty for planning my escape without asking him first. He handed me the box.

"Anna, clean these eggplants for me and cut them into small squares about ½ an inch, please."

"Yes Maharaj," I said keeping my head down, without being able to look him in the eyes.

Stationed by the end of a long stainless steel table I started to peel the eggplants. Brian was next to me. On the other side a handsome young man with brown hair growing down to his broad shoulders, was watching us smiling. His skin was golden brown from the sun.

"Hi, my name is Troy. What's your name, Mother?"

"Anna," I said.

"Do you need some help with the eggplants? I just finished what I was doing."

"Thanks, I can use the help. Are you from New York? I think I've seen you at the Interfaith Centre."

"It's possible, I am from New York, but I live here now. I've been here for about two weeks."

Brian was getting inpatient. "Did you get to see Gauranga?" He anxiously asked.

"Yes, he wants us to meet in the dining hall around one o'clock or so. I think he is planning to leave right after lunch."

"Oh, I can't wait! You better tell Maharaj you're leaving."

"I can't. You tell him, please."

"Anna, you want to get me into trouble? You should tell him. You're scared of him, aren't you?" Maharaj just walked in. I mustered all my courage and looked him in the eyes.

"Maharaj, Brian and I are going back to New York with Gauranga this afternoon."

"What, so soon?"

"I've got a job and I need to make a few dollars," Brian said. "A friend of mine is moving and he needs my help. He'll pay me."

"Anna, I thought you'll be staying here for a while, we need you here."

"I am sorry Maharaj, it's too cold here. Sleeping on the floor, I can never warm up. There is a draft from the door in Nina's room."

"Why are you sleeping in Nina's room? We have plenty of empty rooms. You can pick and choose."

"But Baladev Swami told me I can't have my own room."

"That's only when we have guests and the ashram is full."

"Maharaj, I have to go, but I'll be back in the spring."

"Do whatever you want, remember we'd like you to stay here. You can come here anytime."

"Thank you Maharaj. You don't know how much it means to me to have a place where I feel welcome."

"I know," he said, "remember when you can't stand the heat, you run away. Eventually you must go through the fire, if you want to become gold. We all did. There is no other way."

"I thought I might be ready but maybe not yet," I said.

"You think too much," Maharaj said.

"Please don't be angry with me, Maharaj."

"I rarely get angry, Anna, I just want you to become a devote."

I felt him receiving me with his soul wide open. I could almost touch it. Cool, molten gold. He looked at me with compassion and went to the other side of the kitchen.

"Both of you are going back with Gauranga?" Troy asked.

"Yes," Brian whispered, "I can't wait to get out of here!"

"I know what you mean," Troy said, "I am a prisoner here, they won't let me go anywhere man, they are afraid I won't stay clean. I used to have a little bit of a drug problem."

"I see," Brian said "you're probably better off here."

"I really changed a lot in the last two weeks. Radakund Swami took me under his wings and I didn't want to disappoint him, but sometimes I feel like I am going out of my mind."

"I would if I stayed here for two weeks," Brian said.

"Come now, two weeks is not that long," I said.

"Look who's talking!" Brian said.

"You know what Radakund Swami told me?" Troy said with fear in his eyes.

"What?"

"He said if I leave this place I'm going to die."

"You better stay here," I said "Radakund Swami knows what he's talking about."

"He's just scaring you man," Brian said.

"Who do you want to listen to, Brian or Radakund Swami?" I asked.

"I want to stay here, but I don't know for how long I can take it? I wish I could go back with you guys."

"Come on, man," Brian said, "you live here for free, you do a little work, it's not too bad. I just have a job back in New York but I'll be back. I think that I want to spend the summer here. It's peaceful, just look around you."

"I don't need a free ride, I have plenty of money," Troy said, "and I've got a great car. Did you see the black Cadillac outside? It's mine. Unfortunately, broke down as soon as I arrived here. Maharaj wouldn't let me fix it. He keeps on saying that it's better if I don't use the car."

"I know where your head is at, man," Brian said. "Look me up when you're back in New York. I go to the Native programs at the Interfaith Centre. I like the drumming."

"I play the flute," Troy said, "I am pretty good at it. Maybe we can jam together, sometimes."

When I looked up, Maharaj was watching us with a sad expression on his face. It rather scared me. I knew that Troy was fighting for his life. Troy knew it too.

Lunch turned into a great feast. Brian and I sat with Goranga and other devotes at one of the long tables. They were trying hard to make us stay. However, I was resolute in my decision.

CHAPTER 15

SPIRIT MOUNTAIN

We left around two o'clock. It was a clear day, with the sun reflected on the white snow. It was hurting my eyes and I couldn't look at it for more than a few seconds. The heat in the van was broken. Luckily we had plenty of blankets. It was so cold that I had to cover myself completely, including my face.

"I am going to stop somewhere for a few hours," Gauranga said. "You guys can come with me to warm up a little."

"Where?" Brian asked.

"Not far from here. Some Native friends invited me to a Sweat Lodge."

"It's awesome," Brian said.

"Can we go into the lodge?" I asked.

"I don't see why not."

"I always wanted to try it," Brian said, "it'll warm up my bones."

We drove for about an hour on narrow roads winding around wooded hills, passing through small towns that had a European flavor. Gauranga was meeting his friends by an abandoned stone quarry owned by Pandava Swami. A group of natives from the Lakota Tribe were spending some time on the property at the invitation of senior devotees to held Sweat Lodges and teach local people about the Lakota tradition.

It was a small hill called "Spirit Mountain". The devotees built a log cabin on top of it. Huge blocks of stone piled up haphazardly, were forming small caves where people carved different symbols on the walls. The quarry looked like an immense modern sculpture or an ancient Egyptian tomb.

Faraway from any village or highway, the whole place was enveloped in deep silence. The only sign of civilization was the distant buzz of an airplane that would transport one from the Stone Age, directly into the Twentieth Century. Two lodges were standing next to the quarry. They were constructed from branches bent and weaved together to form half a sphere covered with colorful blankets. It was so dark inside that one couldn't see anything. A small pit lined with stones was right in the center of the lodge. The ground around it was covered with branches and layers of blankets, creating a perfect insulation from the frozen ground. Hanging on long polls around the lodge, four colored flags; black, white, red and yellow waving in the breeze, were representing the four directions. Outside, a large pit lined with stones, was the recipient of the Sacred Fire. Large stones heated in the fire were transported into the lodge, one by one.

A short stocky man greeted us at the cabin. His name was Red-Cloud. They say that his hair sometimes in the sunlight looked red. That is how he got his name.

"Wakan-Tanka," he said.

"Wakan-Tanka," Gauranga answered.

"Please come in, it's warm in here. We were waiting for you."

"I have two devotees with me, taking them back to New York. I hope is okay with you."

"Everybody is welcome here," Red-Cloud said. "We know that you devotees don't eat meat so we cooked some veggies for you but don't expect us to eat only vegetables we'll die of starvation."

"Thank you, I am deeply moved, Red-Cloud." Gauranga smiled. "I owe you one, and I have something for you," he handed a package to Red-Cloud. "It's the best sage. I picked it myself from Colorado last summer. Enjoy it!"

Red-Cloud opened the package a little, took a leaf, squeezed it between his big fingers and sniffed it.

"Ah this is very good, one of the best. Are you sure you don't have some native relatives?"

"I wish I did," Gauranga said.

It was warm inside and I was able to warm up. We sat around an old kitchen table and we eat corn on the cab, Sloppy Joe and lots of bread and butter, as well as jelly doughnuts.

"The jelly doughnuts have no eggs," Red-Cloud said. "We know you don't eat eggs. We'll be ready for the lodge in about an hour. The women and the men go in separate lodges. We've got two of them. I will be leading the men's and Marianne (Snow-Bird) the women's." Red-Cloud looked at me and continued, "You can change in the back room and use one of the sheets to cover your body. Don't worry. It'll be very warm inside. Snow-Bird will tell you everything you want to know about the lodge."

In the back room, several women from the neighboring villages were waiting, covered with white sheets. A tall blond woman came over to greet me.

"I am Snow-Bird. What's your name?"

"Anna," I said, "I am glad to meet you. I've heard a lot about you from Gauranga and brother Ram."

"They are both friends of ours. Good men." She laughed, and to my surprise she looked, more Anglo-Saxon than Native American. "You look at me like you have seen a ghost," she said. "Never mind, it happens to me a lot."

"I am sorry," I said, "but I pictured you differently."

"My mother was Native from the Lakota Tribe but my father was from Sweden. I didn't see much of him around. She brought us up, my brother and me, in the Native tradition. She was a fine woman."

"Snow-Bird, I am very pleased to finally meet you. Would you tell me about the Sweat Lodge? What am I supposed to do?"

"I will, but first I have something that I'd like you to take back to New York for Brother Ram." She gave me a small package. "It's an eagle feather. Be very careful with it. They are very rare, but I know how much Brother Ram wanted this feather.

"Thank you," I said, "he'll be so happy, he thinks highly of you. You're like his second Guru." She laughed and her face lit up like a sunny day.

"Well, about the lodge," Snow-Bird said, "It gets very hot in there. You must let go of your bodily awareness and concentrate on something outside yourself. This is a spiritual ritual. In order to withstand the heat you must pray and send your thoughts to someone that needs healing. In the Lodge during ceremony your thoughts will have amplified power. If you think 'Oh, it's so hot in here, I can't stand it' you won't be able to endure it. Remember to keep your mind away from the body. It'll help you in the lodge."

"Thank you, Snow-Bird, I'll remember that," I said. "Do I take off all my clothes?"

"Yes, wrap your body in one of these sheets. Before entering the lodge, I'll smudge you with sage for purification. We don't want you to bring anything with you inside the lodge except your body. Make sure to leave all jewelry, hairpins, or whatever outside before you go in."

"Snow-Bird, please tell me what's the meaning of the Pipe Ceremony?"

"The Pipe is a sacred act of communion with the whole Universe, inside us as well as outside. This profound experience contains great power. When you find yourself in time of need, the simple remembrance of this experience will help you overcome anything. The Sacred Pipe is the symbol of The Great Everything, which we call Wakan-Tanka and was given to our people by a magical woman. It is said that when she left she turned into a white buffalo and disappeared. She was holding the bowl of the pipe in her left hand and the stem in her right hand. We call her the White Buffalo Woman."

"What is Wakan-Tanka?" I asked.

"Wakan-Tanka is neither male nor female. It's the source of all creation and the center of stillness. He is the breath of all animals, plants, rocks and human beings. It is the Sacred Breath, which connects us all. It gives life to the whole Universe. You'll have to make your own connection to the source. Make it your own experience." She handed us the sheets to be used inside the lodge. "Let's go," she said, "if you feel ill from the heat let me know immediately. You can go out anytime you want."

She took a bundle of sage and started smudging us one by one. I took off my watch and my prayer beads.

"You can keep your prayer beads," she said.

We all covered our bodies with the white sheets and walked by the men still sitting around the table in the front room.

"Ready to go?" Red-Cloud said, "we'll follow you in a short while."

We walked outside in the freezing cold with just the sheets covering our naked bodies. The fire was blazing around a pile of big stones. One of the native men was the Fire Keeper. He had to keep the fire burning and take the hot stones one by one with a shovel bringing them to the entrance.

It was very dark inside and to my surprise not so cold. They warmed it up with a few stones before we came in. We sat in a circle around the center pit. Snow-Bird sat next to it. She had a big bag that contained her pipe and other paraphernalia for the lodge. We kept the floppy blanket by the door open so we could see our way inside. Snow-Bird laid a fur on the ground where she put her simple and elegant pipe carved in white stone, as well as bundles of sage and other herbs. Snow-Bird had two buckets of water, for later in the ceremony. She explained the ritual to us. When the temperature became very high, she would pass around one of the buckets. We were allowed to use only one ladle of water at a time, and pour it over our heated bodies to cool off.

"Conserve water," she said, "we only have one bucket. Take only what you need." In the other bucket, she mixed all kinds of herbs. "This is for the ceremony," she said. "I'll pour this water with sacred herbs on the hot stones, to make steam. It will help us heal and purify the environment." She began singing a monotonous chant. I could not understand a word of it but was making me sleepy.

"We will bring the first stone," she said.

The Fire-keeper brought in a big stone and gave it to Snow-Bird. She was very strong. Took the shovel with the big heavy stone with ease and gently placed it into the pit. She told all of us to pray while she kept on pouring water on the stone. The herbs gave the steam an unusual fragrance. It cleared my head. The air was warming up slowly but I was still shivering. It was very dark inside and she told us to keep on praying. I began repeating my mantra and after a little while, the fire-keeper brought in another big stone. Now the lodge began to heat up. It was good to feel the warm steam enveloping my body, in complete darkness. It felt so safe and secure, the safest place I could ever imagine. One more stone came in, and now was getting very warm. At that point somebody passed me the bucket of water. I poured a little water in my palms and splashed it over my face. It was refreshing and most gratifying. Snow-Bird began invoking the Great Powers of the Four Directions.

"Now we are facing south which takes us into the past, represented by the Moon. Think about the most painful experience of your life. Now imagine you walking away from it and leaving it behind forever. Imagine yourself whole and completely healed from that experience. We must forgive those who hurt us and forgive ourselves for the mistakes we made in the past that hurt others.

Now we move to the west, which represents change, and the Earth. The whole Universe is in constant change. Every season the trees grow new leaves. Each autumn the leaves fall to the ground back to Mother Earth. The death of the body is a gift that we make to Mother Earth of the elements she gave us to make this body. Now it's time to thank her for the body, which is such a miracle.

Next direction is north, representing the flickering stars. Its color is white. We are looking at that which is yet to come, the future. This life is a precious gift we should always cherish. Imagine yourself in a white field of clouds. In front of you, the brightest star emanating sparkles of white light. Now you are walking in perfect balance toward the white light with trust and confidence in your future.

Now we turn to the east and contemplate the rising Sun, a giant golden sphere, ascending into the sky. At this point, we contemplate our immortality, our Spirit, the part of us that lives forever. The World of the Spirit is everlasting. Everything that we see around us is alive in the Spirit World. The stone that gives us heat and us are all equal. Send your prayers to the East to send to you a Spirit Guide that is willing to walk with you on the path of your life, show you the way, and protect you from danger. Your Spirit Guide knows the path. He walked on it before, and will take you to your destination."

When Snow-Bird stopped talking everything fell into a deep silence. A multitude of images of planets, animals and people wearing strange outfits from some forgotten worlds were moving fast through my mind. Strange animals, big lizards, and people were screaming, laughing and crying. A big red planet was coming towards me with such a speed that all I could do was just to sit there and watch. At that moment, Snow-Bird announced:

"I will pass the Sacred Pipe around. We will dedicate it to Peace in the World, and for us humans to learn how to live in peace with each other. The sooner we learn this lesson the easier will be. The more we wait, the higher the price. We are not only hurting ourselves but everything around us as well. When you receive the pipe, bow your head to the pipe and take a smoke. Afterwards you can pass it to the next person. If you don't want to smoke just bring the pipe to your right shoulder and then pass it on."

In the meantime a few more stones came in. It started to get hot. I poured water over my shoulders and the wet sheet felt good on my heated body. I turned my head up to the sky and began to pray. In that very safe place, I was able to bring my true emotions to the surface and feel the depth of my loneliness and alienation from the World. I was entirely alone in the whole Universe.

A silent cry for help came out of my open mouth, and two gigantic birds rushed towards me. Their feathers were all gray and as soft as the clouds. They wrapped me under their wings. The warmth and love that I felt emanating from them was so healing and soothing that my loneliness began to melt away. I was in a trance. When I came back from meditation, I felt completely refreshed and transformed. Somebody out there heard my cry of loneliness and reached out.

I felt a light tap on the shoulder and the woman seating next to me passed the bucket of water. I took a full ladle and poured it over my head. The heat was getting to be unbearable. I remembered what Snow-Bird said earlier about how to overcome the heat and began to pray.

I prayed for the deserts of this world to be blessed with rain. I prayed for all the animals and trees to live a natural life without us ending it in its infancy. I prayed for the helpless people of this world to have their needs fulfilled. I prayed that all beings might have an equal chance to be happy. I prayed to the Creator to soften our hearts that we may feel the pain of others. Then I prayed to the Big Architect that planned us all to take a second look at that Devine Design and see that maybe something went wrong. I heard a voice from the depths of my being.

"Know what you are like. Know what you treasure. Know what you need. Know what kind of world you envision. I am listening! Show me!"

My mind was extremely clear. I thought about ancient civilizations and the many ways they tried to communicate to the Creator. Why didn't they talk to Him directly? Numerous images rushed unto my mind. Colorful circles with geometric designs reminding me of the ancient ceremonial mandalas that Hindu Priests made at the entrance of temples or at fire ceremonies to invoke the cosmic powers of their Deities. At that point I knew that these colorful shapes and designs I was seeing, had a meaning I couldn't understand it, maybe someday I would. It was a language of thought vibration imprinted in those shapes, the entire thought vibration of the whole World. How was I able to communicate to the Creator the true vibration of my heart? Maybe trough symbols, drawings, art or music. Maybe Art was the language to communicate to the Gods. That explained why I could never understand where the need to create was coming from, just as couldn't understand our origins on this Earth . . .

The Pipe came to me. I took the boll in my left hand and rested the steam of the Pipe on my right shoulder. Bowing my head, I addressed the Pipe in my mind. "This is for all beings that are in pain, are abused, exploited and humiliated and for those who are causing pain to others to stop this cycle of violence." I passed the Pipe to the next person. A sense of urgency came over me. Thinking that we were in a place in time that demanded a complete overhaul I felt an overwhelming sadness, wondering if I will ever be happy again. After that, my eyes became heavy and I drifted into a deep sleep.

When I opened my eyes, a bright light blinded me after the complete darkness I have been accustomed to. The flap door was open for the daylight to rush in.

"Wakan-Tanka" she said, "all my Relations!"

"All my Relations," we answered and began to exit the lodge. One woman brought new sheets to wrap around our bodies. The dry, soft cotton sheets felt so good on my skin. Outside, the cool air was refreshing. A thick white fog was lingering on the ground and above us a brilliant, blue winter sky. The atmosphere was crystal-clear. I felt so light that I could walk on air.

The men were still in the lodge. We rushed to the cabin running barefoot in the snow. I got dressed, and sat on the wooden bench in the front room waiting for Gauranga. Everybody was hungry and we had a snack and some sweets. The men began to trickle in, a few at a time. White-Cloud was all flushed. All their faces were kind of pink from the heat.

"Looks like you had a hot Sweat Lodge," I said.

"You bet," one man said, "it was the hottest!"

Gauranga and Brian walked in.

"How was it?" I asked Brian.

"Too hot."

"He wanted to leave in the middle, what a sissy," Gauranga said.

"Look who's speaking." Brian said. "You look like a red beet."

"I feel great," Gauranga said to Brian, "you don't get it, do you?" Looking at me over his shoulder he added, "Mother, get ready, we're leaving as soon as possible."

"I am ready," I said. Gauranga gave me a funny look and said:

"Mother, you better go back where the women are, we have to get dressed."

I went to the back room and waited until Brian came to get me. We all said good bye to the Natives and left for the long drive back to New York. For a while I didn't feel the cold, but slowly my body began to cool off. Soon it got very cold and I was shivering.

"Anna, are you cold? Take another blanket." I covered my whole body with two blankets but the cold was unbearable.

"When we get to New Jersey, I'll take you out for a bite to eat. I know this great diner, open all night. Breakfast is on me," Gauranga said.

"You're a true gentleman," Brian said, "Us local people are not in the habit of being so generous."

"It's your lucky day," Gauranga said, "I want to make up for freezing you in my van for eight hours. Just think of it as an endurance test."

"Aren't you cold?" Brian asked him.

"I am used to it. Really, I kind of like it. Let's chant, it will keep us warm." He started to repeat loudly "Hare Krishna, Hare Krishna . . ." Brian got his tamboura out and we kept on chanting as loud as we could for hours. I forgot about the cold. Brian took over the driving and Gauranga stretched his long legs and fell asleep. Time was passing by slowly and the trip seemed like would never end. We passed through Pennsylvania, and soon I started to recognize the familiar industrial landscapes of New Jersey.

"We are in New Jersey," I told Gauranga. He opened his big blue-green eyes and took a moment to come back to reality. "You said we'll have breakfast at your favorite diner."

"Oh yes," Gauranga said. "Brian let me drive, please."

"I thought you'll never ask," Brian said and they changed places.

After driving for about an hour, we stopped at a diner on the side of the road, classier than most with red tablecloth and white napkins. It was very warm inside and Gauranga ordered breakfast for the three of us. We had pancakes with maple syrup and herbal tea with ginger and honey. The owners were Indian, friends of Gauranga. At the end we split a large piece of cheesecake between us. Everything was delicious and the owners gave us some Indian cookies for the road.

We thanked Gauranga for the great breakfast and went back to the freezing van. It was still dark. After some time, I could see the sky lit up in the distance. It was not the sunrise. It was Manhattan emanating an aura of light. Soon I could see the buildings. Manhattan always looked better from the distance. I was happy to be back to the familiar landscape.

CHAPTER 16

BACK IN NEW YORK

We stopped on 6th Avenue. The first breath of air felt like sticking my head into a carburetor. I refused to inhale, holding my breath until my lungs felt like bursting. My first impulse was to get back into the van and drive away. However from past experience, getting used to it was only a matter of days. A constant buzzing, more like the moaning of a wild beast, was created by the sum of millions of human beings and their activities. That subhuman sound was constantly ringing into my ears.

My apartment was just around the corner. I said good bye to Gauranga and Brian and dragged my overstuffed duffle bag across 6th Avenue back to my apartment. It was in complete disarray. The cats were out of water and their food dried out. My roommate was away, some of her furniture gone and her room full of boxes. It looked like she was in the process of moving out. Luckily I came back just in time to oversee her departure.

I was trying hard to get used to New York again. The roommate moved out and it took a few extra days of cleaning to make the place livable. I had to earn some money, but the job at the Interfaith Center was gone. Since Maharaj left, the devotees were not very eager to help me. Some resented him and me by association. I put up some flyers and found a job cleaning an apartment once a week, in a low income building complex not too far from my house. The apartment belonged to a middle-aged couple and their terminally ill, old mother. She was going to spend her last days at home with the family. They had a nurse taking care of her for couple of hours a day. Since they were both working, the mother was alone the rest of the day.

The apartment was at the end of a long hallway. One day I came to work and found the hallway sealed with yellow tape and a guard stationed by the elevators. I had to show him an ID and tell him where I was going. Somebody had been murdered in the apartment next door. It was an argument about drugs. The tenant apparently owed a sum of money to some dealer and wasn't willing to pay. Two men came to the apartment around four or five in the morning. One of them was dressed in women's clothing. The other one was the drug dealer who expected to get his money. Something went wrong. One of the men took a kitchen knife and stubbed the tenant several times in the stomach, leaving him to bleed to death. The man was able to open the door and drag himself into the hallway. He collapsed and died on the hallway's floor.

When I arrived, the body had been removed. There was blood everywhere even on the walls. The Police put white sheets on the floor for people to walk over. I had to walk over the sheets with blood underneath to get to the apartment. At that point, I wished I had taken the day off. The entire scene shook me. I went straight to the kitchen and began washing dishes. At some point, I heard heavy breathing coming from the old woman's room. She was gasping for air. I called the hospital and they started to give me instructions and walk me through the process of using the oxygen tank.

When I walked into her room, she wasn't breathing. I was still on the phone with the hospital. They told me to check her vital signs, but she was dead. I closed her eyes and called her daughter. She did not seem surprised. I was more shook up than her. I had to wait for her to come home, and for somebody from the hospital to file a report for the death certificate. While waiting I lit a couple of candles and said a prayer and cried. It hit me how alone we all are when we die in such a cold and loveless world.

Soon both of them, husband and wife came home. They were calm and didn't shed a single tear. The woman from the hospital talked about death in a beautiful way. I offered my condolences and left. On my way out, I had to step over the bloody sheets in the hallway. I took a cab and on my way home decided to stop by a little church on 29th street.

It was an old church with a small chapel. People called it 'The Little Church Around the Corner'. The altar was carved in wood with intricate designs and masterfully painted icons. On each side of the altar there were two prayer niches and a beautiful white marble statue of Virgin Mary. I sat on an old wooden bench close to the altar. I didn't know the denomination of the church, but it didn't really matter.

Feeling the impact of that tragic experience, life seemed confusing and empty. Nothing made much sense. Sometimes I was completely engaged in being happy, looking forward to the next portion of happiness, but now the future seemed like a black curtain with nothing behind. Thinking about that old woman, after a life of sacrifices, raising children, struggling to do her best, was baffling how she ended up in a room alone, a burden for her family.

The words of a special being came to mind. He was saying that modern people lost the meaning of life. In the old days everything a person was supposed to do, or whom they should marry, was decided beforehand by their family. In the modern World, everybody had to choose his or her own identity. The suspicion of not choosing the right thing always existed. The modern person was living every second in the middle of an identity crisis.

In the old days, people belonged to groups, religions and countries. They had no individuality. People lived as part of a collective mind. They had a safe, uneventful life, thinking that they were doing something important just because everybody else was doing the same thing. In our modern society, 'meaning' seems to be lost. A person has to create each morning a reason to live for the day, a reason to stay alive, struggle and survive. Without a reason to live, many people would give up at the slightest difficulty. Maybe that's why so many people today are addicted to drugs or contemplate suicide. Drugs could create an illusion of power, wellbeing and safety. When the illusion is over, confronting reality could be unbearable. Nowadays life is confusing, with no clear distinction between right and wrong. In the midst of this agonizing dilemma, one could never find peace. I wished I could accept the good and the bad that came to me, and create a new start each day and a reason to go on living.

On the other hand, it takes courage to follow a dream. Dreams are worlds apart from the logical, material, calculated existence that most of us are forced into by circumstances. In the foolishness and innocence of youth chasing after a dream seemed unquestionably the right path.

How difficult is now to dream the impossible! How brave one has to be, in spite of the experience accumulated over a lifetime, to have the courage to dream. To choose dreams over the cold reality and to say: "I want to be young again and allow my heart to falter at the image of a beautiful dream," is real courage. To let all the years of experience run through the fingers like water, and choose the impossible over reality. After all, a moment of being truly alive, weights more than an entire lifetime of numbness. For a moment I closed my eyes. A sweet, mellow peace filled the air. I sat there, absorbing and being nourished by this miraculous substance of the soul.

That night I dreamed that my house was a small lot of earth about seven by fourteen feet long surrounded by a low fence. The fence had a narrow side door that was slightly open. I was sleeping on a grass mat isolating my body from the bare, cold ground. I woke up wondering if that piece of earth was my grave. Was it my grave from a past life? Maybe many graves existed somewhere in the world, where my body had been buried over hundreds of years in the past. It was ironic that in this life I was afraid of becoming homeless and actually I was the owner of all those graves. What a crazy thought.

A couple of months passed. I wasn't earning enough money to pay the rent so I needed to get another roommate and ended up putting an ad in the New York Press. As soon as the ad came out, lots of people started calling to make appointments for the room. After interviewing many people, I couldn't find anybody I liked. The ad came out on the Wednesday paper. On Friday morning, I received a call from a man with a foreign accent. His name was Helmut. He was from Amsterdam and made an appointment for following day.

He showed up with his girlfriend. He was a journalist and she a student. They owned a condominium in Chelsea. The story was that she was awarded a scholarship to study Architecture in Italy. They had to rent out the condominium because it was too expansive for him to keep it by himself. He wanted to 'save some money'. The whole story made sense and I decided to let him move in.

A month went by and he started to lock himself into his room for days at a time. I could hear him making phone calls at four o'clock in the morning. Every night a strong, smoky smell was coming from his room and I would wake up with a sharp pain in my heart and shortness of breath. I sealed all the cracks in the wall with duct tape but it didn't help. Every time I knocked on his door, he took a very long time to answer. I began to suspect that he might be doing some drugs in his room, maybe crack.

One night he asked me to sell him a couple of candles, the tall glass candles that one could buy at the grocery store. It was peculiar. That night I woke up gasping for air. The smell was so strong that I had to open both windows for fresh air, in spite of the freezing wind.

In the morning I decided to confront him about the drugs and knocked at his door. No answer. I knocked again and he finally told me to wait for a few minutes. I waited for about ten minutes and again I knocked at his door.

"Helmut, I need to come in, open the door right now!" The same story repeated itself. By now, I was getting angry. "I am coming in," I said and propped my foot on the door, forcing it open. A long piece of wood from the doorframe came loose flying towards me. I grabbed it in one hand and walked into the room. He was sitting on the floor. His eyes were red and swollen and he looked like he did not sleep in days. Candles and drug paraphernalia were all over the floor. When he saw me walking towards him, picked up the phone and called 911 telling the police that I was attacking him. I was stunned, not believing what was happening.

"Are you crazy?" I said. "I have no intention to attack you."

"Get out of my room!" He yelled.

"You better get out of my apartment!" I said angrily, and went back into the living room. He closed the door and I could hear him cleaning up all his drugs from the floor. Within less than ten minutes, the doorbell rang. It was the police. Two police officers walked in.

"Did you make the call?" One of them asked me.

"No," I said, "my roommate did."

"Where is she?" The other officer asked.

"Him," I said and took them to his room.

The officer knocked on his door and asked Helmut: "Did you make the call?

Helmut came to the door: "She broke into my room," he said, "and she attacked me with the stick. I want her arrested!" The cops looked at me and than looked at each other.

"Did you break into his room? They asked me.

"Yes," I said, "he was locking himself in the room. I suspected he was doing drugs."

"Did you have a weapon?" He asked me.

"No! I did not have a weapon!"

Helmut picked up the piece of wood. "Officer, she was going to attack me with this," he said and showed it to the cops.

"Were you holding that piece of wood?" The officer asked me.

"Yes" I said, "it came off the door when I forced the door open but I had no intention of attack him." The cops looked at each other. In the meantime, Helmut started to calm down.

"What do you want from me?" He asked.

"I want you to move out of here!"

"Would you give me my security deposit back if I move?"

"Why should she give you anything?" One officer said, "You want her arrested."

"If you drop the charges she'll give you the money back, aren't you?" The other cop said looking at me.

"Of course," I said to Helmut, "I'll give you the security back when you move out."

"Are you going to withdraw the charge?" The officer asked Helmut.

"Yes," Helmut said, unsure and fearful, "you'll give me my money back, promise."

"You'll have your security back when you move out, as we agreed in the beginning."

"Don't go into his room until he moves out," the other officer said to me.

"Understood officer, thank you."

"Don't mention it," the officer said and both of them left.

Helmut locked himself into the room. I had to get out of my apartment and went for a long walk towards Union Square. I was still feeling shaky. Everything happened so fast. Now, that it was all over I realized how close I came to being arrested. It had to be a lesson the Universe was trying to teach me. I had to do something about my anger and uncontrolled temper. It was too dangerous. I had to find a different way to deal with bad situations. I was deeply grateful to that officer, who so brilliantly got me off the hook. Without his help, I could have been in jail. I stopped by the café at Virgin Records and ordered steamed milk with a lot of cinnamon and honey. Second phase was figuring a way to get rid of Helmut. I called Brian telling him the whole story.

"Helmut must go!" Brian said. "I have some friends, Italiano you know, they'll get him out in no time."

"I don't know," I said, "I don't want him hurt. Please, come and stay with me until Helmut moves out."

"If you cook I'll stay over your place."

"You know I like to cook."

"I am kidding, however if you want to I wouldn't mind."

"Brian," I said, "I am not going home alone. Would you please meet me at the café at Virgin Records?"

"Give me about an hour," Brian said. "Leave it to me. He'll be sorry he ever moved in with you."

"See you later Brian, I owe you one."

I sat by the window watching people hanging out in the Union Square Park, just across the street. Some teenagers were skateboarding and jumping over crates, turning and twisting in the air. Amazing what they were able to do with those boards. Occasionally a kid would take a bad fall and then got up like nothing happened. A "Freedom of Speech" red banner was stretched between two polls. Some people gathered around a homeless man that was speaking with animosity, gesticulating with his hands. I was wondering what he was talking about.

Brian showed up and we had more milk and honey. When we arrived home I found a note from Helmut saying that he will be moving out the following Sunday. We both had a sigh of relief. Every day I kept on asking Helmut if he found a moving company. His answer was always vague. Brian and I decided that Helmut was incapable to make moving arrangements. We left him a note that we would help him find a moving company. I made some phone calls and many companies never called back but finally couple of guys responded and seemed reasonable and reliable. They promised to come on Sunday morning at eight o'clock. Helmut always locked himself in his room and when he came out he was literally out of his mind. We tried to talk to him but he was talking to himself as if we did not exist. He said that he had been up for at least a week.

Sunday came and nothing was packed. The movers showed up around ten. We knocked at Helmut's door. We all had to wait for about twenty minutes until he opened the door. I told the movers that he was on drugs but they didn't care. All they wanted was to be paid. When Helmut finally came out, his room was a disaster. We told the movers to begin packing. It took the movers and us the whole day to pack his things. Helmut was acting completely crazy. He would take a box that was just packed and had the movers open it again. He would take everything out of the box, looking for some clothes or his telephone or whatever and the movers had to put everything back into the box. It was exasperating! This went on until eleven o'clock at night when they finally finished packing. Helmut in the meantime, kept on going out every twenty minutes. He was going to do his drugs up on the roof. When everything was out of the apartment, I gave Helmut the security deposit and had him sign a receipt in front of everybody.

The movers were on their way out and Helmut was still lingering around the apartment. I asked the movers to take him along.

"Let's go! You're coming with us, we'll drive you wherever want." One of them said.

Helmut reluctantly counted his money again and finally left with the movers. As soon as he left, I changed the lock.

"Brian, I don't know how to thank you."

"Don't mention it," Brian said. "He is not coming back, don't worry. He is so far gone that probably couldn't find his way back here, anyway. You know what I think?"

"What?"

"I think he'll kick the bucket soon. I don't see how he can survive for too long in this state. He told me that he never sleeps and that he was doing crack, a lot of it."

"I feel bad for forcing him out like this."

"You're lucky he didn't hurt you, you are lucky to be alive! Anyway, better him than you. There is nothing you could've done. If he is lucky, the police will pick him up. Anyway it's over now. Just say a prayer for the bastard."

"Let's go out, I'll buy you dinner," I said.

"Anna, I'll take a rain check. I am exhausted and need to go home."

"Thanks a million Brian!"

"Call me tomorrow," he said and left.

I locked the heavy metal door behind him and felt safe inside my place, finally alone. I didn't sleep well that night, haunted by those crazy red eyes bulging out of his head, focusing on nothing in particular, just staring at something undefined, maybe images of hell.

As time went by the weather was warming up. It was a Thursday morning. I woke up thinking about Maharaj and missing him a lot. I decided to go by the Interfaith Centre that evening. I called Brian to see if he would meet me there for dinner. I arrived late and the program was almost over. Brother Ram was happy to see me. We were just getting ready for dinner after the program, when Troy walked in. He looked like hell. He was shaky and very pale. He came over our table and sat next to me.

"I thought you were in West Virginia, when did you get back?" I asked him.

"About a week after you guys left. I really couldn't take it anymore."

"How are you?"

"Anna, I need you to do me a favor," he whispered, "I need to talk to you, alone."

"Let's go for a walk." We went out into the yard. "You don't look so good, what's the matter?"

"Anna, I am sick. I have aids. I came back to get some medication, but things are not too good. I think Radakund Swami is angry with me for leaving."

"I am so sorry, Troy," I hugged him and he started to cry like a child. "I don't think Radakund Swami is angry. I just think he cares about you."

"Anna, please call Radakund Swami and ask him to give me specific instructions about what to do? I am scared. Please, do this for me."

"I'll call him tomorrow. Will you be here tomorrow evening?"

"Yes," he said, "Definitely, please don't forget."

"Of course, I won't forget. Let's go inside and eat something. Come, you must eat. We went back inside but Troy did not touch his food.

That night arriving home I found a message from Maharaj on my machine. He was coming to New York that weekend, to take a whole bunch of devotees with him back to West Virginia on Monday, and asked me to come along. At the sound of his voice all anxiety disappeared. I was so happy to hear from him. I played the tape over and over.

The following morning I called Radakund Swami in West Virginia. One of the devotees answered the phone. I told him to relate to him that Troy needed to get specific instructions about what to do with his life because he was in a bad shape. The boy put me on hold and went to look for Radakund Swami. I was anxious. He finally came back to the phone.

"Tell Troy to chant Hare Krishna!"

"That's it?" I said, "Troy asked for specific instructions, he's in a bad shape."

"Mother, chanting Hare Krishna is the highest form of worship. Troy was lucky he met the devotees. Chanting is all he needs. It's all anyone needs."

"Thank you," I said, "I'll tell him."

"Oh . . . Mother, Radakund Swami also said that Troy should've stayed in West Virginia."

"We're all coming to West Virginia on Monday, with Maharaj. We'll see you soon. Thank you," I said with a heavy heart. It was a nagging emotion. I was afraid that Troy went back to his heroin habit. That night I went by the Interfaith Center. Nothing was going on and Troy didn't show up. I went home early, called Brian and left the message from Radakund Swami on his answering machine.

Saturday morning I woke up thinking about Troy. I attempted to visualize him but couldn't get a clear image of his face no matter how hard I tried. I was startled when the phone rang. It was Brian.

"Hi Brian," I said "how is Troy, did you give him the message?" There was a silence on the other end. "Brian, what's going on?"

"It's no easy way to say this," Brian's voice was shaky "Troy died last night of an overdose."

"What? No, you're joking, it cannot be!"

"It's true. After he came to New York he was right back to his heroin habit and was selling it as well, you know . . . he had access to a lot of heroin. I didn't want to tell you because he kept on saying he was okay. But, oh God, part of me knew something was wrong. He didn't look good. Remember how well he looked when we met him? He kept on bragging about how well his business was doing. God, how come I didn't see it coming?" I was speechless. "Come to the Interfaith Center tonight, I need to see you." He started to cry. "I couldn't give him the message, his last message. It was too late!" He was crying uncontrollably. "Maybe he would've survived!"

"It's nobody's fault," I said, "it's the drugs, it was an accident. He wanted to live, was asking for help. He wanted to go back to West Virginia with us on Monday. Please don't put this on yourself. You were his friend."

"No," Brian said, "I convinced him to come back to New York. I'll never forgive myself for this!"

"Brian, please! We don't know when our time comes, can be anytime, anywhere under any circumstances. When it's time to go, you're gone, no matter what. It was his time."

"Yes," Brian said, "but he was so young, it's not fair."

"Life is not fair. Not the way it appears to be anyway. Innocent children die every day needlessly. They are hungry. Some die of malnutrition, some of diseases that could be prevented. Look; all the food we throw in the garbage every night, all the restaurants, salad bars, etc. in the city alone, could feed so many hungry people, could save so many children from dying. Can you say it's your fault? What can you do?"

"I don't know," Brian said, "there must be something I can do to put a stop to this massacre of innocent people. I must do something! Otherwise what's the point of living?"

"I don't know, Brian, maybe we can do something. Let's do a ceremony tonight for Troy at the Interfaith Centre. I'll bring some candles and incense. I have a Buddhist prayer they say could point the soul into the right direction. I also have some very powerful Hindu mantras. I'll meet you an hour before the program."

"All right," Brian said, "I'll bring my drums. Troy liked them a lot. I'll see you there, thank you Anna for listening . . . thank you."

He hanged up the phone and I remained motionless holding the receiver in one hand, disbelieving the reality of what just happened.

CHAPTER 17

TRIP TO WEST VIRGINIA WITH BROTHER RAM

On Monday morning Sunrise and Brian left with Cougar and Maharaj in another van. Christina and I took Brother Ram's old van. We were still shaken by Troy's death. It was so unfair that he overdosed just two days before he was planning to come to West Virginia with us.

"It's so weird," Christina said, "something about the timing of his death, only two days before he wanted to give up drugs again."

"People die all the time," Brother Ram said. "It's good for him he'll have a better karma next life."

"What are you talking about?" Christina said angrily, "he was only twenty two years old."

"I don't want you girls talking about Troy anymore. He was a drug dealer. Who knows how many people died because of him? Just worry about your own souls."

"You are so callous, so hardened, you have no compassion," Christina said.

"Christina," Brother Ram said, "we have a long journey. If you don't want to drive with us, there is still time to get off and ride with Cougar."

"I am sorry," Christina said, "I didn't mean to blame you. I am just hurting. He was a friend, and died and nobody cares!" She started to sob and I gave her a hug.

"I care," I said, "but we have to go on. Life is never fair. That's why we're here, to get out of this mess." Christina stopped crying and fell asleep on my shoulder.

We drove in silence for a while, and the van kept on breaking down. Something was definitely wrong with 'Thunder', Brother Ram's favorite van. He just kept on insisting that the van was okay and just needed a little fixing. When we tried to mention something about it, he would categorically refuse to take it to the shop saying that he can fix it himself. In the meantime the van would stop dead in its tracks every twenty minutes. Every time it stopped, we had to wait for the motor to cool off before we could start it again. We were in for a very long ride.

After driving like this for a good fifteen hours we were still in Pennsylvania and exhausted. The back of the van was full of things that Brother Ram was bringing from New York. He removed the back seat to make more room and replaced it with a small make shift seat that he took from an old car. At each turn, the seat would swing from side to side and Christina and I had to change places every so often, while Brother Ram was driving. It was already dark. Christina was losing her patience.

"I am hungry and tired," she said, "You should've fixed the van before we left. What were you thinking?"

"All right," Brother Ram mumbled, "I know a camping ground somewhere around here. Let's camp out tonight."

"Good," Christina said, "we can grab something to eat first."

"There is some bread from this morning you can have," he said.

"Oh no, I am really hungry."

"Me too," I said.

"What would you girls want to eat French or Italian?"

"I wouldn't mind having a Pizza," Christina said.

"It's almost ten o'clock. Nothing is open around here except the truck stop we just passed."

"Let's go back," Christina said.

"I am not going back! If you want to go back, you drive!"

"I'll drive," she said. The van stopped again and we had to wait for it to cool off. Christina moved into the driver's seat. "I never drove a van."

"There is always a first time for everything. Piece of cake, just make sure nobody is behind you when you stop short."

Christina started the motor and she became all excited. "I can't believe I am driving this van," she said and made a U-turn.

"Are you crazy?" Brother Ram said, "We can get a ticket!"

"There is no one in site, what are you talking about?"

"You never know, they can hide at the intersection."

"Do you think they came here on purpose to wait for us?"

"You always must have the last word. Learn some humility," he said.

"Oh, please, it's not my fault that I have to drive this piece of junk."

Annoyed he said: "If you don't like it you can walk!"

"You holly people, it's not becoming to get angry," I said, "life is too short."

"There is the Truck Stop," Christina said all excited and pulled into the parking lot.

Brother Ram handed me a twenty dollar bill.

"Get whatever you want," he said.

I went inside and except from junk food there wasn't much to choose from. I ended up with rolls, potatoes chips, cottage cheese, and some juice. Back to the van, they were still arguing. He didn't want to drive anymore, neither did Christina.

"Brother Ram," I said, "since you know where the camping ground is, you can drive tonight. Tomorrow, we'll see."

"How come you don't drive?" He asked me.

"I never had to drive. I can't have a car in the city. Where am I going to put it, in my living room?"

"Okay, I'll drive but I don't want to hear you girls complaining about Thunder anymore."

"No more complaining," Christina said.

We drove around for about an hour before we found the camping ground. It was in some national park in Pennsylvania. Except from couple of picnic tables and a garbage can, the place was all wild. Christina and Brother Ram laid their sleeping bags under the picnic tables. I put mine out in the open so I could look at the sky. In New York one could never see more than one or two stars. It was a bright night and thin clouds were moving fast across the sky creating endless patterns in the moonlight.

Brother Ram started a campfire and finally we sat around it and ate ravenously. Christina played some songs that she learned from some hippies at the Rainbow, on her old beat-up guitar. Later, he played Hare Krishna chants and we sang along and played the cymbals. The fire was painting orange and red designs on their faces in contrast to the dark blue sky illuminated by the cool moon rays.

"It's time to go to sleep," Brother Ram said, ending my contemplation. "We'll get started real early, tomorrow."

I crawled into my sleeping bag and watched the clouds parading in front of the moon. I tried to see all sorts of figures in the ever-changing shapes of the clouds. Unusual sounds were coming from the woods. I kept hearing footsteps, but in spite of it, I fell into a deep sleep. Suddenly, a light rain woke me up. Now it made sense why they slept under the picnic tables. I had to take all my stuff inside the van. The back of it being full, I could only sit in the front chair and stretch my legs, but it was impossible to lie down. It was difficult to sleep in the van. In a while I decided to go back outside so I could stretch my legs. The rain stopped but the grounds were still wet. I took two garbage bags and laid them under a tree. The ground was not so wet because it only rained for a short time. I put the sleeping bag over, and finally was able to stretch my tired body, falling into a deep sleep.

Christina woke me up, hysterical.

"Brother Ram left! He took the van and left," she said . . . For a moment, I did not know where I was, but soon everything came into focus.

"Are you sure?"

"Of course I am! I've been up for about an hour. There is no trace of him or the van."

"Maybe he went to get some food or something. He'll be back soon, I wouldn't worry."

"I'm worried," Christina said.

"I think I'll sleep some more, I was up most of the night. It rained, you know?"

"It did? Oh look, the ground is still wet. I'll wake you up when he comes back, if he does."

"He better be!" I said.

The sun was out and it started to warm up. I fell asleep. When I woke up again the sun was at the zenith. Christina was sunbathing and Brother Ram still gone.

"Hi Christina, what time is it?"

"About twelve thirty," she said, "I don't know what to do? What if he doesn't come back?"

"Do you have any money?"

"About forty box. How about you?

"I have twenty dollars. I don't think is enough to get us to West Virginia."

"It would be if we hitch a ride," she said.

"I don't want to hitchhike around here, it's too dangerous."

"I hope we don't have to," she said, "let's give it till three o'clock. If he doesn't show up we'll have to do something."

"I hope he shows up soon," I said, "if it comes to worst we have enough money to get to Philadelphia. The Krishna Temple is very nice. We'll be able to figure a way to get back to New York."

"You're a genius! The devotees from Philadelphia go to New York all the time. We can always get a ride with somebody."

"Let's wait till three o'clock."

"I'm going to get some sun," Christina said, and taking off her blouse lied on the grass. I felt calmer and started to read from one of Christina's books when we heard a motor approaching.

"There he is," I said

"Not so fast, it doesn't sound like Thunder."

"What?" I was a little apprehensive. A police car just turned around the corner. They came closer and got out of the car walking toward us.

"Good afternoon officer," Christina said

"Good day girls. What are you doing here?"

"We camped out with our friend but he left early in the morning and didn't come back yet. We're waiting for him," she said in a sweet voice.

"What kind of car was he driving?" The officer asked.

"It was a blue van, kind of old looking," Christina said.

"We saw a van that looked like your description by the garage. I think he might be doing some repairs. Was anything wrong with the van?"

"As a matter of fact, yes," Christina said. "That van is a piece of junk. Would you be so kind to take us to the garage?"

"No problem," the officer said. "Gather your things and get in the back of the car."

I packed my sleeping bag, put on my shoes and we sat in the back of the police car. She looked at me with a mischievous smile. I had to control myself not to burst into laughter.

"He should've told us where he went," I said to Christina.

"Where are you girls from?" The officer asked.

"We're coming from New York, trying to make it to West Virginia. We're not having much luck." The officers looked at each other and smiled. We drove for not more than five minutes.

"Here we are," the officer said. "There . . . Is that the van you're looking for?"

241

"Yes," Christina said, "it's Thunder all right. I told him to fix it before we left."

"Thank you for the ride," I said.

"You're welcome," one of them said. "If you girls need any help, call the police station. Here is the number," he handed me a card with the phone number.

"Thank you. I hope everything will be okay."

"We hope so too," they said and drove away.

We walked to the van and saw Brother Ram inside the gas station. He was eating from a large container of ice cream and waved to us with a big smile.

"Shame on you," Christina said. "We thought you abandoned us. We were trying to figure how to get back to New York. Luckily the cops came by and gave us a ride. They saw your van and brought us here. What's wrong with you? Why didn't you say anything?" She was angry but he didn't care.

"Here," he said, "have some ice cream."

"I am hungry," Christina said.

"Here we are again," Brother Ram said disappointed.

"I am hungry too," I said

"All you girls think about is food."

"Look who's talking," Christina said, "you probably stuffed your face the whole day."

"That's not so," he said, "I wanted to get the van fixed. Who knew how long was going to take? Lucky if they'll finish it by tonight. Let's have something to eat. Everything closes early around here. There is a diner a few miles down the road. Dinner is on me, if you forgive me."

"You're forgiven," I said, "let's go!"

"I've got to talk to the mechanic. Why don't you girls go first, I'll meet you at the diner?"

"No," Christina said, "we'll wait for you here!"

"Don't be silly, girls. Go and order me some pizza."

We walked by the side of the road mindful of the incoming traffic. Occasionally a car would pass by but the road was quiet empty.

"Wait a minute," Christina said, "I want to get some money from him."

"Good thinking."

She ran back to the gas station and I sat on the side of the road. I was tired and famished but happy that we found Brother Ram. In a short while, Christina came back.

"He only gave us twenty dollars," she said disappointed.

"That should be enough, how much do you think you can eat?"

"A lot, I am so hungry, you have no idea."

We walked about half mile to the small diner where among other things they served pizza and a good assortment of deserts. We ordered a whole pie and had couple of slices left over, which we carefully wrapped in paper and put in Christina's bag for later.

"Maybe we should give the slices to Brother Ram," I said.

"He doesn't deserve it."

"You're right, how about some dessert?" I asked Christina and her eyes lit up.

The desserts looked scrumptious. They were displayed in an old glass case that turned around. It was hard to decide. Cristina ordered chocolate cake and I ordered a slice of cheesecake with strawberry topping. As we were waiting for the desserts, he walked in and joined us at the table.

"We already ate," Christina said.

"How could you, why didn't you wait for me?" He was a little annoyed. Then calmed down and smiled, "I don't care now you have to wait for me. What did you girls eat?"

"Pizza," Christina said.

"Was it good?"

"You bet," I said.

The waitress came with the desserts and when he saw the chocolate cake, had a fit.

"You know you're not supposed to eat chocolate. It's bad for you, in the mode of ignorance. It's poison for your mind and soul."

"It's fine with me," Christina said, "this is not going to make me more ignorant than I already am."

"Maybe it will, and will ignite your passions."

"I hope so, I'm going to eat it and you just make believe you didn't notice."

"You're impossible. I pity the man will marry you."

"Never mind, I can be very charming if I want to."

"Unfortunately that doesn't happen too often."

"Don't you want to look at the menu?" I asked and handed him the oversized menu.

"Thanks," He said, "I get a little grouchy when I am hungry. Sorry!"

"Apology accepted," Christina said and dipped her fork into the huge slice of chocolate cake. Brother Ram was watching her fascinated. She took a piece of creamy chocolate and pointed the fork to his lips.

"Here, try a bit. At least you must know what you're missing."

"Get out of here!" He said grabbing her arm, "that's why Pandava Swami tells us to stay away from women. They try to make you fall into temptation."

"A little chocolate . . . What about all the crimes committed by men? The murders and rapes committed in the name of religion and justice! Who are committing those crimes men or women?"

"The women are the instigators. They are always behind the men that are committing those crimes."

"Nonsense, that's such a cope out!"

"What's happening with Thunder?" I asked.

"It'll be ready tomorrow morning." Brother Ram said relieved.

"Tomorrow morning? Where are we sleeping tonight?"

"Good question," he said, "maybe we should go back to the camping ground, since I don't think there are any motels around here."

"That's about two miles from here," I said.

"Do you have another suggestion?" he asked a little annoyed.

"I don't know, I'll think about it."

Brother Ram ordered four slices of pizza; two plain and the other two with vegetables topping. My cheesecake was delicious, very soft and creamy.

"Is that good?" He asked.

"Excellent," I said, "Would you like a bite?"

"Just a little bit."

I gave him a big piece. He rolled it on his tong, savoring it.

"Oh, this is good cheesecake. Did you offer it to Krishna?"

"Sorry, I forgot."

"It figures, I should've known better. Now I have to take on all the karma from the cheesecake."

"You can handle it."

"Anna, nobody can handle karma but Krishna. We must chant double rounds tonight before we go to sleep."

"Not me, "Christina said, "I offered my food."

"That doesn't count," he said, "Krishna doesn't accept chocolate cake."

"How do you know, did you ask Him?"

"Don't be ignorant, it's written in the scriptures."

"I want to see where it says that Krishna doesn't eat chocolate cake."

"It's not so simple, we are suppose to offer to Krishna only food in the mode of goodness."

"You're right, but is not much of a sin, is it?"

"Is not up to us to judge, karma is too complicated for our little brains to comprehend."

Brother Ram's order came, and in a minute it was all gone.

"I am still hungry," he said

"Have some cheese cake," I suggested.

"No. It might have eggs in it."

"Let's ask the waitress."

There were eggs in the cheesecake and we all had herbal tea with plenty of honey. Brother Ram slipped a few packages of honey in his pocket, stood up and stretched his arms behind his back.

"It's unusual to find honey in those diners," he said. "Let's go now. I need a good night sleep. We've got a long drive tomorrow."

We left and walked back to the garage, arriving just in time before closing. We took the sleeping bags from the van and began our way back to the camping ground.

"Did you get the flashlight?" I asked Brother Ram.

"Yep, and my knife, just in case."

We were walking by the side of the road when we heard the siren of a police car. The officer rolled down the window.

"It's everything okay? You didn't get your van fixed?" he asked.

"The van will be ready tomorrow," I said, "we're going back to the camping ground."

"Why don't you guys stay at the motel?"

"We didn't know there was a motel around here. Where is it?"

"Only a mile from here, just go north and pass the gas station."

"Thank you officer, we need a good night sleep. We're going to the motel," Christina said, turning toward Brother Ram.

The police car took off and we turned around and started walking the other way.

"You sleep on the floor." Christina said to him.

"It's okay with me, I don't like beds anyway."

"What's wrong with sleeping in a bed?" I asked Brother Ram.

"That's where people die, they procreate and they spend time when they're sic. No thanks."

"You're sick," Christina said.

"Watch your thong, Lady!"

"We'll sleep in the bed. We're not as pure as you," Christina said and we kept on walking. It was getting dark.

"You guys have any money?" Brother Ram asked. We both answered at the same time.

"Forty dollars," I said.

"Twenty dollars," Christina said.

"Well, it's twenty or forty?"

"Twenty," we both said.

"Give me twenty dollars for the hotel." Christina gave him a twenty-dollar bill. Brother Ram stuffed the money into his pocket and we continued walking by the side of the road. I was tired and the walk seemed too long. We passed the gas station and kept on walking until finally arrived at the motel.

The façade covered with imitation wood paneling was dark and depressing looking. All rooms were lined up at the edge of a parking lot. One could park right in front of the door. Brother Ram went to the lobby to rent a room for the three of us. We waited in the car. He came back dangling the key to the room. Christina and I dived on the double bed that occupied most of the room. He slept on the floor. By the side of the bed, I noticed a small metal box. For a quarter the bed would shake for five minutes. It reminded me of the seventies. Christina had a mischievous grin.

"Anna, do you have a quarter?"

"You don't want to . . . okay," I said, "here is a quarter, I hope it works."

We waited until Brother Ram fell asleep, than she put a quarter in the slot. The bed started to shake, making the most unbearable screeching noises. He was startled, not knowing what was going on and grabbed his flashlight looking around the room. When he saw the bed shaking, he thought it was an earthquake. When he finally realized what was going on he become furious. We were laughing under the blankets.

"That's enough," he said, "off the bed, both of you! On the floor! You had your chance, now it's over!"

We did not budge. He threw the blanket on the floor and grabbed Christina's feet pulling her off the bed. She was laughing hysterically. I rolled on the floor hugging both pillows. Brother Ram jumped on the bed and stretched diagonally taking over the whole bed. By now, the bed stopped shaking. We slept on the floor and Brother Ram had the whole bed for himself. In the morning, he stepped over us to get to the bathroom. He was in a good mood chanting while taking his usual cold shower.

"Get up girls, the van should be ready. Hurry up, we wasted too much time."

"Whose fault is it?" Christina said.

"Christina, don't start again, my patience is wearing thin."

"Okay," Christina said, "let's go."

We walked to the garage and the van was ready. I have never seen Brother Ram so happy. Thunder—his baby—was running better than ever.

CHAPTER 18

BACK IN WEST VIRGINIA

Christina and I slept most of the way. It was already dark when we arrived at the ashram in West Virginia. Many vans and cars were parked by the Golden Temple.

"Something is happening at the temple," Brother Ram said.

"Let's go and see," I said.

"I am too tired, you girls go."

"Let's go," Christina was all excited. "Brother Ram, would you please leave our bags in the office?"

"Yes your Majesty," he said "don't dance too much."

"It's never too much," she smiled.

We walked to the temple in the dark. Entering the hallway, we heard the magnificent voice of Radakund Swami in a fast tempo. We left our shoes in the antechamber. My heart started beating fast at the thought of seeing Maharaj again. Christina was nervous as well. We both looked at each other and burst into laughter.

"Cover your head," she said.

"No way, live me alone," I said, straightening up my clothes.

We walked in the beautiful temple, with floors covered in colorful marble tiles, skillfully cut and arranged in amazing patterns. Walls and columns had marble panels bordered with gilded bas-reliefs, and the ceiling was painted to look like the sky, with elaborate floral bas-reliefs in bright colors and gilded in gold. The whole temple was like a jewel. The most attractive Radha and Krishna Deities stood on the imposing altar. Radha was wearing a dress made from silk flowers stitched together in different shades of purple. Everybody was dancing and jumping around with Radakund Swami singing and playing the harmonium. When he looked at me and smiled, his little eyes became even smaller almost appearing to be closed. People dance was frenzied. It was one of those inspired moments when Radakund Swami wouldn't stop, speeding up the tempo. The room was full of people I have never seen before.

"They are devotees from Washington," Christina said.

Her eyes lit up with excitement. With her nostrils dilated, she looked like a young deer, ready to take off. We danced for a while. Rejuvenated, I become aware that I was experiencing a magical moment, dancing barefoot in a marble temple after the sunset, on a hilltop in West Virginia with my heart full of love.

The music stopped unexpectedly and everybody kneeled on the floor and bowed to the altar while the curtains were closing, allowing the Deities to enjoy their own pastimes in privacy.

Maharaj took the mike to make some announcements. Between other things, he mentioned that the cook left the community that morning and they were searching for a new cook. I wished from the bottom of my heart to get that job, knowing that I wasn't qualified and my chance to get it was slim, when Christina grabbed my arm with a spark in her eyes.

"Anna, do you want the job?" she whispered in my ear.

"You mean the cook job?"

"Yes. Maharaj just told me to ask you."

"I was just thinking about it . . . Of course I do!"

"You got it, let me tell him."

That night I cleaned the floors in my room and burned some incense. After turning the lights off, I went up on the roof. The moon was almost as bright as the sun; a night sun. I sat for a long time bathing in the moonlight, soaking in the magic of that night.

My morning routine was simple. Right after meditation, I skipped the program in the temple and went to my room to sleep an extra couple of hours. By ten o'clock, I was in the kitchen getting ready to cook lunch. After burning some incense and chanting some mantras, I would take a basket to the vegetable garden, and filled it with ripe tomatoes, basil, sometimes zucchinis, cucumbers and pumpkins.

The sun was already hot with a cooling breeze coming from the valley. The fragrance of fresh grass was permeating the crystalline air. From the garden I could see down in the valley and over distant hills. A small barn was inhabited by Devendra, the gardener. He knew everything about plants. He was not just the gardener but also the community doctor. Devotees came to him for herbs to cure all kinds of ailments. There was a special area in the garden just for medicinal plants. He used to teach me about the healing properties of herbs. Sometimes he had a bag of greens, he collected earlier for me. We sat in front of the barn and talked for a while before I went back to the kitchen. He was one of the few devotees I could honestly talk to. That morning the garden looked different with several tables in front of the barn, and chairs cut from tree trunks. Devendra was all excited.

"Anna, I am opening the 'Sunset Café'. I need some help, would you be interested in waiting at tables? I'll pay you. I cannot pay more than $ 2.50 per hour plus food and fresh tomatoes anytime."

"I'll do it. Evenings are boring anyway, when do we start?"

"Tonight . . . I am going to serve fresh mint and chamomile tea, a sandwich with tomatoes and basil picked from the garden and fresh French fries. I'll charge one dollar for the fries, one dollar for the sandwich and fifty cents for the tea."

"What a great idea, I'll be back tonight, you can count on me."

"Come right after the evening program."

I couldn't wait to go to the garden that evening. Word spread quickly in the community and people came. The café was full. We had to sit some people inside the barn. The whole thing started when Devendra found in a discount store nearby, a machine to cut potatoes in curly spirals. The machine was very inexpensive and Devendra bought it. Now his curly French fries were a total success. The bread was freshly baked by a devotee in the kitchen's stove during the afternoon. Sometimes it was still warm. After the first night's success, he raised my pay to $3.50 per hour. I was working two hours every night. We added a few more tables. A family of devotees began baking cookies, and we started to sell cookies as well. From the café one could see the breathtaking sunsets every night. One morning when I went to the garden to fetch vegetables, Devendra looked pale.

"Anna, I am thinking about leaving the community," he said.

"Why? Everything is going so well, the café is booming."

"I know," he said, "but I am depressed. I've been depressed for a long time, I miss something. I don't know what. I need to try something else."

"I had no idea you were so unhappy."

"I didn't want to bother you with my problems. I've been drinking beer. It's against the regulations, you know."

"Beer it's the worst thing you can do for depression," I said.

"Anna, please don't tell anybody!"

"I won't! You're my friend, the only person that I can honestly talk to. I'll miss you a whole lot."

"I can't stay here anymore, I have to hide my drinking and lie about it. That makes me more depressed."

"I understand. Many times I want to leave and go back to New York. When are you leaving?"

"Soon," he said, "for now I'll move into the nearby town. I found a job baking for the health food store, and we'll see . . . Tonight is our last night at the café."

I was sad to see Devendra go. That evening the café was full. He didn't tell anybody. Maharaj and a few devotees came to the café for dinner. I was very nervous and knocked a cup of tea on the table. The tea spilled all over Maharaj. I thanked God that it didn't burn him, but he laughed.

"Anna, where did you learn how to be a waitress?"

"I am sorry Maharaj," I said.

"Don't worry. Just bring me another cup please."

"Yes Maharaj, right away."

I cleaned the table and brought him a fresh cup of tea together with the tomato sandwich and curly fries. They all enjoyed the food. The night was perfect. Not too hot, with a faint breeze bringing a subtle fragrance from the rose garden. It was the last night at the café, and that made me sad. After everybody left I helped Devendra clean up, said good bye and gave him my phone number in New York, where he could leave a message on my machine and let me know where he was.

Before returning to the temple I went for a walk in the woods, on the path going down to the river. When I came back everybody was asleep. It must have been around nine o'clock. My evening ritual was a long walk followed by some quiet moments in the temple. The doors to the temple were open. The lights were off in the entire building, except for the hallways. I walked into the temple being careful not to make any noise and sat on the floor in front of the altar. I took my beads from under the shirt and chanted quietly for a while. My eyelids grew heavy and I was falling into a peaceful state of rest half-asleep and half-awake. Every night I had a special visitor that sneaked into the temple through the back door. A stream of light from the hallway would project his elongated shadow on the floor and the little head with big eyes would pop up through the door. It was a little raccoon that, just like me, enjoyed the peace and quiet of the temple late at night. He would look at me from the doorway with distrust, then, carefully walk across the floor, and sit still like a statue watching me. When he got tired looking at me he would inspect the whole temple, making sure everything was in order, and he would leave the same way he came in. After the raccoon left, I knew it was time for me to get back to my room.

Close to the entrance, outside the temple, a large open area was consecrated to fire ceremonies. Four columns supported a roof covered in wood shingles. On the ground, a square pit lined with bricks for the ceremonial fire was surrounded by wooden benches. During the day devotees gathered in that area. On Sundays, tables were set to sale all kinds of things to the visitors; from tee shirts to candles, books and incense, etc. Maharaj and a small group of new devotees met there every morning to chant and meditate. From that place one could see the valley opening wide with little hills disappearing at the horizon. White mist was enveloping everything. At sunrise the mist would retreat into the valley and dissipate slowly. Emerald drops of dew remained on the grass for a while longer.

I woke up at 3:30 every morning. The temple was steeped in darkness, and an unearthly silence was pervading the surroundings. Even the birds were still sleeping. In my room, a cool breeze was coming through the window and a feeling of peace pervaded my inner being. I would light up a candle and contemplate the shimmering flame flicker in the dark.

It took an act of faith every morning, to descend the stairway to the temple. I still can hear the wood under my feet making a deep cracking sound amplified by the morning silence. I tried to make my steps lighter by balancing my weight on the entire surface of the foot and holding my breath.

In the temple, devotees were sitting and chanting on their beads, whispering the mantra. Some very soft and others loudly, each keeping a different rhythm. The whole temple was vibrating like a beehive. I walked across the temple room to the front door, being careful not to disturb anybody, and stepped outside with a sigh of relief. Black silhouettes of devotees were sliding like shadows across the walkways surrounding the temple. The air was imbibed with a fresh mountain fragrance that could be sensed only in the early morning hours. With each deep breath a rush of energy traveled through my whole body. I was eager to arrive to the meditation place. Some devotes were already there. Maharaj was sitting motionless at his usual spot. I sat on a bench in front of him. The air was neither too cool nor too hot, and I was gradually sinking into a state of stillness where all self-awareness was absorbed by a never-ending abyss.

Emerging from the deep, I become aware of his presence near me. When I opened my eyes, he was covered in an orange shawl, his body gently swaying from side to side. I focused my attention on his forehead, trying to penetrate into his being and see the enchanting worlds of Krishna where he roamed freely in his meditation.

A soft vibration started to pulsate gently, overcoming the big void inside my chest and loosening the tight grip I had on the World. It seemed that at the root of my existence was an immeasurable desire to be me, to be able to see and touch the World. This desire was so powerful that left at its own accord would consume everything. Nature was weak by comparison. My soul was attracting the World into being and kept it in perfect balance. The Earth and all its objects suddenly became immaterial like the projection of a movie on a screen. This worldly desire was life itself. It was expanding throughout my whole being beyond the limitations of this existence. It was there when I was born and it will be there when I will depart. The World was materializing like a dream for me to experience its beauty. There was deep intimacy between my soul and everything around me. The beauty that I perceived was not of the senses. It was a beauty felt directly into the heart. Each object had its own vibration in the centre of my being.

The morning silence was broken by a few birds at first, and soon by a whole symphony. Each, singing in their unknown language and together creating a perfect harmony. The sunlight slowly began to penetrate in every dark corner still sleeping. The whole nature was coming back to life, the beginning of a beautiful day in West Virginia. The sky was without a cloud. A light breeze was bringing the sweet fragrance of freshly cut grass and wild flowers from the valley. The meditation was over.

After meditation I rushed to the kitchen to get an early start. Only about twenty devotees were having lunch that day. Most of them had to go and raise money for the community. I cooked the usual cracked wheat with ghee, soup and salad with fresh tomatoes and basil from the garden.

My plan for the day was to explore the surroundings and find a quiet place for meditation away from the ashram. After I finished cooking, I put a shawl into the backpack and a book with chants dedicated to Lord Shiva, my secret Deity.

I walked uphill on a narrow road, curious where it took me. On the side of the road, large areas were fenced in, and most of the houses looked uninhabited. Suddenly a dog appeared from behind a fence. It was a young German Sheppard. He came running toward me waging his tail and started to lick my hands and roll on the ground full of joy. He wouldn't let me go, leaning against my legs and watching me intensely with his beautiful brown eyes. For a while I sat on the ground next to him, to catch my breath. It was like meeting an old friend. I wondered if he remembered me from some past life. When I left he followed me for a long time. Finally I had to tell him to go back home. He stopped and sat on the ground watching me go away, with his ears erect as if he was trying to hear the sound of my steps.

"Good Bye, my friend," I said not knowing that it was the last day of his life. The following morning he was shot to death for attacking a neighbor's chickens. As he disappeared from view, the path I took led me to the main road. Few cars and some bikes were passing by. I was walking against the traffic.

"Mother Anna," somebody called. Gauranga on a bike stopped on the side of the road. "Where are you going, Mother?"

"Just for a walk, I am looking for a place to meditate."

"Mother, if you walk about a hundred yards to the right, you'll find a small lake. We call it Brindavan Lake. It's a nice quiet place."

"What are you doing now . . . would you like to come with me?"

"I have to work on the new temple down the road. I promised I'll sand the floors this afternoon otherwise I'd love to show you around."

"It's all right," I said, "I'll be okay by myself. See you tonight at the temple."

"Hari Boll," he said and went on his way.

After I crossed the road, hidden under a canopy of trees the lake appeared covered in lush vegetation. Many small yellow and purple flowers were growing from the shallow waters. In the center, between high marsh grass and the round leaves of water lilies, patches of water were reflecting the brilliant blue sky. I sat by the side of the lake to meditate. The tall grass was reaching up to my shoulders. I closed my eyes, but my mind was restless. After a short while, I got up and cut my way through the tall grass uphill. When almost on top, I encountered a barbed wire fence and crawled under it.

A wide meadow spotted with granite boulders opened in front of me. Some were quiet tall, like sentinels watching over the kingdom. In the middle of it, the burned trunk of an old tree was standing alone, witness of a violent thunder that descended without warning splitting it in half. As I approached that spot, I became aware of another presence. I sat next to the tree facing the valley. Many layers of wooded hills were melting into the horizon, ranging from the brightest color to a faint, almost transparent bluish green that looked more like clouds. I was in a kind of reverie and suddenly I sensed this enticing fragrance and a tall person walking towards me barely touching the ground.

Unusually dressed, he was wearing a garb of loosely woven grass fibers in earthly colors and rows of beads made from all kinds of grains and seeds as colorful as the rainbow. His golden hair had small crystals braded into it that shined in the sunlight. There was a white light coming from his forehead that made everything look pale by comparison. His eyes were changing colors. Sometimes they were brilliant blue, other times they will turn green, from the lightest green like the color of new leaves in springtime to the dark green of mountain forests in midsummer, or a deep brown like the earth.

As he sat by me, my self-awareness disappeared and a sense of complete freedom filled my whole being. We talked for a long time but I cannot recall much of the conversation. I think he asked me about my life. All I remember is that I asked him what "pure love" was. He said that pure love sprang directly from the heart and had no reason or object. He also said that a healthy ego was naturally even and smooth like the still waters of a lake. It did not occur to me to ask who he was. It seemed that I already knew him. At a certain point, I heard a loud cracking noise coming from the burned tree. It startled me and I looked to see what happened. Half of the trunk had fallen to the ground. When I turned around, my handsome friend was gone. All that remained was the flattened grass, a reassuring sign that the whole thing was not just a product of my imagination. The apparition seemed so normal at the time that only couple of days later I realized that I witnessed something unusual.

Later that evening I walked to a lake that was stretching in front of the ashram. It was getting dark. In the gentle breeze, small ripples were waving intricate embroidery on the water. Three deer were grazing leaves from the young trees across the lake. They would adventure in the shallow waters from time to time to drink. I kept very still, listening to the evening symphony of sounds. The night was clear. A blanket of stars covered the sky. Millions of them, some very bright and some so faint that at times they would disappear for a while and then flicker again. Everybody retired to their rooms. The whole nature was slowly falling asleep. I sat in a gazebo watching the sky and the lake, delighting in the soothing embrace of the moonlight. Two swans were floating like phantoms in perfect silence. I wondered what were they doing up so late.

On my way back, I stopped to see a young cow by a little shed built especially for her close to the temple. She was a beautiful healthy cow and everybody spoiled her. I used to see her every night before sleep. She was waiting for me close to the fence leaning her head on a cardboard box. I went closer and she started nudging me with her big nose. Then she rested her head on my arm, happy like a child held by its mother.

CHAPTER 19

RAINBOW GATHERING

Back to the temple, the lights were on. A few vans were parked in the front, and a whole bunch of devotees just arrived from Columbus. Christina was talking to them.

"Hari boll, what's going on?" I asked.

"We're on the way to the Rainbow". A young girl said. Her hair was braded and she was wearing an Indian vest over an old pair of jeans.

"Hi, I am Anna, what's your name?"

"Sabrina," she said, "we're leaving tomorrow morning."

"How come I didn't know anything about this?" I asked surprised. "Can I come with you?"

"Yes, there is plenty of room," Sabrina said.

"Where is the gathering?"

"What planet are you on?" Sabrina said.

"I must be from another galaxy. Nobody tells me anything around here."

"In Colorado, up in the mountains, the most spiritual place on Earth," she said all excited. Christina pulled me to the side.

"Anna, you can't go with them, you must get permission from Maharaj!"

"Where is he?"

"I don't know!"

"Maharaj is coming with us, isn't he?" Sabrina asked.

Christina was a little hesitant.

"Yes . . ." she said, "he's coming, we're all going. Who's going to cook if you leave?" She asked me.

"I don't know, I am not the only cook around here. Let them find somebody else."

"Just come with us," Sabrina said.

"I don't have much money."

"Don't worry, if you stay in Krishna's camp, you don't need any money, especially if you help in the kitchen."

"What do I need to bring?"

"Well, I don't know, it gets cold at night. It's about ten or eleven thousand feet up in the clouds. Someone just called me and mentioned something about a snow storm the other day."

"Wow, it's almost July!"

"Well, I think over there snows all year around."

"You know," I said, "I made up my mind. I am going with you guys."

"Yes!" Sabrina said all excited. "Brother Ram is taking the school bus, we'll ride with him."

"It's perfect," I said, "he's my friend."

"We'll see you early in the morning."

"Thank you, Sabrina."

"Hey, you're always welcome to the Rainbow."

I went to my room disappointed for being kept in the dark about the trip. They didn't want me to go. For some reason I didn't belong, it was hard to know. I began to doubt Christina's friendship and felt betrayed. After spending a long time figuring out what to take I packed all my stuff, and felt too excited to sleep.

In the morning, I went outside to chant. Brother Ram was getting the bus ready, in the back of the ashram, behind the kitchen. It was an old school bus painted in bright colors with flowers and clouds, as well as pictures of Krishna and many religious symbols.

"Hari Boll," he said with a big smile. "Anna, how are you? Long time no see."

"Hare Krishna," I said "Brother Ram, I want to come to the Rainbow with you. Is there any room left in the bus?"

"Plenty of room, did you ask Maharaj?"

"No. I don't want to ask him. What if he says no?"

"You know what?" Brother Ram said, "just bring your stuff. You're coming with me."

"Thank you, I already packed everything."

I made sure the door to my room was locked, and dragged my bags to the bus. All the benches in the back of the bus had been removed.

"Where are the benches?"

"It's a long story . . . we needed a special license to drive the bus, and I didn't have enough time to get it, so we turned it into a van. Had something to do with the number of seats, I took some of them out."

"Very clever," I said, "you never stop to amaze me."

"Look," he said all excited, "I built these benches on the side so we can sit more people. Anna let's make sure we have enough food for the road. About seven or eight people are ridding with us."

"The cooler is kind of empty, I'll get whatever I can."

"We can buy some corn down the road from Brother Sam." He looked at me and his eyes were as bright as the sky. "Anna, I am glad you're coming!" On my way to the cooler, I ran into Maharaj.

"Hari Boll, Anna," he said.

"I'm going to the Rainbow, Maharaj," I said quickly and he was surprised.

"I didn't know you wanted go, who are you riding with?"

"With Brother Ram, in the bus."

"Oh, the old bus, I hope it won't brake on the road . . . Anna, we're going to cook for lots of people at the Rainbow. We're taking two vans full of supplies and hundreds of people eat at our camp. Will you help in the kitchen? We need as many cooks as we can get."

"Of course, Maharaj, I am looking forward." I felt a hundred times lighter.

More people were gathering in vans and cars. Brother Ram and I carried all the supplies to the dusty bus. I tried to clean it but couldn't do a very good job, and decided to burn some sage and incense to purify the atmosphere. It took us the whole day to get everything together. Around six o'clock in the evening we finally left.

Sabrina and her boyfriend showed up. He was from the Czechoslovak Republic visiting the United States for the first time. He wanted to make a movie about the Rainbow Gathering, armed with an old video camera. Sunrise and the girl he was seeing were also coming as well as Brother Ram's two teenage daughters. Sleeping bags were layered on the floor in the back of the bus, where four or five of us could sleep. One person had to stay awake at all times to keep the driver from falling asleep. It was going to be a long drive from West Virginia to Colorado. We were planning to drive the whole night and following day, after which, we would drive during the day and camp at night.

Brother Ram estimated the entire trip would take four or five days, maximum.

We drove through Ohio the whole night and Indiana the next day. We decided to camp out in Indiana, than we drove through Missouri and camped out during the night. We were running out or food so we stopped in a small town in Kansas where we encountered a lot of hostility from the locals. The town was super clean and well kept, with small houses. People lived in trailers as well. Each dwelling had a bit of a garden in the front, with neat flower arrangements and freshly cut grass. We couldn't find much at the convenience store so we eat some junk food and kept on driving. We wanted to get to Colorado and out of Kansas as soon as possible. After driving for about twelve hours on wide roads stretching before us with no end in site, the terrain began to change from hills to mountains. We were getting close to Colorado.

Soon we were driving through the tall mountains of Colorado. It was a breathtaking spectacle. Vast mountains with rocky cliffs and brilliant snow patches surrounded us. The sky was deep blue with myriads of vibrating sunrays into the clear air. Brother Ram stopped the bus by the side of the road to gather fresh sage, abundantly growing everywhere. The sage in that area was the best in the whole country. I collected enough sage to make some bundles that I could use to barter at the Rainbow where money exchange was not allowed.

The Czechoslovakian fellow filmed the whole trip, dozens of cassettes, which he couldn't keep in order anymore. He was hiding couple of bottles of rum in his backpack drinking in secret. Everybody knew it because he was drunk all the time. Brother Ram would not allow alcohol in the bus but he decided to let this go. Sabrina was distancing from him more and more.

"I don't like this guy," she said to me. "I don't know why I brought him? He's a nasty drunk. He's not my boyfriend, anyway."

He was loud and totally out of control. Finally, Brother Ram told him if he didn't behave, we would leave him on the side of the road. He got scared and was quiet for a while.

After driving the whole night, we finally arrived in Paonia early that morning. Brother Ram filled the tank with gas and all of us chipped in a few dollars. I was left with about twenty dollars for the rest of the trip, but at the gathering I didn't need any money.

From Paonia we drove to the Rainbow site. It was in the White River National Forest, by the Overland Reservoir. The Bus Village, where we had to park the bus and leave all the cars was on the left of the Reservoir. There was a small boat going across the lake, only for kitchen equipment, supplies and people in an emergency. We had to carry our luggage around the lake and up the mountain to the Krishna Camp, which was about a mile away. Some devotees were already there. They arrived several days in advance to clear the site. Our camp was by the Main Meadow, the center of the gathering. More than thirty kitchens were serving food for everybody. I had to sleep in a large tent with eight or nine girls. It was the women's ashram. After unpacking, I put my yoga mat under the sleeping bag.

It was a cold, sunny day. I had a hard time adjusting to the altitude. Our tent was at the edge of a meadow under a pine tree. I went for a walk to investigate the surroundings, following a small river spotted by big rocks.

Upstream, I found a beautiful area with lush, thick grass surrounded by trees. Some rocks were piled up reminding me of the Zen tradition where three rocks on top of each other represented the Buddha. I decided to make this spot my temple and lay on the grass in the warm sun, with a curtain of trees protecting me from the chilling breeze. I fell asleep and when I woke up, the sun was hiding behind the mountain and it started to get cold.

Back to the camp, Brother Ram was setting the kitchen. There was a lot of activity with many devotees and hippies busy, getting the kitchen ready for the next day.

The cold night was unbearable. I wore everything I had but couldn't warm up. Early in the morning when I went outside, the grass was covered with a layer of frost. By the kitchen, a few hippies were sleeping close to the fire. They kept it going the whole night. The ashes were still hot with a layer of red coal underneath. One man's hair was covered by frost. I woke him up and he shook his head.

"Man, it's cold," he said, "fire's almost gone."

He put a few logs in the fire blowing into the hot coals to kindle it, but it didn't work. We had to gather small twigs and some paper to rekindle it. A big pot of boiling water was always on the fire for everybody to drink. The water came from the river and the sanitation regulations required us to boil it. One could find those big pots of boiling water in every kitchen. I made some chai and we sat around the fire drinking the delicious hot chai, when Sabrina showed up running.

"Anna, come to the tipi, Radakund Swami is leading the meditation, come quickly!"

I felt dirty and disheveled but the river was so cold that I did not dare bathe in it. Some folks would dive right into the freezing waters, but as far as I was concerned, not in this lifetime! I left my cup by the makeshift kitchen and followed Sabrina to the tipi.

It was a huge tipi that Brother Ram brought all the way from New York. He had the polls tied right on top of the bus. The tipi was a tall cone shaped structure, round at the base with a small opening on top. Inside, Radakund Swami was leading a fire ceremony. He sat in front of the fire. The rising smoke would escape through the hole on top of the tipi. He was chanting mantras and pouring ghee into the fire. The tipi was full of people seated on the floor, shoulder to shoulder.

A young girl sat next to Maharaj. They were talking to each other and he was very interested and enlivened by her. About seventeen or eighteen years old, she was pretty, well built and sun tanned. Her curly, blond hair was covering her shoulders. I could tell that she was fascinated by Maharaj and seemed happy to be sitting next to him. Her face was beaming with joy. Wishing that I could seat next to him, I was overwhelmed by a dreadful feeling of envy that took over my being. I wanted to sink into the ground and disappear. I sat all the way in the back and tried not to think about him, but he was in the center of my mind. Part of me knew that life had so much more to offer than this elusive vision I was chasing, constantly running after a mirage which was preventing me from enjoying the present moment. Ashamed of my worldliness and lack of spirituality, I pulled the shawl over my head and covered my face, not wanting anybody to see how I felt.

For a split second, Radakund Swami's eyes looked directly into my heart and smiled. I felt that my secret was out and everybody knew about my attachment to Maharaj. I was learning a painful lesson about worldly attachments. As volatile and impermanent as they were, had the power to enslave the souls of all of us. With roots so deeply planted in the core of our nature they were almost impossible to eradicate. On the other hand, running away from happiness was a weakness in itself. It was a dilemma I didn't know how to solve.

Everybody was silent, listening to Radakund Swami's Sanskrit mantras. Somebody was burning sage and frankincense. Suddenly Radakund Swami began chanting the syllable Ohm repeatedly. Few of us joined in, and soon everybody was chanting in unison, starting each O in a low tone and escalating it as loud as we could, ending it in a humming sound. The sound vibration was getting stronger, expanding towards the sky and like the waves of an ocean advancing over the distant tops of mountains through forests, villages and cities, covering the whole World. For a moment the tipi took off, propelled by the tremendous energy released from this magical syllable, projecting us into space on a trajectory to Krishna's World. After the chant we all sat in silence bathed in that sweet vibration.

On the way back, Sabrina and I decided to walk to the Bus Village. It was about one mile away, a step closer to the 'Civilized World', with portable showers and kitchens where one could grab something to eat anytime. All of the meals were free. Sometimes one had to barter something like beads, jewelry, food, etc.

From our camp we had to trek on a narrow path between unusual rock formations around the Overland Reservoir. At a certain point a flat area opened up on the side of the road, covered with grass and purple flowers. As we passed by that area, I felt my energy being drained and my life force sucked out of me by some unknown source.

"Are you okay?" Sabrina asked.

"A little lightheaded, I think I'm going to faint."

"Just keep on walking," Sabrina said grabbing my arm so I could lean on her, "we have to pass by this spot. People say that the natives used to trap all the bad spirits in this place. You are more vulnerable. We must get to the other side quickly!" She dragged me behind her and after we passed that area, I immediately started to feel better. "Oh, thank God you're getting some color in your face. You were white like a sheet of paper. We have to get something to protect you from all those bad spirits. We'll find something at the Bus Camp."

As we were approaching, we could see the cars and the tents in the distance. Some campers had showers and people were lining up. We waited on line and took a shower with warm water. It was such a luxury. Afterwards we went to one of the kitchens and had corn bread with lentils and beans soup. It was delicious.

"I know a medicine woman, her name is Alanda," Sabrina said, "let's find her. She'll give you a remedy for the bad spirits."

We walked to a van painted purple with many crystals hanging in the windows. Alanda was an older woman. Her hair almost white and her face still young. She had clear, blue eyes and a kind smile.

"Alanda," Sabrina said, "this is my friend Anna. She almost fainted when we walked by the Spirit Grounds. She needs some protection."

Alanda took my hand and held it in between hers. "Anna" she said, "I'll give you an amulet to wear around your neck. It's a combination of herbs to keep the bad spirits away. You must always ware it, especially when you pass by the Spirit Grounds. You're very vulnerable to negative influences. This will help you overcome some of the bad spirits. You come from such negative environment that I am surprised you were able to survive it!" She stroked my cheek and hugged me.

"Thank you, Alanda," I said.

"You must give me something to free the karma between us, anything you have on you. Give me one dollar." I had two dollars on me and handed it to Alanda. She took only one. "One dollar is enough, Anna, we don't use money here, but since you don't have anything else, I'll take it . . . You don't have much money, but don't worry. You'll always be provided for. There are many beings in this Universe that care for you, only you cannot see them. They manifest sometime in your life as good friends or animals. The worst you already left behind. You'll never have to repeat your past again. The person you chose to be your physical mother was not really your mother. Your real mother travels throughout the Universe. She comes from Planet Altea. She planted you into this world for a purpose."

"Why?" I asked. Alanda looked at me surprised.

"I don't know," she said, "someday you'll find out. Anyway, you're not the only one. Many of us are visitors here."

"I never belonged anywhere and I am always searching for a home, so far I didn't find it. I'll keep on searching."

"Your home is not here," Alanda said. These words were too familiar. I put the amulet around my neck. It was hanging right above my heart. "I want you to meditate on a place that you can call 'Your Home'. Imagine what kind of place it is, what it looks like and who you'll encounter there. It'll give you a new sense of belonging and security you never had before. You need to know who you really are so you can live in harmony."

"Thank you, Alanda. I'd like to keep in touch with you, how can I see you again?"

"I travel around. I don't have a place. If you need me, we'll meet again." After we hugged and said good-bye, we left.

"Wow," I said to Sabrina "this was intense. I don't know how to thank you. She really knew so much about me."

"I go to see her sometimes, when I need advice," Sabrina said. "She is always right on target." We walked by the Spirit Grounds and miraculously I felt all right.

"This thing works." I said to Sabrina. She looked at me intensely.

"Anna, I've got to tell you something. I am in love with a man, but he doesn't know it. I met him for the first time, two years ago at a gathering. He lives in New York, but he came here a few days ago. He stays in a big tent with some of his friends, up by the Meadow. Please, come with me . . . I want to see him but I am too scared to go alone."

"Okay," I said, "let's go now."

"Thanks, thanks," she jumped, clapping her hands "I'll help you cook later on. Maybe he wants to come and cook with us. His name is Michael. He has the most beautiful hair I've ever seen! It grows down to his waist. I know he is my soul mate. I just have to make him see it."

We climbed to the top of the Main Meadow and started to see fewer and fewer tents pitched in that area.

"That's the one," she pointed to a large tent that looked like it came from a discounted military equipment store, painted with many planets, stars and people of different intergalactic races. Sabrina was very nervous. We walked in the tent and they were still sleeping.

"Good morning, time to get up!" Sabrina yelled.

"Sabrina, is that you? I can't believe it!" Michael's voice came from the far corner of the tent.

"Come let me give you a hug." His shiny hair was covering his chest and shoulders. He had nothing on but a string of beads around his neck. She ran to him, stepping over some sleeping bodies and they hugged ecstatically.

"I am so glad to see you again," Sabrina said "I missed you the whole year."

"I missed you too," he said, "I told you to come back to New York with me, it's your fault."

"I'll never leave you again," Sabrina said and started to cry. He stroked her hair and she calmed down. "I came with a guy, I just didn't want to come here alone, but he is not really my boyfriend. I am thinking about you all the time, I can't get you off my mind." Michael was looking at her smiling.

"Come and stay here with me," he said, "I'm not letting you go this time."

"I am sorry I forgot to introduce you. This is Anna, from Krishna's Camp. We just went to get some medicine for her. She was attacked by the bad spirits at the Spirit Grounds. The medicine really works, doesn't it Anna?"

"Yes, it sure does. Nice meeting you too," I said. "Sabrina told me about you."

"We are going to the Krishna's Camp to help in the kitchen," Sabrina said, "will you join us?"

"Yep, but first I'm gonna take a deep in the river. I'll see you by the kitchen."

"Great," Sabrina said and stroked his hair, "never cut this hair!" He smiled. We left and Sabrina was floating in the highest Havens. "I've never been so happy in my life, Anna. What do you think of Michael?"

"I think he loves you too."

"I can't believe he wants me to stay with him. This time I know it's for real. Last year I didn't think he loved me and was afraid of getting hurt, but now I just know. Thank you Anna for coming with me, you gave me the courage to look for him. I was afraid that he might be with another girl."

We ran down hill jumping over big rocks on the dusty path. At the camp, everyone was busy in the kitchen making lunch. Brother Ram and Maharaj were there. They looked at us.

"Where were you?" Maharaj said, "we're making a big feast today. Tomorrow is July 4th, the big celebration and we have to leave the day after. Pandava Swami wants us back in West Virginia as soon as possible."

"We went to see a Medicine Woman down by the Bus Village," Sabrina said, "Anna needed some medicine against the bad spirits from the Spirit Grounds."

"Let's get back to work," he said, patting me on the shoulder. Many of us were in the kitchen including the new girl that Nandana Swami liked. He looked at me.

"Anna, this is Daffodil. Daffy and some of her friends are coming back to the temple with us!"

"Hi Daffy," I said. Sabrina gave me an 'all knowing' look and then turned to Maharaj.

"I am not going back, Maharaj, I am going to New York with a friend."

"New York? I can't see you living in New York," Maharaj said, "such a hellish place!"

"Not for me," she said. Maharaj looked her up and down intensely.

"It's not good for you, you're not strong enough!"

"What do you mean?" She said. He closed his eyes for a moment . . .

"It's going to happen, anyway . . ." He mumbled.

"What? What's going to happen?" Sabrina asked. Maharaj shook his head like he was trying to get rid of a bad dream, and then he was back to his usual self.

"Nothing, let's get going here, we must hurry."

We started chopping vegetables and rolling dough for the Chapattis. Michael joined us and Sabrina couldn't take her eyes off him. We stayed late into the night, chanting and dancing around a big fire that Brother Ram kept going. We took turns in the kitchen, cooking. Many people were sitting on the grass eating.

The following morning I woke up early. It was the morning of the Fourth of July, Independence Day. The hot stones I put in the sleeping bag kept me warm the whole night. Outside, the sky was clear and by the position of the sun, it was no later than seven o'clock. The blades of grass were covered with a thin layer of frost. It was still quiet cold. Brother Ram already started the fire for our improvised stove. He was all smiles.

"Hari boll, Anna, come and have some hot chai, it'll warm you up."

"Thank you for suggesting the hot stones," I said, "they really worked. It was warmer in the tent and I got a good night sleep."

"It's an old Lakota technique to keep warm in the winter. It works. I used some hot stones in the tipi last night myself. It got quiet cold."

"When is the meditation starting?"

"At twelve noon, sharp. We need to be there by eleven. Anna, I need some help cooking. People will start gathering to eat around nine o'clock."

"What do you need me to do right now?"

"You can start the chapattis. The dough is in these containers. I prepared it earlier. You make little bolls of dough, flatten them out and then fry them on the hot stove on each side. You've done this before?"

"Of course," I said.

"We need couple of more people for the chapattis, but finish your chai first." I sat on a box next to the fire. The chai tested better than ever. "Did you take a bath in the river, yet?"

"No Brother Ram, it's too cold."

"Nonsense," he said, "the cold water will invigorate you. You know, you can't cook without a bath."

"Okay," I said, sipping the delicious chai when Maharaj came by.

"Hey, Hare Krishna, you're up early, today."

"Yes, Maharaj," I said.

He took some chai in a thermos and said: "Start cooking right away!"

"Anna has to take a bath," Brother Ram giggled.

"Forget about the bath, this is a special day, we need to hurry! Grab a few hippies to help. They never take a bath, anyway."

"I'm going to smudge them with sage," Brother Ram said. Maharaj looked at me with his radiant smile.

"I have to take this chai to Radakund Swami, he likes it hot. Keep up the good work."

Brother Ram smudged me with the smoking sage that made me feel much lighter. Some kids started gathering around the fire to warm up.

"Who wants to help with the food?" Brother Ram asked. Three men and a couple of girls volunteered. "Whoever helps may go in front of the food line."

Few more people volunteered. We were frying the chapattis. Some were cutting vegetables and some were making more dough for more chapattis. A man dressed in a skintight suit tie-dyed in bright colors came with a box of apples.

"We're donating three cases of apples, fresh from the farm. We just arrived. Anybody wants to help carry the boxes?" Some people went back with him and returned with two more cases of apples.

"Let's bake them." Somebody suggested and everyone started cheering. We scooped the apples, filled them with some sugar and put them on the stove right on top of the burning coals.

"How about the corn?" I asked Brother Ram.

"Oh the corn, I forgot all about it. Yep, we're going to have a feast. Anyway, today is our last day." We opened a few large bags of corn and started husking it.

Some kids with guitars were singing Rainbow songs. A long line of hippies was already forming. They were patiently waiting for us to start serving the feast. We started serving around nine and kept on cooking until eleven.

"Okay folks," Brother Ram said,—the line was still long—"everybody comes back after meditation. Don't worry nobody will go hungry."

The sun was much stronger now and it warmed up a lot since the morning. Hundreds of people were climbing the narrow dust road leading to the centre of the Main Meadow, on top of the mountain. By the time we arrived

I was completely out of breath. The high altitude did not help.

The plateau opened widely in front of us with concentric circles of people holding hands, from the smallest with maybe thirty people to the widest, with hundreds of people. Many of them camped out for one or two weeks waiting for this moment, but some came just for the day. The meditation was dedicated to 'World Peace', with people from all walks of life, an unforgettable site. I made my way toward the centre and ended up in the second row. The sun was blazing and it was a beautiful warm day. We were all holding hands.

The meditation began at twelve, when a huge gong was struck three times. I looked around at the hundreds of people with their eyes closed, praying. Suddenly a woman in the front row began to sob loudly and a bunch of people surrounded her in a hug of consolation. Someone else began to cry in the same manner.

I felt waves of pain and sorrow welling up from deep inside me. It was such sadness, that I started to cry uncontrollable. Soon I found myself surrounded by people, hugging me and trying to commune with my pain. It was as if I felt the pain of the whole world. These people knew, they also felt it, it wasn't a happy occasion. Our prayers were rising up to the sky towards God, the one God manifested in different forms in each of us. We all perceived Him in different ways, but He was there listening to our prayers, behind the blue sky and in the depth of our souls.

The many people hugging me shared my pain and eased my suffering. When I calmed down, a girl put some beads around my neck and somebody gave me a yellow bandana to wipe my tears. I rejoined the circle and closed my eyes. I had a strange vision; 'The whole sky was black with hundreds of luminous zigzag patterns of thunder. Thunder was striking as far as I could see. A continuous roaring sound coming from far away was shaking the ground under my feet. It felt so real, that for a moment I thought the end of the World was near. I was stunned by this image. Was this an answer to our prayers? Was it an omen?

When I opened my eyes the sky was blue, the sun shining and the World blessed with peace. You couldn't find a place more serene than this glorious meadow, eleven thousand feet up in the sky. The meditation lasted one hour. The circles of people looked like strings of colorful beads decorating the Earth. On my way back I encountered a little girl handing out transcripts of 'The Declaration of Independence' with children's drawings on it. By the time I arrived closer, they were all gone.

"Do you have another one, please?" I asked. She showed me her empty hands smiling but a man next to her handed me his copy. I was moved. "Thank you," I said, "this means a lot to me."

I began reading it as I was descending the dusty road on my way to the camp. 'We hold these truths to be self-evident, that all men are created equal, that they are endowed by the Creator with certain unalienable Rights, that among these are Life, Liberty and the pursuit of Happiness.' My eyes filled with tears and I had to stop reading.

We continued serving lunch and cooked the whole afternoon. The long line of hippies waiting for food never seemed to end. Brother Ram was playing the harmonium and chanting in his beautiful voice. Many other musicians gathered around him, and soon we had a huge orchestra. Some people were dancing.

Sabrina showed up with her new boyfriend. She was wearing tie-dyed black tights and a skimpy tee shirt with clouds painted on it, exposing her beautiful body. Her big gray pensive eyes gave her a calm expression. She started to dance, and her body was swaying like a willow in the wind. Everybody was watching her. In awe, Maharaj was captivated by her exquisite dance.

That night the cold was unbearable. No matter how many hot stones I put in the tent and in my sleeping bag I couldn't warm up at all. In the morning I felt ill. I was feverish and my throat was hurting so much that I could hardly speak. I went outside to the kitchen to warm up by the stove, but the kitchen was gone. Brother Ram was packing the tipi.

"Anna, would you help me with the tipi?"

"Brother Ram, I am really sick with a cold or something."

"Here, some warm milk," he gave me the thermos, "don't touch the thermos with your lips just pour it your mouth. That's the way we drink in the Vedic tradition."

"Okay," I said, but some milk spilled on my sweater.

"Anna, you are like a kid, what am I going to do with you?"

"I'll go pack my things," I said and went back to the tent.

The other girls already packed their bags. One of them looked at me.

"You don't look too good."

"I have a cold. I am not feeling well at all."

"Here," she said, "I have some herbs that a Native Shaman gave me. It's very strong medicine, take just a little. You'll be well in matter of hours. It'll make you feel worst in the beginning but later you'll feel much better. Trust the medicine."

"Thank you." I took the course powder wrapped in some cloth, and put it in my pocket. "I am going to eat something before I take it." I said and went outside.

Brother Ram was almost finished packing the tent.

"Anna, we have a lot of food left over from yesterday, over there," he said pointing to a bunch of boxes and plastic containers. "I was going to leave it here for everybody, but why don't you take some for the road."

"I can't carry all that, I'll just take a few chapattis." I felt better after eating. The day was rainy and very cold. All my clothing, couldn't keep me warm. "I am going to the bus to warm up," I said.

"Wait for us in the bus," Brother Ram said.

I started dragging my duffle bag downhill toward the Bus Village. The backpack was heavy. A group of hippies were walking by.

"Do you need some help?" One of them asked.

"Yes. I can't carry this bag all the way to the Bus Village, it's too heavy."

"Don't worry, I am a strong guy, look at me," he flexed his muscles and laughed. "I know you from Krishna's Camp. Here people help each other. This is our World, a better World."

"Thank you," I said, "I appreciate it." We walked in the misty rain down the slippery path. The door to the bus was closed. It only needed a little push to open. We got in, finally sheltered from the rain.

"You're going to West Virginia?" He asked.

"Yes we are going to the ashram. Where are you heading?"

"We don't know yet, I guess we must go somewhere."

"Why don't you come with us? You can spend the summer in West Virginia."

"It sounds good to me," he said, "can we all come?"

"I don't see why not, we'll ask Brother Ram when he gets here."

"By the way, my name is Condor. What's your name?"

"Anna." I said.

"You're all awesome," he said, on his way to get his friends. I sat in the bus waiting for them to come back.

We left around five o'clock and Maharaj was driving the bus. Two vans were also coming with us. Maharaj had me go in one of the vans with three devotees. The driver was a young, skinny red haired man, the nervous type that was talking incessantly. The heat was on in the van. I thanked Krishna for that. The two vans were supposed to follow the bus all the way to West Virginia. I was so sic that I didn't really care about missing the opportunity to ride with Maharaj. At six o'clock it was already dark and still raining a cold rain that felt more like late fall than summer.

We drove on a narrow mountain road that was endlessly stretching in front of us for three hours without encountering a soul. There were no villages, no gas stations, no cars, nothing. By now, it was completely dark outside and the van started to make some funny noises. We were the last car in the caravan. Soon, the van just stopped. The driver said:

"Let's wait for five minutes. It does this once in a while."

We waited about five minutes but the van wouldn't start no matter what we tried. It was completely dead. Stranded on this road to nowhere in the dark, with nothing to do but wait and pray, we thought that we might end up spending the whole night in the car. After about a couple of hours that felt like an eternity, we heard a motor approaching. It was Maharaj with the bus. They finally realized they were driving in the wrong direction, and decided to turn around. We were relieved and thanked Krishna for what seemed to be a miracle.

"All of you get in the bus!" Maharaj said. The man with the van didn't want to leave it behind. Nandana Swami was annoyed. "Either you come with us or we have to leave you here. This is the middle of nowhere, you better come. There is absolutely nothing around here. Deal with it tomorrow, we have to drive back to where we started on this road."

We all squeezed into the bus. It took us another three hours to get back to where we started. We were exhausted after driving for such a long time, but Maharaj didn't want to stop so we kept on driving.

I reached for the medicine the girl gave me, wondering if I should take it, and decided that anything would be better that the way I was feeling. Soon my stomach began convulsing at regular intervals, every four or five minutes. It was like I had an entire chemical plant inside me. My whole body curled up into a ball and my mouth will fill up with saliva. I thought I might be dying. This lasted for couple of hours and slowly I began to calm down, curled up on the narrow bench and fell asleep.

When I woke up, we were in a small town endowed with a public bath. The men were gone to take a shower. Miraculously I was feeling better. The medicine worked. After they came back we continued driving till evening.

Sabrina's old boyfriend, the Czechoslovakian guy, came back with us. We called him Chucky. He was stoned all the time and lost his camera at the Rainbow. At a certain point we stopped, right before entering a tunnel. Chucky went into the woods to pee. We left, and only after about twenty minutes, realized that Chucky was missing. We forgot him, and couldn't find a place to turn for another four or five miles. When we arrived, he was waiting on the side of the road and I've never seen anybody so frightened.

Maharaj was tired and we all took a room at a Motel. The Swamis slept in the bed and the rest of us took turns sleeping on the floor. It was a luxury to stretch my legs. The following day we were back on the road early in the morning and stopped only for lunch.

We drove for forty-eight hours straight. The drivers were shifting, but Maharaj was doing most of the driving. By now he was exhausted. It was difficult to sleep on the benches, so I put my duffle bag at the end of the bench as an extension to stretch my legs a little. It was late at night and one of us had to keep him awake. I was talking to him but he was constantly falling asleep. Out of nowhere, a police car showed up and the siren went on. We pulled to the side of the road and two officers told Maharaj to get out of the bus. They gave him an alcohol test, and then told him to get some sleep because he was too tired to drive.

Brother Ram took over the driving, but he was exhausted as well. Most of us were taking turns sleeping on the pile of sleeping bags in the back of the bus.

The landscape started to look more familiar. I began to recognize the rounded hills and dense vegetation of West Virginia. Soon we arrived back to the ashram. In spite of the seven hours lost when we took the wrong turn we still made good time. I went to my room and lay on my mattress, so happy to be back.

CHAPTER 20

DESCENT

One afternoon I went to the gift shop in the temple. An older devotee from Mexico was running the store. Her name was Lalita. Every time I stopped by, she used to give me something. Sometimes a picture, a candle or some incense. Often I would bring her cookies from the kitchen. She never went anywhere and one could always find her in the shop. I was feeling lonely and wanted to talk to somebody. Lalita worked all day long and kept the shop very clean, organized, and always smelling like incense. She used to make beautiful clothing for the Deities or string prayer beads while she sat in the store. Occasionally someone would buy something.

"How are you, Mother Lalita?"

"Oh, I have much to do, you like these beads?" She showed me a pair of delicate, blue crystal beads.

"Beautiful . . . Do you have a nice candle for my room?" She picked a pink candle with dried flowers pressed on the sides, and gave it to me. "How much is it?"

"Nothing, just take it!"

"No, you'll go bankrupt that way, please tell me how much?"

"Just give me whatever you wish."

I gave her two dollars and sat on the chair next to her.

"Are you okay?" I asked.

"Yes, but I want to talk to you . . . Can you keep a secret?"

"Of course," I said, "I don't have many friends around here to talk to anyway."

"I am thinking about leaving, going back to Mexico. I'm getting old and things around here are too much for me. I have family over there. My daughter and grandchildren are there but my son is here. I am afraid to leave him alone."

"How old is he?"

"Twenty-four . . . but he needs me."

"Mother Lalita, your son is old enough. I left home at nineteen and never went back. You must do what's good for you. He's the one who should be taking care of you now."

We both heard a noise at the front door. Somebody was coming. It was Mother Yeshoda.

"Hari boll, Anna," she said, "I was looking for you all over the place. My husband and some young devotes will be going to the prison to give a small program to a swami serving a life sentence. They would like you to come along."

"Right now?"

"Yes," she said, "they are meeting in the parking lot by the temple."

"I'll be there in a few minutes. See you later, Mother Lalita."

I took the candle and went to my room to change. Mandal, Yeshoda's husband and two young devotes were waiting for me downstairs. I jumped in the back of the van and we drove to the town nearby.

We approached the prison. It was a massive stone building that looked like a medieval fortress. The walls about thirty feet high had long and narrow windows guarded by heavy iron bars. It was impressive. We went in and a guard searched the men, and called for a woman guardian to search me. She took me into the ladies room and checked everything. I had to turn my pockets inside out, than she checked the seams of my clothes and even the bottom of my feet. We walked through two gates to the visiting room. A musty odor in the air made me sneeze, and the carpet was coarse and stained.

The Swami was sitting in a chair facing us with a blank face completely lacking any expression. His glance was cold and distant. He had a protruding forehead, and sunken eyes deep into the skull. In spite of the heavy atmosphere we all sat on the floor chanting, and later danced in a circle for what seemed to be a very long time. I was extremely self-conscious to be the only woman dancing with these men, under such unusual circumstances. I tried not to show how disturbed I felt. After the dance, he talked for a long time. He decided to testify against Pandava Swami at the coming trial and received recent threats on his life because of that decision. That's why the guards searched us so thoroughly. He told us that the cell in which he lived was only 5 by 8 feet. He was able to have many spiritual pictures and an altar in the small cell, and was happy to always be so close to Krishna. He considered his imprisonment to be a blessing.

I couldn't wait to get out of there. After one long hour a guard told us to leave. I walked out, wondering why they asked me to come along. That night I was worried and decided not to go to the prison program if they asked me again. That decision gave me some peace of mind and I was able to fall asleep. When I woke up it was still dark. Someone was banging on the door shouting:

"Fire fire, everybody out!"

I dragged myself down the smoky stairway holding my breath. The ground floor was full of smoke. Many devotes were standing outside, as well as a fire truck and a couple of police cars. The fire had been put out. It started with one of the devotees walking around the temple doing his morning chant, when two men from a nearby village sneaked from behind and knocked him over the head with a bottle. He fell down, hit his head on the pavement and lost consciousness. The two men entered the temple and set the shower curtains on fire in the bathrooms, and the wooden cabinets in the kitchen.

Mother Yeshoda was busy that evening and luckily decided to spend the night in the office. The smoke woke her up and she discovered the fire. She was able to put it out by herself. In the meantime, the police and fire squad arrived, and soon apprehended the two drunken men. It was a miracle that the temple didn't burn to the ground. Being built out of wood, it could have ignited like a match. About two hundred people were sleeping in the temple that night, most of them Indian devotees visiting from Canada.

We hang around outside the temple for a while and then people started to go back to their rooms. The fire truck left as well. Only the police cars remained. I went back upstairs to my room and collapsed on the mattress.

The following morning I couldn't get out of bed. I felt dizzy and the whole room was spinning. Every cell of my body was hurting. Mother Yeshoda knocked on my door at a certain point to see why I didn't show up to cook lunch. I didn't answer and after a while, she left. I slept most of the day and could not eat anything.

In the evening, I barely made it to the cooler to fetch some milk and rice left over from lunch. The temple was quiet. Everybody had gone to their homes. I went outside the back door to the parking lot and sat on a milk crate, looking at the clear sky with sparkling stars. The milk was rich with a sweat taste. The bright moon was bathing my face with its cool rays. I prayed to the sky to illuminate my mind and show me what to do.

My mind became quiet and detached. In a moment of clarity, I realized that my life at the ashram was over. I knew that soon I would be leaving this place. A shadow emerged from the dark advancing toward me. It was Maharaj.

"Hari boll, Anna," he said, "Are you okay?"

"No Maharaj, I woke up ill this morning. I don't know what's wrong, my head is spinning and my whole body hurts."

"Lots of bad spirits are trapped in that prison. You might want to take some of the holly water tomorrow morning from bathing the deities, and drink it. It'll chase away the bad spirits."

"Maharaj . . . can I ask you a favor?"

"Yes of course, anything."

"I want to get in touch with Sabrina. I know she is in New York. I want her to go by my apartment and see what's going on." The expression on his face suddenly changed.

"You didn't know? Sabrina died about a month ago. Right after she went back to New York after the Rainbow."

"What? I don't believe it, can't be true . . . what happened?"

"She died of an overdose. She was in a coma for four days, but they couldn't save her"

"Oh, Maharaj, she was such a wonderful person, but why? It's not fair!"

"Anna, the ways of karma are too complicated for us to understand. See that falling star?" He pointed to a falling star in the brightly lit sky. "She was like that, a spark in the infinite sky."

I could see her supple silhouette waving in the sun, dancing in the rhythm of the wind, with her profound grey eyes, like the deep see during a storm.

"I'll miss her," I said.

His eyes were sparkling in the moonlight and I thought they were full of tears, but it was too dark to tell. I sat in silence, looking at the sky, aware that we were so lucky to be there, in that moment when the odds were so infinitesimal for us to exist in this world.

"I am afraid to sleep in the temple, Maharaj, we're all so lucky to be alive."

"Krishna will protect us," He said, "don't worry."

"I can't, I want to go back to New York."

"We all had a bad day. It's already in the past."

"Maharaj, why do you stay here?"

"I love Krishna," he looked at me, but was rather looking through me.

At that moment, I felt a wave of love sweeping through my whole body. I became speechless. He remained there standing before me, looking intensely at something, maybe another world that only he could see. After a while, he turned around and disappeared into the night. My whole being was so full of love that I felt immobilized. Waves of bliss were overflowing from my heart, embracing the grounds, the trees, the roof of the kitchen brushed by the moon rays and the whole sky. I knew that he gave me a glimpse of his love for Krishna.

I walked through the garden. The big, thick leaves of comfrey had a luminous silvery glow in the moonlight. Everything looked like a dream in Wonderland.

The following morning I dragged myself out of bed and packed all my belongings. My body was stiff and every joint hurting. I carried everything downstairs and made a call to find out the bus schedule. There was a bus leaving from a town nearby in couple of hours. I didn't have enough money for the ticket. I sat by the entrance in front of the temple waiting for a miracle. Gauranga drove by and stopped short.

"What are you doing here Mother Anna?"

"I'm not well and don't know what's wrong. I don't have enough money to go back to New York," I told him the story with the prison and he looked worried. "Mother, how much money do you need?"

"About eighty dollars," I said. He pulled a small bag from inside his shirt and handed me a hundred dollar bill.

"Don't worry about it," he said, "Krishna will take care of it. Do you need a ride to the bus?"

"Yes please, I do."

"Come, take the money and get in the van." He helped me put all my things in the van. "You have a lot of stuff, Mother," he said.

"It's not as much as it looks. Thank you Gauranga, you don't know how I appreciate you doing this for me." My eyes filled with tears.

"I know," he looked at me with a sad expression.

This spiritual journey was coming to an end. Torn between the pain of separation from my transcendental love and the liberating feeling of freedom, I was going to embark on a search for my own truth, a journey of a lifetime.

We drove by the clear, blue lake, further and further from the ashram on my way back to New York, my curse and my blessing.